A DEATH UNDER SAND

C.W. Stimpson

A DEATH UNDER SAND

FICTION4ALL

PREFACE (OR IS THIS A FOREWORD?)

Maybe it's just an Introduction...

Well, here it is. It took a long time, but I finally got down on paper just about everything I wanted to say about the business that started in the dump that Sunday afternoon. It really was never meant to be this long, but I think I caught a dose of whatever the writer's version of verbal diarrhea is called. Writer's diarrhea, I guess. Can we change the subject?

When the dust (sand, really) had finally settled on the affair, we thought we would hear no more about it until the court case came up. Boy, were we wrong. First the local paper got a hold of it and Mickey Dombrowski's dad, who works for the paper, came around with a photographer and asked all kinds of stuff. We were closely chaperoned by a woman from the D.A.'s office, who wouldn't let us say much beyond our names and what we had for breakfast that morning. The photographer took a couple of shots and the two of them went away scratching their heads. The next day we were all over the front page surrounded by columns and columns of total fiction that made us look like

Arnold Schwarzenegger and Sly Stallone on Speed. After that it got really silly.

First, we couldn't walk ten feet at school in any direction without either some little kid wanting to hear the story 'from our own lips' or some big kid wanting to see how tough we really were. And of course Tony and Liddy, after everything that had happened, were really pissed that they weren't getting the same kind of attention. Then I guess someone at the *Sentinel*, the big city paper, got wind of the story in the local paper and sent down a couple of guys. Same deal—we weren't allowed to answer most of what they asked. Same result— suddenly we were boy heroes on BMXes (no kidding, they actually used that somewhere in the story).

Not long after that we got to be featured artists in what they call a 'media circus', which is a pretty good name considering the number of clowns involved. One Wednesday no fewer than *three* different TV stations sent down to Gretchyville their big outside broadcast trucks, complete with cameras, lights, sound equipment and squeaky blonde reporters. They waited in the parking lot of the school half the morning, until Chief Bonaventura ordered them out, but that wasn't the end of it. When I stepped off the school bus that afternoon I could see them camped out across from my house. It was another two hours and three interviews before the last of them wound in their satellite dishes and headed back to the city. A few hours later I was treated to triple coverage of myself looking embarrassed on national TV.

Well, as a result it dragged out for a few more days at school until almost everybody got tired of it. Then, when even Colin 'Brainpan' McGovern had given up nudging me, winking and exclaiming "way to go, Petey!" and Deborah St. Pierre had stopped sitting on my desk, crossing her legs and laughing at everything I said, Mr. Wyszynski got it all started again.

Mr. Wyszynski is our English teacher, and has always had a keen eye for literary talent (that is to say, he always likes the essays I turn in. I've never thought much about it—I just enjoy the writing part). One day when I really thought it was all over he was announcing a menu of topics, one of which we were supposed to choose as our title for that weekend's essay. As he announced away he was strolling around the classroom, and by accident or design stopped in front of my desk just as he was finishing the list.

"...except for you, Mr. McLeod" he concluded ominously. "I would like you to work on a different topic entirely. Since the media has lately been treating us to some rather egregious examples of hyperbole, I would like you to take as your essay assignment an objective narrative of the escapades of the Gretchyville junior detective force." He waited for the laughter to subside around him, then continued.

"I would like you to concentrate on salient features of the case, maintain a strictly orthodox chronology, and speculate briefly on different contingencies that might have arisen. Any questions?" None had yet formed in my mind, so he took the opportunity to reach under my chin and close my mouth for me.

For the next few nights I tried to come up with something close to what he had asked for, but found myself putting in more and more of what seemed important to me. The result was that, when it came time to hand in the finished essay, I had barely covered the description of the crime that was at the center of attention that week in September. I pleaded for an extension and was granted one without too much fuss. But for the next three weeks the same thing happened, and I finally felt obliged to show him some evidence of my progress. When he read over what I had written he maintained a thoughtful silence for one whole agonizing minute, then handed it back and looked me closely in the eye.

"Mr. McLeod, I am going to relieve you from completing this assignment as a normal weekly essay. From this point on, you will write and hand in essays that I assign in the usual way, but I would also like you to continue writing on *this* topic in the style in which you have started. I hope and trust

that you will be able to complete this—
uh...*magnum opus* by the end of the Spring
semester."

The end of Spring semester was so far over my
mental horizon that it might as well have been half-
way through another lifetime, so I promised
faithfully—and rashly—to comply with his request.
In fact, the damned thing took up nearly all my
spare time for the next six months, but Wyszynski
did not pressure me for it. And when, three weeks
before semester's end, I finally walked into his class
with a bag full of typed sheets and presented them
to him, he merely raised an eyebrow and murmured
some mild words of encouragement. I didn't expect
to hear anything more on the subject for several
days, so I was surprised—not to mention thoroughly
embarrassed—when he burst into the classroom five
minutes early the following day and called me out
into the corridor.

Outside, Wyszynski launched into an
enthusiastic discourse about what I'd written,
waving the mass of papers around like a signal
flare. I was so stunned to see our normally sedate
and unflappable English teacher in a state of high
agitation that I did not understand everything he
was saying, but I gathered that he thought my
efforts worthy of showing to a friend of his in some
unpronounceable firm—publishers or agents, I
guess. Of course, as he reminded me in almost the
same breath, there was work to be done in

'rectifying' and 'normalizing' much of the grammar and phraseology, but he would be only too pleased to assist me with those tasks. Now it was beginning to sound less like an embarrassment and more like hard work. Finally, he pointed out that I would absolutely *have to* remove those passages featuring Miss Mireille of the French Department, but that I could leave untouched those in which Mr. Bamberg and Mr. Creel appeared.

So, partly to appease Mr. Wyszynski and partly because, frankly, I had begun to feel that our part in Gretchyville's hottest news item in years *should* be recorded in some way—I went along with his suggestions. There were times, I will admit, in the process of 'rectifying' what I'd written when I dug in my heels and insisted on leaving certain passages the way they were, and times when it became too much effort to argue and I let him fool with it the way he wanted, but overall I think it tells the story—the *real* story—pretty much the way it happened. I know there are folks in town and at school who are going to take issue with some of the stuff I put in about them, and when I realized that what Wyszynski had in mind was a hard-cover book staring back at me from the shelves of the *Autumn Leaves* bookstore on Main Street I was all for taking that stuff out, but he promised me that if it was honestly felt and expressed, it should remain in the book. All except the stuff about Miss Mireille.

A DEATH UNDER SAND

So here it is. It's a story about a few bad folks, lots of good folks, and *some* folks who sat on the dividing line. Mostly it's about Robert and me, and if you're one of those people I know who has a problem with Robert and me being friends, just take the book back to the store. I don't want your money. Oh yes—and it all happened, just the way I wrote it.

Peter McLeod
Gretchyville

SUNDAY, 1:30 PM

It started with a weird experience.

Then it got weirder.

I don't mean weird like asking your little sister to get you a soda from the fridge and then she actually gets you one. Or weird like your mom giving you twenty dollars and telling you to get whatever you want from the videogame store. I mean weird like seeing something really ordinary in a place where it absolutely and completely *does not belong*, and that's just the start of a whole chain of events that sucks you in deeper and deeper and nearly drives you crazy. You know the kind of thing I mean?

Maybe I'd better explain, before you all think *I'm* weird. It happened up at Silver Hill (the town landfill or, to be really precise, the Gretchyville Waste Management Facility. The dump, to you and me). There were four of us: Robert Juneau, Tony Newburg, Liddy Giraldi and me, all with our BMXes. You can get into the landfill on a BMX if you take Overlook Road up to Birch, go up Birch as far as old man McDermott's place, then cut through his yard into the woods. There's a path leading off to the left that runs down the hill and comes out at a gap in the fence just wide enough to take a bike, although you have to duck going through to avoid the top wire. One time Tony forgot to duck, which is why his forehead looks the way it does.

Anyway, the four of us like to get over there early on Sunday afternoons when the wind's in the right direction (when it's not, the smell's enough to make you wish you'd skipped lunch); there's one whole part of the dump they've hardly used yet, and it might have been made just for BMX meets. There are steep little hills, gullies, mounds, cliffs and straight-aways...even a couple of mini-ramps we made out of some plywood dragged over from some other part of the dump. It's not the same as being at the skatepark the Town built last year, but hell, that's all the way over in West Gretchyville where the rich kids live, and it's always full of tiny tots falling off their roller blades and skateboards. Real monochrome. We usually spend a couple of hours at the dump; we'll fool around freestyle for a while, then mark out some trails and do timed runs. Robert often wins, even on his secondhand Viper, which the others find a little boring. It doesn't bother me; Robert and I have been best friends since second grade, and I know he doesn't have too much else going for him either at school or at home. So when he wins I feel almost as good as when I do (which is about one time in ten).

More often than not we stay at the landfill until one of the bulldozer drivers spots us, which usually happens when Tony tries to get radical by trying a superman tailwhip off a cliff. As soon as they see him up on the high ground they come lumbering over in the 'dozer, cursing us out and looking like they want to bulldoze us all into a pile with the old fridges and box springs. We really don't mind at that point, because no-one has the energy for any more racing. We don't exactly panic to get out of there, either; at the speed the 'dozer goes, we're not in any great danger of being caught and plowed under the tracks. It's a bit like being chased by the mummy, you know: if you can work yourself up to a strolling pace you can get clean away.

So most days we just head back through the fence and ride down to town looking for something to do. Not that there's a whole lot of entertainment to be had in the seething metropolis of Gretchyville outside of tourist season; as soon as the students start abandoning their summer jobs and traipsing back to college in late August, Crazy Golf and Water Land shut their doors, quickly followed by most of the arcades and ice cream parlors. That's the trouble with living in a second-string tourist town on Cape Cod: what little there is to get excited about around here is put on almost exclusively for visitors. Come late September the adults are looking around for sources of income and the kids for sources of fun; neither group makes out too well.

In any case, Tony and Liddy don't usually stick around for more than an hour after we get back to town. She'll start dropping progressively less subtle hints, which usually have to reach Condition Orange before he gets the message; (you have to understand that Tony hasn't quite figured out that he's the main reason Liddy hangs with our group at all). When he does finally get it, the two of them disappear in the direction of his place, leaving Robert and me. That suits both of us. We always seem to want to do the same things, and we don't have to argue for half an hour like you do in a big group before you do anything. So we'll ride down to the beach, or hang around the schoolyard, or check out the unfinished houses in the new development, or just do whatever we feel like. We usually end up at my house or his apartment and stay until someone's mother decides she doesn't want to feed one extra mouth tonight. We've become good at taking hints.

Anyway, that's how our Sunday afternoons tend to go. We don't spread it around too much; it's one thing to have a reputation at school, but it ought not to be for unnatural acts. We're already pushing the envelope—three guys and a girl doing stuff we probably should have grown out of a year back— but what the hell; we're in our final year at the Junior High, so nobody there can tell us to grow up. When we get to Gretchyville High next year we'll probably get into other stuff, but for now we like being who we are and doing what we're doing.

But what happened that sunny, mild day in late September was different—and weird. We'd been freestyling for about half an hour when I suddenly felt bored, and for no particular reason started to ride toward the active side of the dump. Robert saw me going and called after me.

"Hey Peter, where you going?"

I dropped my left foot and skidded to a stop, the rear wheel swinging around in a shower of sand.

"Just looking around. You want to come?"

Robert nudged his BMX forward over the edge of a steep hillock. He came down the slope in a rush, almost disappeared from view behind a low ridge then shot out over the ridge, airborne. He landed pedaling, and was still accelerating as he passed me.

"What you waiting for, man?"

I tried to think of a suitably cool response, but couldn't manage that *and* get my Cozmo back up to speed. Robert and I rode together across the landfill, keeping to the low ground and steering away from where the seagulls were swarming above the fresh garbage; it was too early in the day to want to bring on an attack by the Great Yellow Mummy. Somewhere near the middle of the dump we reached a wide, flat, unprotected sandy area. It was an area we knew about, and usually made a point of avoiding. It was as if someone had graded a strip of land a couple of hundred yards long for roadbuilding then changed his mind, leaving a dead straight avenue pointing right into the dump. The problem with this place is that there's nowhere to hide once you get into it. The other end of the avenue is close to where the 'dozer turns around, and if anyone appears at that end while you're in it they just can't miss you. So what does Robert do? He just rides right on out into the avenue without even slowing down, that's what.

I was about fifteen feet behind Robert and had been about to stop at the edge of the avenue to check for signs of life. That seemed pointless now, with him halfway across, so I just kept going. Even so, as I broke out into the open I glanced quickly to the side, the way you do when your car crosses railroad tracks and you look down the line just to make sure you're not about to get crushed by a ninety-ton diesel. Just then something made Robert turn his head and look down the avenue too, so we both caught sight of the man at the same time. He was no more than fifty feet away. He must have been one of the sanitation workers, with his grimy orange overalls and big boots. He was standing almost in the middle of the avenue facing directly away from us, one hand in his pocket and the other holding a long metal rod. I felt my jaw drop as I tried to figure out what he was doing there, all on his own in the middle of the dump and facing back the way he'd come! Understand that neither Robert nor I were so fascinated by this guy that we were about to stop and make his acquaintance if we could help it, but what we were looking at just didn't make sense.

C.W. STIMPSON

A more important question than who he was or what he was doing, though, was whether he was going to turn around in the next few seconds and see us. If he did, and if his gumboots didn't slow him down too much, he could pretty easily get between us and our way out through the fence. So far he hadn't heard us, and we'd both stopped pedaling the moment we saw him; the only noise we were making came from our tires as we coasted over the packed sand. Even that was loud enough. And at the rate we were running out of speed we'd have to start pedaling again before we reached the other side, which we couldn't do without creating some kind of graunching noise. How could he fail to hear us?

But Gumboots didn't move. As we teetered across the avenue, getting slower and slower with each second, he continued to stare in the opposite direction without showing any sign of life. I began to wonder if he'd had some new kind of heart attack, one that left you stone dead, standing up. Robert said later he'd thought someone had dumped a storefront dummy there, which made some kind of sense, I guess: where else in town would you throw a dummy when you were done with it? Finally we had to start pedaling again or fall over sideways, but even that noise didn't disturb him. We rode out of the avenue, necks twisted three-quarters around to keep him in sight, and into a place we call the crater.

A DEATH UNDER SAND

The crater was one of those peculiar features you find in a landfill (trust me, I'm an expert). It had once been the area set aside for old oil tanks and engines—anything that might still have some oil or gasoline seeping out of it—but the brains of the dump must have changed their minds after having used it for a short time. They'd bulldozed great walls of sand around it, presumably so it wouldn't spoil the beauty of the rest of the dump, and left it looking like a big shell-hole. Inside this hole were several rusting engines, furnaces and oil tanks, some half-buried in the walls. A narrow gap had been left in the wall facing the avenue for some reason—maybe the bulldozer driver lost interest before finishing the job—and it was through this gap that Robert and I were now passing. The moment we were safely inside the crater, with a high wall of sand between Gumboots and us, we stopped pedaling and braked gently to a stop. Slowly and silently we swung ourselves off the bikes, wheeled them behind a rusted-out oil tank close to one of the crater walls and laid them down in the soft sand. Then we flattened ourselves on our bellies, wriggled forward and peered through the ragged holes rusted into the sides of the tank.

A minute passed. We kept our eyes fixed on the gap, waiting for the man to appear.

Another minute. I could feel Robert beginning to fidget and knew what it meant. It would be just like him to jump up and run to the gap to see what was keeping the guy. And knowing Robert's luck he'd run right into him. I felt that we'd already pushed our luck too far.

Another couple of minutes had passed when, as I expected, Robert started to lever himself up. He was on one knee, with a hand on the edge of the tank, when I suddenly grabbed the back of his shirt and pulled him back beside me. Gumboots had chosen that moment to saunter out into the gap.

A DEATH UNDER SAND

SUNDAY, 1:40 PM

We lay there together, side by side, trying to slide out of sight between the grains of sand underneath our sweating bodies. Or will ourselves into another hemisphere—or at least a couple of hundred yards away. Nothing worked. We even gave up trying to spy on the intruder; I don't know what Robert was thinking, but I had the most irrational feeling that if I put my eyeball to one of the ragged holes in the side of the tank Gumboots would somehow be able to see clear through it and figure out our names, addresses, and telephone numbers. So we just waited.

Another minute had passed when Robert squirmed around and faced away from me toward the center of the crater. He started edging toward the outer end of the tank, and I knew exactly why. Robert is the kind of person who won't—or just can't—let things happen to him. He had no intention of letting Gumboots blunder onto us while we lay there straining weeds between our teeth; he wanted to be able to see the danger coming at him so he could stand up and face it, or jump on his Viper and ride away from it, or grin his stupid, lopsided, toothy grin at it—anything rather than just lie there and let it hit him when *it* wanted to.

You have to know Robert; he's not capable of facing life any other way. I've seen him go out and

create a far worse reputation for himself than he
ever needed to, just because he wouldn't let Mr.
Bamberg (our math. teacher, aka Dumberg) get
away with one of his unenforceable threats.
Dumberg had announced that he was going to
march anyone who hadn't done their math.
homework down to Prideaux Pond and throw them
in, and Robert, who you just *knew* hadn't even
looked at his homework, walked to the front of the
class and told him in a voice loud enough to be
heard by the thought police in the corridor that, no,
he had *not* done it. All the weenies in class held
their breath, waiting for old Dumberg to carry out
his threat, but I knew what Robert was doing. He
wasn't just calling the guy 's bluff: it wouldn't have
bothered him much if Dumberg really had been fool
enough to throw him in. He didn't think he would,
but it was more important to Robert not to let the
old tyrant find out for himself about the homework
and get him on the defensive; he was going to face
his punishment head-on no matter what it was. As
it turned out, he took the guy by surprise. You
could see the math. teacher trying to compute how
to get out of this one with some dignity, and not
doing an A+ job of it. He finally told Robert to sit
down and that he would "deal with him later",
which of course he never did. As for Robert, I
would bet my life he had forgotten about the
incident before the end of class; it was never a test

of strength for him, just his way of dealing with the world.

Perhaps Dumberg was no contest, anyway. I know for a fact that Robert reacts the same way when the police come to his door looking for his father. You don't see him hiding in the house for fear that the neighbors will see him through their twitching curtains; he's out there daring the police to treat him the same way they treat his old man. When they finally drive away he waves them off like old friends, then looks right back at the neighbors' curtains as if to say "Yeah? What are you going to do about it?" It's one of the reasons I like him so much, as different as we are. He takes no prisoners, and I often wish I were even half as tough.

So when Robert started to pull himself across to the corner of the tank I let him go. I had a sense that, even though he had allowed me to pull him down a minute ago, he wouldn't let me do it a second time. He would shake off my hand with an irritated gesture and I would be reminded that, friends as we are, I was not allowed to interrupt the staring contest he was having with life.

I watched nervously as Robert inched closer to the edge, his left shoulder and cheek almost scraping along the discolored metal. As he reached the corner I was half-expecting to see him pull back suddenly in alarm and make a grab for his bike, indicating that Gumboots was practically on top of us. Instead, he stayed in position, his nose butted up against the tank edge and his body perfectly immobile. Whatever else Gumboots was doing, he apparently was not about to loom over us like the giant in *Jack and the Beanstalk*.

After watching for a minute Robert drew back and wriggled toward me. Pointing with his thumb back over his shoulder and grinning, he whispered:

"He's poking the sand with a stick!"

"What?"

"That's all he's doing, just walking around poking with a stick!"

I stared at Robert for a moment, trying to figure out whether it was him, me or Gumboots who had lost his marbles, and finally decided I had to check this out for myself. I crawled off around the opposite side of the tank and peered out across the crater. Sure enough, there was Gumboots about thirty yards away with his back to us, apparently attacking the opposite wall of the crater with the metal rod I had seen him carrying. He would drill into the sand with it as far as he could, then retrieve it, move along the wall a few feet and repeat the process. What was going on here? Had he dumped a refrigerator here a long time ago, and only just realized he'd left a TV dinner in the freezer compartment? Or was he looking for a suitable location in which to build his dream house? These were not questions we were likely to get answered any time soon.

But if the object of his search wasn't obvious, one thing was: the more he moved from left to right along the crater wall, the closer he was coming to finding he was not alone in his little world. Not that we couldn't have moved quietly in the opposite direction to keep the oil tank always between him and us, but we couldn't have taken our BMXes along with us without making some kind of noise. And if we left them where they were, he would soon see them and realize that they weren't dump fodder—they were too new and clean, even Robert's, and their owners would have to be somewhere nearby. I started to turn back toward Robert to alert him, and almost bashed foreheads with him. He had crept up behind me and had obviously seen the danger exactly as I had seen it.

"What are we going to do?" I half-mouthed, half-whispered urgently. Robert's reaction was typical. He watched Gumboots spearing the sand once more, then shrugged.

"Let's just mount up and get out of here" he whispered.

I turned back again to assess Gumboots' progress. It was already too late to get to the bikes without being seen, and the man was still close enough to the only exit from the crater to cut us off before we could get up to speed. This would be exactly the worst time to move, which of course made it Robert's first choice. I could see only one possibility. Since, purely by chance, he was working the side of the crater opposite to where we were hiding, Gumboots had his back to us most of the time. He had another twenty or thirty yards to go before the wall curved around enough to bring us into his field of vision, and by the time he reached that point he would be as far away from the exit as he could get. If he missed seeing the bikes until then, we at least had a chance of getting to them, mounting up and getting up to speed before he could react and reach us. It also meant, unfortunately, that there could be no subtlety about our maneuver. The moment we broke from cover for the bikes we would be in full view, and any hitch from that point on—like getting a front wheel turned around or snagging the bikes on each other— would probably deliver us into Gumboots' tender care.

Well, if we were that klutzy, I reasoned, we probably deserved to get caught. But I felt it was the only option we had, and turned back to Robert to explain; to his credit he understood quickly and agreed without argument. Now we just had to get our timing down. Gumboots was moving ponderously around the inside of the crater, getting closer all the time to the spot I had mentally selected as the 'go' point (as in, when he gets there we GO!) Finally, when he was within a couple of yards of it and busy poking at the sand again, I slapped Robert lightly on the back and we launched ourselves out from hiding.

A DEATH UNDER SAND

For the first few seconds Gumboots was too busy with his sand sculpture to notice us, but as soon as we started to pick up our BMXes he must have caught the movement out of the corner of his eye and swung around in surprise. Until then he obviously thought he was the only living soul in that half of the dump, and suddenly here were two kids within a few yards of him. The time it took him to process this information through the marshmallow bag between his ears gave us an extra couple of seconds' lead-time. We were able to turn the bikes, get one pedal underfoot and push off in the right direction before he even found his voice. And when he found it, all that came out was a feeble "Hey…"

Robert accelerated around to the right of the oil tank while I headed for the small space between its left edge and the crater wall. I knew the space was wide enough for me to pass through, but since the tank blocked my view of the ground beyond, it was not until I came out on the other side that I saw the rusty coil of wire directly in my path. My front wheel, still accelerating, ran over the wire and compressed it, but I knew exactly what would happen as soon as the wire emerged from under the wheel. It sprang up and immediately became entangled with my pedals, chain and rear wheel. I had no choice: I had to stop and free my bike before the wire became so enmeshed that it would not move, which would mean abandoning it.

C.W. STIMPSON

With a curse I jumped off and threw the bike on its side, hands grabbing for the loose end of the wire. Precious seconds went by as I worked the twisted, springing metal free from the exposed workings of my Cozmo, all the time expecting the arrival of Gumboots with a heavy hand and a lecture in which the expressions 'trespassing', 'in trouble', and 'name and address' would feature prominently. Long before I was finished Robert had disappeared through the gap to safety, which was good—there was no point in both of us getting caught.

After what seemed longer than a Friday afternoon Social Sciences class with 'Mr. Creosote' Creel, I finally got the last loop of the wire free. Somehow I managed to combine the actions of putting the bike on its wheels and throwing myself onto it—I was lucky I didn't throw myself clear over the far side of it and land on my face—and I was back in motion. I headed for the gap, amazed that my path was still clear, and as I accelerated into it I allowed myself a quick glance back into the crater.

What I saw was my second big surprise of the day: Gumboots was still standing in the position he had reached when we made our breakout. Unlike all the other dump workers we had encountered, he had not even bothered to try to catch us. In fact, his behavior was as unlike that of his colleagues as I had ever seen. There was no truculence, outrage or hostility in his look, only uncertainty and defensiveness; if I had to identify any reaction on his face I would have to call it guilt. He seemed to be trying to conceal the rod behind his back, while his pudgy face, framed by overgrown sideburns of black wiry hair, had the same expression I'd seen Scott Hurling use the time his locker burst open and spilled all those missing workshop tools at Mrs. Brandt's feet. It was as if we had caught Gumboots doing something he wasn't supposed to be doing or being somewhere he wasn't supposed to be, instead of the other way around.

Even so, this was not the time to stop and engage the guy in deep and meaningful conversation. I turned forward again and pedaled fast through the gap, across the avenue and back to where I had last seen Tony and Liddy, and where I assumed Robert had also headed. I found them soon enough, in a tight group on the edge of a wilderness of tree stumps. The others were listening attentively while Robert, standing astride his BMX, was talking rapidly and gesturing behind his shoulder with his thumb. As I came into view Tony looked up, caught sight of me and interrupted Robert's story.

"Here he is!"

Robert and Liddy looked toward me, relief showing on their faces. As I pulled up beside Robert he shot a glance behind me, as if expecting to see Gumboots in full pursuit, then looked at me with concern.

"What happened to you back there, man?"

"I got my bike snagged on a wire; it took forever to get it free."

"So how come you didn't get caught?"

"I-" I turned in my seat to look back the way I had come, then turned back to the group.

"I don't know. He didn't chase me" I finished lamely. The others regarded me with suspicion. I think they would have disbelieved me altogether about Gumboots had Robert not already told his story.

"So what happened—he just lets you work on your bike and don't say nothin'?" Liddy, with her hard-edged Italian accent, could make "hello" sound threatening; her question made me feel I was under the lights in an interrogation room. She folded her arms defiantly across her skinny chest, her dark eyes narrowing. I never know quite how to take Liddy; half the time she's pure tomboy—and for much of that time she comes on tougher than most of the guys around her—but then, without warning, she'll find some really wide feminine streak inside her, usually when Tony's around.

"What does it matter?" asked Robert. "We'd better get out now before he changes his mind. Maybe he's just a slow thinker." He pointed his bike towards the outer edge of the dump and pushed off. The rest of us followed him, falling into single file along the foot of the steep sandy scarp that marked the limit of excavation in the dump. Tony was behind Robert, with Liddy next in line. I came last, frequently snatching backward glances, and soon we were passing back through the fence and toiling up the path that led through the woods toward Birch Street. We came out onto Birch and started to freewheel down the hill. As was our habit we descended without braking, limiting our speed by snaking backwards and forwards across the road, skier-style. You can do this on Birch fairly safely because, since there aren't too many houses up there yet, there's not a lot of traffic. None of us has yet been squished by an SUV with a lead-footed driver.

We had almost reached the intersection with Overlook when, without warning, Tony hit the brakes of his Mongoose Brawler and jammed his uphill foot on the ground. Liddy missed putting tire marks on his foot by about three inches and screeched to a halt cursing and swearing. I managed to miss both of them and ended up further down the hill with Robert, scrabbling to come to a stop.

"This is STOOPID!" shouted Tony, banging his handlebars with the flat of his hand. "It's not even two o'clock and we're leaving because Robert and Peter met some guy who doesn't care if we're there or not and who can't move fast enough to catch us!" He snorted in disgust and looked hard at me, as if challenging me to explain why we were not back in the dump right now, enjoying ourselves. I opened my mouth to speak, but Robert beat me to it.

"Hey, Tony, come on!" he shouted back up the hill. "It's over. They'll have the Dump Special Forces crew out by now, bloodhounds and all. So we do something else today and come back next week."

Tony shook his head in irritation, then looked around for support.

"Liddy?"

"I'd just as soon stay; what's the worst can happen?" asked Liddy, predictably. Robert looked at me, the only one of the four who had not declared himself one way or the other.

"Peter? What you want to do?"

I considered the question. It should have been easy, according to our formula:

We have fun.

Dump crew sees us.

Dump crew chases us (kind of).

We leave.

But something about the formula was wrong this time. One of the ingredients didn't match. It was Gumboots; try as I might, I just couldn't cast him as the villain. The idea of that stumpy, lost-looking guy in overalls trying to intimidate us into leaving, or collaring one of us and reporting us, just didn't fit. As I mentally replayed the incident in the crater, and especially the last few seconds of it, the truth—or at least one possible version of the truth—began to dawn on me.

A DEATH UNDER SAND

Gumboots was not supposed to be in the dump any more than we were.

SUNDAY, 2:00 PM

"Come on, Peter" said Liddy impatiently, scraping a couple of strands of dark hair off her right cheek and shoving them behind her ear. "I don't want to stand around here rest of the day."

"What d'you think, man?" asked Robert. "You were there right enough. You want to give him another chance at us?" I turned and looked squarely at him. It was not fear that was driving Robert; he had simply worked the formula through to what was, to him, its logical conclusion. True, it had come to a head today sooner than on most days, but so far as he was concerned the formula had run its course, we were done for the day at the dump, and he had already moved on. But of the four of us, Robert was the only one who had seen the interloper yet had not seen what I had seen in his face. He did not know what I knew, which was that Gumboots was not a threat and may have been no more eager to confront us than we were to see him again. I knew we could go back to the dump right now.

"I think it will be OK to go back" I replied.

"Yeah!" shouted Tony and Liddy in unison, pumping their fists. Robert gave me a look I won't forget for a long time, one that seemed to question how well I really knew him at all. He had a reputation at school for being fearless, which even held good in our little group; if anyone was going to be the first to try something new, untested or even dangerous, it almost went without saying that it was going to be Robert. And having found himself with the reputation, he seemed to go to great pains to maintain it; it was something he could call all his own and bask in, even as his grades were disappearing through the pavement. So to be the one member of our group appearing to chicken out, when Tony, Liddy and even I were voting to head back into the great unknown, was not a trivial matter for him. It was a direct assault on one of the few things he had going for him in his life, and my decision to side with the other two instead of supporting him must have counted as betrayal. He probably considered that I was not so much a member of the attacking army as the traitor who unlocked the city gates to let it in. He swore and shook his head.

"You wanna talk about stupid" he muttered. But when he moved, it was to turn his BMX back up the hill toward the dump. Whatever the outcome, and however much he disagreed with the decision, he must have realized the futility of continuing into town to look for solitary entertainment on a Sunday afternoon.

With more effort than elegance the rest of us sorted ourselves out and turned our bikes around. Slowly and in ragged formation we made our way back up the hill, each one standing on his pedals and leaning way forward over the handlebars, buttcheeks in the air and grinding. We reached McDermott's yard, crossed it for the third time that day and soon were on the path, dropping down toward the fence. As the gap came into view, it suddenly occurred to me to sound a note of caution before crossing into the dump.

"Hold up at the fence, guys" I called. The four of us came to a halt in line abreast, a couple of feet short of the fence.

"Let's just check it out before we go down."

Straddling our BMXes, we scanned the scene below us. A yard or two beyond the fence the ground fell away sharply, turning quickly into the coarse sand that is no more than two feet below the surface at any point in Gretchyville. About twenty feet below us the gradient leveled out, creating a kind of narrow, uneven perimeter track running three-quarters of the way around the dump. Beyond the track commenced the dump proper—acres and acres of molded sandy landscape looking like nothing so much as an attempt by the Board of Selectmen to create the world in miniature, right here in Gretchyville. There were hills, plains, plateaus, canyons, narrow gullies steep enough to look like fjords, and saturated areas that could have been oceans separating great continents. In a few places some particularly determined vegetation—a rough kind of beach grass whose seeds had probably been blown there from the nearby edge of the real ocean—had taken root in the unpromising soil, and in this world view peculiar to the four of us appeared as tracts of virgin forest. And there, near the farther side, were the great mountain ranges: one consisting wholly of wheel rims, another of kitchen appliances, yet another of metal bed frames, all reflecting pinpoints of sunlight to show where their icy glaciers flowed and their snowy peaks jutted skyward.

And it was ours. Our planet, our scaled-down world with its very own topography. I really could not tell you how or when or with whom the notion started that this was a baby world and that it was *ours*, but I know that it was shared by all of us as if it were one of Mr. 'King Dick' Richard's immutable laws of physics. A long time ago one of us must have compared one of the piles of rusting metal to an Alpine peak, or one of the flat, exposed stretches to an African desert, and from that moment we gave the same treatment to every part of the landfill that could be likened to some geographic or topographic feature. And the more we did this, the more the place became ours. So far as we knew, no-one else ever treated Silver Hill as their private play area, so the chance that some other kid or group of kids was as familiar as we were with the whole place was pretty remote. When one of us identified a pile of abandoned mattresses as a line of ancient chalk cliffs, no-one was going to come along the next day and decide it was a high-rise development in a badly planned city. And it was doubtful whether the landfill workers had the same perspective as we did, let alone the rampant imaginations. Besides, they *had* to be here; it was their job. This miniature world was ours simply because we—and no-one else—chose to come here, chose to give its various parts planetary proportions, and chose to use it as our world-size adventure playground, meeting place and racetrack all in one.

Once, we even named a spot after a man-made landmark. Liddy had been leading us through a section of high ground that bordered our normal operating area when we found ourselves looking into a fifteen-foot-deep chasm, at the bottom of which were some old and broken pieces of household furniture. The chasm was bridged by a couple of pieces of corrugated iron loosely joined at the midpoint, and it was our consensus that this piece of accidental engineering deserved the name of The Golden Gate Bridge. Of course, Robert— being Robert—immediately tried to cross it, and although he made it safely across, the metal groaned and sagged under his weight to such an extent that I was obliged to throw my weight on one end to prevent bridge, bike and boy from disappearing into the depths. We concluded that our version of the span that crossed San Francisco Bay might take the weight of a thirteen-year-old on a good day, but an adult—or even a thirteen-year-old on a BMX— would really be pushing his luck attempting to cross.

A DEATH UNDER SAND

On occasion, the operation of the dump by the Public Works Department would require that some section of it be remodeled by the great yellow 'dozer, which in turn would require us to adapt our thinking. When a pile of last year's Christmas trees and the pool of muddy rainwater adjacent to it were covered over with a flat-topped mound of sand, it was easy to rationalize as a natural planetary cataclysm: a tropical rain forest bordering the coast had suddenly, in consequence of an earthquake so massive that it actually changed the area's climate, become a high and arid desert plateau bordered by dry, steep-sided wadis. When you are as much into fantasy as we were, that kind of adaptation is a piece of cake.

A whole minute passed as we watched for signs of life. Somewhere close to the dump entrance, on the opposite side from where we stood, the 'dozer was busy with its resculpting duties. A little further to the left but still a good half-mile away a pick-up truck or car would occasionally pop into view, then disappear again, as it made its way to the household dumping spot *du jour*. Apparently they were using the Great Rift Valley today, judging by the location of the duty flock of gulls, which always glided and drifted over the point of greatest activity in the dump. I myself could never see what attraction it held for them, unless this were a renegade flock who had simply got sick of their diet of fish and were branching out into restaurant refuse and household food peelings. It didn't matter; besides the gulls and the good citizens with their carloads of junk, nothing was moving down there. Gumboots was nowhere in sight, and for all we knew had buried himself in the sand of the crater.

"I don't see nothin'" declared Liddy finally, with an unmistakable tone of impatience. "What we waiting for?"

By way of an answer Tony pushed himself forward into the gap, remembering to duck his head as he passed through. A couple of seconds later his figure dropped rapidly out of sight as he passed over the lip of the escarpment and descended without a pause into the steepest section of our route. The decision had been taken. Liddy followed close behind, leaving Robert and me alone on the high side, the safe side, the legal side of the fence. I shot a quick glance at Robert. His expression was that of a high diver mentally preparing himself for a dive he had never attempted before, and knowing how unlike Robert it was to be so over-cautious, it disturbed me. I needed to break the mood.

"It'll be fine" I asserted, launching myself across his front toward the gap. As I crossed the fence line I could hear him behind me starting to move, but his single word of response came out flat and without confidence.

"Sure."

Over the edge we went, dropping and accelerating toward the perimeter track along which

A DEATH UNDER SAND

Tony and Liddy were already cruising. As we did so the more distant features of the dump—the buildings by the entrance, the oil-recycling shack, the dark blue dumpsters belonging to Gretchyville Waste—fell below our rapidly contracting horizon. By the time we reached the level of the track that horizon consisted of only the nearest hills and ridges.

Robert and I caught up with the others and the four of us wound our way in single file around the track. Before long I knew where Tony was heading; it was a particularly deserted section which had not yet been used for any kind of dumping, and thus would be unlikely to endanger our bikes with half-buried household artifacts. It was a spot we had used as our operations area several times before, and whose topography was well suited to our trail riding needs. Tony soon peeled off from the perimeter track and headed straight for a steep, short incline that ended in a long ridge. He hit the incline at speed and let his momentum carry him all the way to the top, where enough of his speed had washed off for him to be able to drop his feet into the sand and come to a rapid halt.

"OK," he announced, as the rest of us caught up with him. "My turn to lay out the trail."

This came as a surprise to me. Design of our competition course was a job that we neither left to an individual nor took in turns; more often than not it was an impulsive, uncoordinated effort by the group (I would say 'team', except that it would imply the functioning of some kind of collective, organized brain, which in our case would have been a definite overstatement). But it didn't take me long to realize that this was Tony's way of restoring order to the fractured afternoon. Tony was someone for whom it seemed to matter that plans, once made, were followed without deviation, a character trait that I had imagined was restricted to adults. Certainly it was true of my dad, to the point where arguments on the subject between him and my mom had been, for a long time, a regular feature of our home life. Life was at least quieter when he left.

But the same planning disease seemed to have affected Tony Newburg, and I knew from experience that he was more upset than any of us over the interruption in the day's activities. He was not going to be satisfied until we had had our afternoon of BMX racing and quit at the appropriate time, not a minute before. Most kids of our age were nothing if not flexible, but Tony had to have everything in neat packages, with each package planned and executed in the right order at the right time by the right people before the next package was opened.

Without waiting for a response Tony proceeded to mark out the trail over which we would be racing that afternoon, creating turning points with whatever came to hand—rocks, splintered fragments of wood, metal palings—or just by gouging a deep 'X' in the surface with his heel. The course he marked out was unusually extensive, running several hundred yards in a counter-clockwise direction around the periphery of the dump and passing out of familiar territory into a section virtually unknown to us before reversing direction. It provided several opportunities for radical moves, such as getting airborne off the edge of a precipice or descending a particularly steep slope at speed.

When he had laid out the trail to his satisfaction Tony led the rest of us on a guided tour. His course started at the elevated spot where he had proclaimed his role as designer of the day, then ran the length of the ridge before jogging left into a serpentine path that ran in a series of valleys between head-high bluffs. After climbing and descending several dome-like mountains it then followed the line of another ridge, higher than the first, that described a long crescent ending at the perimeter track. Tony stopped at the point where this ridge plunged steeply down to the level of the track and waited for us to catch up to him.

"So now you gotta go down this slope, turn right at the bottom and back to that last mountain" he instructed. I could see exactly where he meant us to go from the marks he had left during his exploratory run. They led in a series of sweeping curves down the steep extremity of the ridge, then turned right in a confusion of tire scrapes and sneaker prints before returning to the track. As I perched on my seat at the very end of the ridge I noticed three things almost simultaneously: first, that the slope was steeper than most of those we were in the habit of tackling; second, that this part of the ridge seemed to have been constructed more recently than the rest of the immediate area, to judge by the color and consistency of the sand; lastly, that Tony's deliberately extended route must have brought us back into a more heavily worked region of the dump, as evidenced by the tortured pattern of caterpillar track marks no further than ten yards from the foot of the slope.

None of these observations gave me cause for alarm. If a slope was too steep and too long to be taken in a straight line without spilling head first over your handlebars at the bottom, you could always serpentine your way down it as Tony had done. On most slopes it meant losing time but keeping your teeth, and this slope was at the high end of the time-losing, teeth-saving category. So far as the construction date of the ridge was concerned, it seemed—at the time, at least—to be of no more than passing interest, and the presence of the earth mover's tracks meant nothing so long as the machine and its driver were nowhere in the neighborhood.

But as I looked more closely at Tony's route I could see that his extravagant path down the slope had kicked up unusually large volumes of sand, both from the sweep of his rear wheel as it had tramped outward at each turn and from the impact of his inside-of-the-turn sneaker as he had dug his foot in while turning. It occurred to me that the sand must be particularly loose or soft on the slope below us.

Tony was still at the head of the line, so was first to launch himself downhill. He tried to follow his original set of tracks but found himself sliding and displacing even more sand than on his first run. I was right; for some reason the sand on the slope was more loosely packed than anything we had encountered so far. Tony somehow floundered his way to the foot of the slope, more in the style of a kid on a scooter than a BMX rider. At the bottom he pushed out a few yards into the perimeter track, turned, stopped and looked back at the marks of his passage.

"Jeez" he exclaimed, his pudgy, freckled face registering astonishment. "Newburg scores low marks for artistic interpretation." In an automatic response the rest of us half-covered our mouths with our hands, so that when we spoke our voices had the quality of a barely adequate ice rink PA system.

"Three point two" I intoned.

"Three point seven" continued Liddy.

"*And* the Italian judge gives two point nine" added Robert triumphantly.

C.W. STIMPSON

"That's got to be a disappointment for Newburg" I concluded in my breathless idiot sports announcer voice. But if Tony was suffering any kind of disappointment, it didn't last.

"Come on down" he called, and as I was at the head of the line it was clear that the command was directed at me. I pushed forward and negotiated the slope with about as much style as a high school teacher's second-best suit. At times my wheels were digging in to the surface a full three inches, and as I reached the bottom I brought with me a minor avalanche of loose sand. After me came Robert, who abandoned the whole notion of pedaling and descended in a straight line, controlling his speed by splaying his feet out and digging both heels deep into the sand.

By now the slope looked like an Olympic giant slalom course after a day's skiing, if you can imagine it as only ten feet high and dirty yellow in color. I couldn't conceive how Liddy could get down it without pitching into one of the jagged trenches made by an earlier rider. As it turned out, Liddy had evidently decided to follow Robert's example and accordingly launched herself over the edge, slipping her butt forward onto the crossbar and dropping her feet to the ground.

Now Lydia Giraldi has a lot of good qualities. Not included in these is the kind of physical self-possession that seems to come naturally to Robert. Liddy was less than a third of the way down the slope when she lost her balance, and trying to recover actually managed to kick the front wheel of her 415 Pro out from under her. It was an untidy tangle of bicycle, kid, and several square feet of sand that continued the downward journey. Half of Liddy was trapped beneath her bike while the other half flailed around, trying to latch onto something that would arrest her progress and succeeding only in displacing even more sand. To the helpful accompaniment of derisive laughter from her good friends, Liddy and all things attached to her arrived together at the foot of the slope.

Liddy's good friends now awaited her reaction, which according to habit should have included equal parts body English and language Italian. In truth, invective was the only kind of Italian that Liddy knew, having learnt it from older brothers and visiting Italian cousins. But having entertained us, Liddy now surprised us. As soon as she had disentangled herself and struggled to her feet she turned and stared back up the slope, a look of genuine wonder on her face.

"Now what the hell was *that*?" she asked of no-one in particular. Still sniggering, I took it upon myself to respond.

"I'd call it a land-based wipeout." Liddy made an impatient gesture.

"No, I mean—there's something there, something hard. I came down on it."

"I think it's called your butt" suggested Robert, which started the three of us off again.

"Shut up, man, I mean it" Liddy retorted, starting back up the slope on foot. "That's why I slipped; there's something hard and smooth under the sand. I came down on it."

By now she was half-way up the ravaged slope, shoveling sand away with her hands.

"There, look! There is something there!" she cried. "See it?"

All at once I could see what Liddy was talking about. Where she had been feverishly scraping with her hands a fragment of smooth, hard material was visible below the surface. I could not yet see enough of it to determine whether it was natural or man-made, but in another few seconds she had scraped away enough sand to enable all of us to see what it was. The early afternoon sunlight reflected directly off the smooth glass panel into our eyes. This was what had caused Liddy to slide all the way to the bottom—a sheet of glass, just a few inches below the surface, which the rest of us had very nearly uncovered with the violence of our own descents. By the time she had demonstrated her own unique slalom style there must have been less than an inch of sand covering the panel.

Liddy continued to scrape away at the sand still covering the panel until she had exposed an area of some two square feet. Suddenly her hand froze in mid-swipe. Briefly she bent close to the glass then raised herself and turned toward us, mouth dangling open in amazement.

"Hey guys" she called, with awe in her voice. "It's a car!"

Every Sunday the Gretchyville Times runs something they call "The Kid's Page" and fills it up with features like *Did You Know?* and *Fun Facts About Our History*. There's always something in the bottom-right corner called *Photo Quiz*, consisting of a photograph of some unidentifiable portion of a familiar object like a mosquito's wing, a printed circuit board or a monkey wrench, usually blown up and turned to some unexpected angle. The caption below the photo would invite you to guess the identity of the object but I rarely had the patience for it, usually skipping ahead a couple of pages to read the answer. Only then would the photograph take on meaning. There would be a moment, suddenly arrived at, when you would understand the context of the mysterious object in the picture: a series of huge rings would become the threads of a machine screw, or a confused mass of rope-like shapes would be recognizable as the frayed end of a length of electrical wiring. So it was with Liddy's find at the moment of her declaration. All at once it was obvious that the glass panel was the tailgate window of a coupe or fastback. Eighteen inches further down, where her scrabbling footsteps had made a particularly deep gouge in the surface, the glint of exposed metal showed us where the chrome of the rear fender was located. It was now as clear to me as if the entire car were free of the sand and visible to our eyes. Somebody had driven the car up to the end of the ridge then deliberately buried it, extending the ridge line as they did so.

Tony, as usual, was a little slower on the uptake.

"I didn't know they let you dump cars here" he said, looking around for other automotive evidence. "I thought they had to go to the auto salvage place on the Cold Harbor Road."

"They *don't* dump cars here" I replied, still staring at the car dumped in front of me. "When have you ever seen cars brought in here?"

"Well..." Tony paused as he began to search his meager memory banks. "There's *that* one" he finished lamely.

Suddenly Robert spoke up.

"Peter's right. They can't dump cars here. Something to do with the oil, and the gas and....stuff.... That thing's not supposed to be here."

To Liddy it was evidently intriguing to be perched on top of this piece of contraband on wheels. Working with both feet she pushed away more sand, revealing a patch of bright red metalwork at the edge of the rear window. Scrambling over to the other side of the glass panel she probed beneath the surface until she located the car's right-hand flank. She seemed to be trying to gauge how deeply the car's body had been buried, and apparently found the answer she was seeking. Suddenly she turned to us.

"Hey guys! Let's dig it out!"

"What you going to do, girl?" asked Robert. "It's a dead car. You going to drive it around town?"

"I don't think it *is* dead. Look—it's not old, it's not rusty" she responded, continuing to sweep off great volumes of sand. "I think this thing's new."

Now we were all intrigued. Laying our BMXes down we drew near to Liddy, who was still digging away furiously. I was sure that she had *not* considered what she would do with her discovery if and when we excavated it, but then neither had I, nor in all probability had Tony or Robert. But that was wholly beside the point. Old or new, the car should not have been there; if, as Liddy thought, it *was* new, then we had quite a mystery on our hands. Why would anyone take a perfectly good car, drive it around to this unloved side of the town landfill, then go to the effort of completely burying it?

It now looked less likely than ever that we would get back to BMX racing today, but somehow that didn't seem important to anyone—even Tony. He and I joined Liddy on the slope, tearing at the surface with our hands and feet, while Robert detoured several yards to pick up a three-foot strip of corrugated iron. Using this in the manner of a snow shovel he succeeded in displacing twice as much material as any of the rest of us could. Before long the rear end and parts of the flanks of the car had been exposed, and since Robert and his improvised shovel were working on the left side of the vehicle, more of that side emerged from its secret grave than the right side.

Soon I jumped down beside Robert to help him scrape the last inch of sand away from the side window. Cupping our hands around our eyes to shield them from the sun's glare we bent forward to within an inch of the glass for our first view of the car's interior. The only light penetrating this space came from the tailgate window, now almost completely uncovered, and from that part of the left rear window not blocked by Robert's body and mine. A few seconds passed before our eyes adjusted to the gloom inside and we were able to make out details. On the rear seat lay a pair of canvas bags, one closed and the other torn open. Strewn around them were the bag's contents: hundreds, perhaps thousands, of dollar bills. From the seat and the floor a host of dead presidents stared up at us, but they were not the only ones. A middle-aged man was also staring fixedly at us from his position between the front passenger seat and the rear half of the car, his chest covered with blood and his eyes dead and sightless.

SUNDAY, 2:20 PM

I could actually hear my heart beating. I could feel my throat tightening, my mouth drying out . I could sense the absolute stillness of my friend as he stood beside me, and knew that it matched my own. Down there, within a few feet of where we stood and separated from us by a single layer of glass, was something neither of us had ever seen before. It was violent death. And although I knew exactly what I was looking at, some part of me refused to believe it. I kept waiting for the man to blink or snort himself awake or give a sudden crazy grin and yell "April Fool!", all the time knowing that he wouldn't, he couldn't, he wasn't going to yell anything ever again. I just kept willing him to do it because nothing in my entire life had prepared me for this reality, and I would have taken the sheer impossibility of a live, sleeping man hiding out in his buried car over this real but lifeless horror before us.

For a timeless moment, then, all that existed in the universe were the thing in the car, me, and the space between us. As an overpowering nausea gripped me, even the awareness of Robert by my side faded, along with the sounds of Liddy and Tony digging away a few feet from me. It was as if the man's face were filling the far end of a tunnel of swimming, swirling light, and I were being forced to stare down the tunnel from the near end. I was conscious of nothing else but his broad, fleshy face, the lank hair falling away from his brow, a mass of dried blood centered around a pair of hideous holes in his chest... and those eyes. The eyes stared out at a point somewhere beyond my right ear, but saw nothing in the sky behind me. They seemed fixed in contemplation of whatever their final view of this world had been—in all probability the person responsible for the stilling of their owner's heart. The far end of the tunnel closed in until it encompassed nothing more than those eyes. The tunnel walls became brighter and more opaque and my ears were filled with a whirring sound, growing in volume all the time and threatening to drown out my wildly beating heart. I couldn't even feel the rest of my body, and wondered abstractedly for a moment whether I was on the verge of fainting.

"Any time you two want to lend a hand would be just fine." It was Liddy's voice, filtering through the sound in my ears and, if not jogging me back to reality, at least nudging me out of the tunnel. One by one the sensations of the here and now returned to me. I backed away from the window and looked around in confusion. Almost immediately my gaze locked with Robert's and I read in his face, with the eyes bulging in his cheeks and his mouth dangling slackly and stupidly open, the same shock that must have been painted all over mine. In that moment he and I shared a terrible secret, but would share it for only a few seconds more. In fixing our eyes on one another each of us was trying to draw strength and resolve from the other, which we would need if we were ever going to be able to live with the meaning of what we had seen.

Our continued state of inaction had not gone unnoticed by Liddy, who tried a second time to get our attention.

"Er—guys" she called. "What's up? Taking a lunch break?"

I broke my eyes away from Robert's and turned toward her. I tried to say something and made a noise that didn't even sound like speech, let alone English. It didn't matter. Looking from my face to Robert's and back again, she immediately understood enough to drop her bantering tone.

"What's the matter?" she asked. "What happened?"

"It's—" I began, but couldn't finish. Robert was completely mute. But Liddy didn't wait for either of us to find our voices; hooking her fingers into the rain gutter above the window, she swung the upper part of her body out and brought her face down until her nose touched the glass, giving herself a perfect, if inverted, view of the car's interior. A moment later she stiffened and gasped.

"Omigod…"

A moment later, Tony cleared enough of the right-hand rear window to afford him a clear view into the motorized tomb. His subsequent shocked cry was loud enough to carry clear across the car to where I was standing. For a few seconds more there was no movement and no other sound from any of us. Then Liddy slowly raised her head, presenting her pale mask of a face to Robert and me with an unanswerable question forming on her lips. But it was Tony who spoke first, calling out in a barely controlled voice possibly the least useful observation he could have made.

"He's dead!"

"Who's dead?"

The four of us snapped around suddenly at the sound of a man's voice coming from behind Tony. Not ten feet away stood Gumboots, a wild look on his face and his hands clenched into fists. He must have heard us excavating the car and had come up on us unseen while our attention was focused on its contents. Now there were five of us rooted to the spot, since Gumboots seemed to have surprised himself almost as much as us by his outburst. I don't know how long we would have remained in that frozen tableau had Robert not energized it with a single bellowed syllable.

"MOVE!"

We moved.

Liddy came down off the roof of the car at speed, landing close to where she had left her bike. Robert and I took off like a pair of dragsters for the perimeter track and our own bikes. As Tony started in the same direction, Gumboots himself came to life and moved after him. What followed looked like a re-enactment of the tortoise and the hare invitational, since Gumboots, at maximum waddle, had zero chance of overtaking a fifteen-year old with afterburners firing. But then, we all know how that fable turned out.

Liddy, being nearest to her BMX, was first away and out of danger. Robert and I, as chance would have it, had left our machines pointing away from the direction of Gumboots' approach and were able to reach them, sweep them into an upright position and carry them along with us with only the briefest delay. But Tony had two strikes against him: not only was his Brawler nearest to Gumboots, it was also pointing in the wrong direction.

From my relatively safe position I watched the debacle unfold. Tony managed to get his bike upright and pointed toward safety, and even took a couple of steps with it, but it wasn't enough. Gumboots' outstretched hand reached just far enough to clamp itself onto his shoulder, and was not to be shaken off. With a desperate effort Tony somehow managed to keep moving, but it was obvious that he was not going anywhere without his wheezing, orange-suited attachment.

"What did you kids do? What did you see?" he cried, his voice barely under control. "You better tell me—right NOW!"

Suddenly it occurred to me that we had little reason to be trying to escape. With the discovery of the dead body our crime of trespass had lost its importance, but we had still reacted as if the worst thing on the day's agenda was a punishment for being where we shouldn't have been. Our escape reaction had been instinctive, and had taken us in an instant from our horror-stricken confrontation with death to an every-man-for-himself descent into flight. I don't know what was going on in the other guys' minds, but I had reacted to Robert's shout automatically, with no other thought but to escape someone who, I already suspected, was not even a threat.

I had just decided to respond to the man's questions when a hunched shape whirred past me in a blur of sound and motion, passing within a couple of inches of my starboard ear. It was Robert, doing that which he did most, if not best—acting from the gut. At the sight of Tony in trouble he had reversed direction and was now accelerating hard toward him. As he passed me, he snapped his air pump out of its holder and brandished it above his head like a helicopter rotor. It was sheer madness, but it was also pure Robert. Was he actually planning on attacking the guy? No, of course not. He hadn't *planned* anything. He had simply and impulsively set himself in motion, and would learn the results of his actions at about the same time as everybody else.

A DEATH UNDER SAND

Those results were not likely to benefit Tony *or* Robert. Gumboots may have been slow, but he was a solidly built adult and could handily take care of a kid of Robert's size. The likeliest outcome, it seemed to me, was that Gumboots would end up with two prisoners instead of one. But even if there had been time to shout a warning I knew that Robert would not have heeded it, so I saved my breath and watched the development of what I was sure would be debacle Part Two.

Robert bore down on the struggling arrangement of man, boy and bicycle with a wild yell. Gumboots saw him coming and took a step back to brace himself for the assault, while maintaining his grip on Tony's shoulder. Disaster in about two seconds, I thought.

And then the miracle happened.

In stepping back to present his profile to the wildly pedaling Robert, Gumboots had positioned himself with the back of his knees almost touching Tony's rear wheel. Suddenly Tony gave another violent wrench, causing Gumboots to take a further backward step. The back of his calves contacted the rear wheel and stopped, while the rest of his lumpy body continued moving just far enough to cause him to overbalance. In an instant he changed from a threatening, oversized adult presence to a toppling pile of orange clothing with waving arms. In falling, he let go of Tony's shoulder with one hand, but threw his other hand out in a futile attempt to restore his balance. As luck would have it the flailing hand came into contact with the rotor blade of the human helicopter known as Robert Juneau, and knocked the air pump clean out of his grip. But it made no difference to where Gumboots was going, and he hit the perimeter track with his back and a one-syllable curse as Robert flashed past him. Tony's bike went down with him, but as Tony had managed to remain standing he was able to retrieve his machine and pull it upright.

To his credit, Robert would never have tried to claim that he had engineered Gumboots' downfall. But only Robert could have been so completely unaware of how lucky he had been not to end up where Gumboots was—lying on his back in the dirty sand with the breath knocked out of him.

Tony wasted no time in mounting up and continuing his flight, and by the time Gumboots was vertical again the two of us were in motion and heading toward the spot where Liddy had thoughtfully placed herself as strategic reserve, a good fifty yards away from the scene of the action. But for Robert, rejoining us was not going to be so simple. His mounted charge had taken him well past Gumboots, who was now squarely positioned between him and our escape route. Robert skidded to a halt some twenty yards beyond the man, while Tony and I caught up with Liddy further down the track in the opposite direction. We all held our positions and watched carefully for Gumboots' next move. True, he was between Robert and the fence, but unless Robert lost complete control of his legs, he was in no danger. It would be relatively simple for him to detour into the heart of the dump and find his way back to the fence unseen. In fact, I wondered why Robert had not already started this maneuver.

But perhaps it wasn't necessary. Gumboots seemed to have lost his aggressiveness, perhaps as a result of his ignominious fall. He stood there looking confused and irresolute, alternating his gaze between Robert, the car, and the rest of us. He seemed to be trying to decide if it was worth the effort to keep chasing us, or perhaps to understand why he had been chasing us in the first place. And finally it all seemed too much for him.

"Ah, the hell with you punks! I don't care what you do—get out of here!" he shouted in disgust, flapping his arms at us in a dismissive gesture as he started for the car.

"Hey mister-" started Liddy. I twisted around in my seat to face her.

"Don't bother, Liddy" I said. "He'll find out soon enough."

Gumboots reached the car and dropped to his knees close to the center of the rear bumper. Immediately he started scraping the sand away with his large coarse hands from the spot where the license plate must have been. Sure enough, within a few seconds the lighter colored metal of the plate began to show through. In fact, I thought I could see two plates, one overlaying the other, but from my angle it was impossible to be sure; in any case, in the next instant my attention was drawn elsewhere. Robert was in motion.

Now, if Gumboots had been faking, or if he now changed his mind about leaving us alone, the worst escape route Robert could have taken would have been the direct one, straight past the scene of his jousting routine and on to join up with us. It would have taken him within a few steps of the man, who could have closed the distance with relative ease and collared him.

Guess which route Robert took.

Fortunately for Robert, Gumboots must have meant it. As my friend sped past him, wisely not pausing to retrieve his pump, the man was engrossed in trying to wrench the license plate off the car. Robert reached us a few seconds later, halted and leaned in to within a foot of Tony's face.

"I think *now* would be a good time to leave, right enough, Tone?"

Without waiting for a response Robert moved off again. Nobody disagreed with him this time around, and we all fell in line behind him as he made his way back around the perimeter track. We were almost out of sight of Gumboots and the car when an anguished scream from behind us brought us all to a skidding, turning halt.

"JIMMY! NO—OH GOD NO!"

A DEATH UNDER SAND

Face pressed close to the window, Gumboots was standing at the spot where Robert and I had stood when we had our first glimpse of the car's interior. It was he who had uttered the high-pitched, despairing scream and who screamed again now, the sound echoing off the face of the nearby scarp.

"JIMMY...OH WHY...JIMMY...OH NO NO NO NOT YOU!"

The man collapsed against the side of the car. From his lips came a sound that seemed to have fought its way up from some point unconnected to his physical body, from some chamber in his soul where all the misery and agony a person can feel are generated. It was neither shout, nor cry, nor scream, for those are sounds we make when we still have some fragment of control over what we do, and understanding of what we are. But at this moment, control and understanding were so far beyond this man that it was difficult even to recognize him as one. It was less a man than a creature, emptying its lungs of all its air and its being of all its pain in a single, awful, incoherent wail. The animal noise poured from the slumping figure, the hollow moan of one who had lost more in an instant than he could recapture in a lifetime, and it flowed toward us over the broken ground as black and as empty as space. I heard Liddy, only a few feet behind me, catch his breath involuntarily while Tony turned his color-drained face toward mine with fear in his eyes. And all I could think was that I would never, as long as I lived, rid my brain of that wild and agonized noise, dredged up from some unthinkably lifeless place.

The remnants of that noise died, finally, in the air, leaving an aching silence that was almost as painful to endure. None of us could stand that silence for more than a few seconds. From behind me I heard Robert's voice, now quite devoid of its former sarcastic tone.

"Come on, you guys."

We hardly needed persuading, and once more four sets of pedals were put into motion. But we were still accelerating when a new noise from behind us brought us to a halt once more. It did not come from Gumboots; in fact, it did not even come from inside the dump. The angry shout had come from the tree line overlooking the perimeter track, directly opposite the position of the car.

"Get out of there! Get out of there, damn it!"

Again we came to a skidding halt, eyes scanning the trees. After several seconds my eyes fell on the figure of a man half-hidden by trees and brush. I could see little of his face; what was not obscured by foliage was hidden under a long-peaked baseball cap and made indistinct by what appeared to be heavy stubble on his cheek and chin. And although the car and Gumboots were now hidden from us by an intervening ridge I could see that he was looking directly down at them. His voice came again, in the same angry tone.

A DEATH UNDER SAND

"What the hell you doing with the car? Get away from it now! NOW!"

The response was immediate. We heard Gumboots bellowing in incoherent fury before he burst into sight, running clumsily across the perimeter track toward the half-concealed newcomer. As he reached a point half-way across the track we saw him suddenly jerk backward as if struck in the chest by an invisible hammer. At the same time the sound of a sharp, explosive report reached our ears, followed in quick succession by two more. At each one the unseen hammer struck Gumboots' upper body, propelling him backward across the track. He stayed upright for a second or two, swaying slightly, then crumpled limply to the ground without a sound and lay still, his arms outstretched and his face upturned to the sky.

SUNDAY, 2:25 PM

Tony, Liddy, Robert and I were like statues. I think I had actually forgotten, temporarily, how to breathe. I certainly wanted to believe that my eyes were lying to my brain, that I had not just witnessed a cold-blooded murder, that the man I had dubbed Gumboots was still alive somewhere in the universe and had not been reduced to this obscenity of unmoving flesh in a town landfill. But what chance did I have? No amount of denial on my part could cancel out the horrors of the last few minutes, and nothing was going to breathe life back into the husk that used to contain Gumboots. Less than ten minutes ago I had seen what death looked like; now I had seen what killing looked like, and I wanted more than anything in the world to be away and out of there and never return.

But before any of us could make a move there was a minor landslide right below where the newcomer had been standing. We saw the boundary fence shaking as he somehow slid underneath it, then he came into view scrambling down the bluff in a small shower of sand. He did not stop at the foot of the bluff but ran the few steps over to the inert body sprawled on the track. In his right hand he carried a heavy-looking handgun, which he aimed at the body as he approached it. For a few seconds he remained standing over the body with the gun pointed directly at Gumboots' chest, then—apparently satisfied with his work—he slipped the weapon under his jacket.

If it had been shock that had paralyzed us a few moments earlier, it was pure fear now. Gumboots' killer had not seen us yet—his path from the fence to his present position was such that we were outside his direct line of vision—but it was clear that if any one of us tried to move or made any kind of sound he would become aware of our presence at once. And would have to deal with the fact that there were four eye-witnesses to his act of murder.

The man was as physically different from Gumboots as could be imagined. He was tall, thin and gangly, and gave the impression of having a lot of energy compressed within his lean body. He was dressed completely in black from his tight-fitting jeans to his T-shirt, biker's jacket and cap. His hair, too—or what we could see of it—was dark; an untidy spray of it was escaping from under all sides of his hat, and the thick stubble on his cheeks and chin seemed to merge with his straggling mustache. He appeared to be wearing dark cowboy boots, now so coated with sand from his descent into the dump that I could not make out their color with any certainty. And in contrast to what we had seen of Gumboots' behavior, he seemed to move with self-assurance and cold deliberation. Certainly he had not hesitated to take the other man's life, and nothing in his subsequent actions suggested panic or remorse.

He raised his eyes from the dead body to the car, and had moved a couple of steps toward it when he suddenly jerked around. I saw Tony give an involuntary spasm of movement, and felt my own hands tightening on my handlebars, but it was not toward us that the man had snapped his head. He was looking intently at the ground in the middle of the track, and at something that had caught his eye there. Slowly he retraced his steps, then bent down and picked up the object.

It was Robert's pump.

The man inspected his find closely and unhurriedly, holding the shiny metal cylinder in his right hand, then brought the other end down into his left hand and held the pump like a cop wielding his nightstick. Then he began to inspect the ground around him. I could imagine what he was discovering, and what conclusions he was drawing: the area where he was standing was covered with our sneaker marks and bicycle tracks. He was putting two and two together, and any moment now would get the right answer.

Slowly the black-clad man raised his head to stare down the perimeter track, but in the direction away from us. For a long moment he was perfectly still, as were we, as was Gumboots, as were the seagulls and even the clouds in the sky, or so it seemed to me. I had the most extraordinary feeling that I was in a video that someone had frozen on the screen with the 'pause' button. The moment seemed to go on forever.

Without warning, then, the man snapped around and in a split second took in our presence; throwing the pump aside, he reached into his jacket. That was all the impetus we needed. Four of us moved off with an acceleration we had never before achieved. No shout came from behind, but within a couple of seconds came something far worse.

He was shooting.

I only heard the first shot. When the second one came, I actually heard the sound of the bullet passing my head as well as the shot itself. I wondered, in a spasm of fear, whether the third would be the one I would feel.

"He's shooting at us!" Tony, his mind as sharp as lasagna, filled us in on events in case we had missed anything. The rest of us were too busy grunting with effort and willing our BMXes into hyperdrive to respond.

When several seconds passed without another shot I took a quick, desperate glance over my shoulder and was surprised to see that the man was nowhere in sight, hidden from us by a ridge on the inside edge of the track. When he had first seen us we were more than a hundred yards away, and the range together with our erratic movements must have kept us alive until we could take advantage of the niceties of dump design. We continued pedaling hard around the track until our exit from the dump came into view.

"Don't stop!" gasped Liddy to Robert, to whom the notion had almost certainly not occurred. Snapping our machines into lower gear we headed obliquely up the scarp toward the hole in the fence, with Robert leading, followed by Liddy, me and Tony. I saw Robert's and Liddy's heads bob down as they passed through the fence, then they were safely into the woods. As soon as I had passed through I stopped and pulled off to one side, then looked back quickly in the direction we had come.

"What are you stopping for?" asked Tony in a breathless, panicked voice as he passed abreast of me.

"Nothing" I responded quickly. "Keep going. I'll follow you."

Tony passed me and continued up the path while I scanned the part of the dump we had just left for signs of movement. There was nothing to be seen on the track, nor was there any movement from the active side of the dump to suggest that someone was coming to investigate the shooting. What noise had not been deadened by the sand had probably been drowned out by the activities of the bulldozer and all the vehicles making their contributions to the landfill.

I didn't stay more than a few seconds before starting up the path in Tony's wake. I caught up with the others by the time they reached Birch, which we descended at speed in a tightly spaced single file. In contrast with our earlier transit, we steered a straight course down the hill; no-one was in a mood now to zigzag, play stupid games or even talk. We came out into Overlook and turned, as usual, in the direction of town, but had not traveled more than two hundred yards when Tony suddenly pulled off into an undeveloped lot, scrabbled to a stop and stumbled off his Brawler toward the trees. For a wild moment I wondered if he had, after all, been hit by a bullet and was reacting as slowly to it as he did to most things. I called urgently to Robert and Liddy, then stopped and followed Tony into the lot. By the time the others had reversed their course and reunited with us, however, I knew what the problem really was.

Tony was hanging tightly with both hands onto the trunk of a scrubby pine tree and leaning into it with one shoulder. His back was to me, but I did not need to see his face to understand what was happening. I could see his shoulders jerking spasmodically, and very soon he vomited copiously into the weeds. For almost a full minute Tony emptied himself, and even when his stomach had given up all its contents his body continued to heave and retch painfully. I was impatient to put more distance between us and the dump and kept shooting nervous looks back towards it in case we had been followed. I knew, however, that I could not hurry Tony in his present condition. Finally he straightened up, turned and leaned his back against the tree, then slid down it onto the ground. Robert, Liddy and I gathered in a loose semi-circle facing him.

"You OK now, Tone?" Robert asked, with genuine concern in his voice, but received no reply.

Looking closely at Tony's slumped figure, I knew what was happening. My Uncle Cameron is a flight attendant with Appalachian Airways, and whenever he comes to visit loves to gross me out with stories of his first aid training. What he told me one time came back to me now as I watched what my friend was going through. Having distributed his guts on the ground Tony now sat on it, his elbows on his knees and his head cradled in his hands. Through his outspread fingers I could see the unnatural pallor of his face; it reminded me of the color of my mom's white tablecloth after I'd put it in the wash with my jeans. From every part of his face, from under his hairline, from his neck and from the exposed skin of his arms the sweat poured freely. But just as it was not the heat that was making him perspire, neither was it cold that made his entire body shiver so violently that he could barely keep his elbows from slipping off his kneecaps. Uncle Cameron had described the effects of shock on a person so vividly that I could be in no doubt about Tony's condition.

A second nugget of grossness that Uncle Cam had treated me to concerned hurling, or, in his favored terminology, bugling. He told me once that it could be contagious, that once one passenger in an airliner started playing tunes in his airsickness bag it tended to spread, often to passengers who wouldn't otherwise have had a problem. I guess he knew what he was talking about, since Liddy now proceeded to give us a demonstration. With no preamble she pushed between Tony and me en route to her hurling tree of choice. Her display could not match Tony's in length, but scored higher on bulk and sound effects. When she was drained she too collapsed against his tree, her symptoms mirroring Tony's.

One look at Robert's mystified face told me that he did not understand what was happening.

"They're in shock" I said simply, wondering when—or if—our turn would come. Robert did not look as if he were about to go tree-christening, and despite everything my own lunch felt fairly secure in my belly.

"What do you mean—'shock'?" asked Robert. I spread my hands in a helpless gesture.

"It's...I don't know, it's—like—a nervous condition. When something really bad happens it might not affect you right away, but when you've had time to think about it you suddenly get an attack of the shakes and throw up and sweat like a pig, and all kinds of other stuff. Like these guys."

Robert's face became solemn.

"When something really bad happens" he repeated.

I knew what Robert meant. To this point, what had happened to us today was about as bad as anything I could imagine. Our initial scare in the crater was as nothing compared to what followed: we had seen the remains of some mysterious crime and the awful reality of sudden death; we had had our close encounter with Gumboots and endured his outpouring of misery; we had seen murder done before our eyes and finally had been, briefly and terrifyingly, the targets of a killer. Any one of those might have been a bad enough 'something' to put a person into shock, but we had had no time to react properly to any of them. They had come so fast upon each other that the only reaction we had been allowed was flight. And now it was all catching up to us—or to Tony and Liddy, at least. Robert and I still showed no sign of succumbing to that condition, and perhaps we wouldn't. But I was beginning to get the feeling that there was a time-bomb ticking away somewhere inside me. I needed movement and activity to keep my mind on the present, not on the immediate past.

"Come on, guys. Snap out of it" I said crisply. "We've got to keep moving. He might still be following us."

Liddy, who was holding herself tightly by the arms in an attempt to control her shivering, spoke up in a thin, breathless voice.

"He...he tried to kill us."

"I know, Liddy, and he might try again."

I had no idea whether the killer had even left the dump, of course, but I needed to get our two trembling Tarzans up and moving quickly, if only for my own sake. The last thing I wanted right now was to join them, incapacitated, among the weeds. I made a silent, gestured appeal to Robert, who quickly retrieved Liddy's and Tony's BMXes and wheeled them over.

"Peter's right, guys. I know you're feeling like hell, but at least you're alive. Let's not give him another chance at us."

Tony shook his head, looking miserable.

"Can't move" he moaned. I could not help feeling sympathetic. Whenever I've lost a load the last thing I want to do is move around, much less get on a bike and pedal through town. But Robert was insistent. He thrust Tony's machine at him.

"Look man, you've got nothing left to throw up" he shouted, suddenly brutal. "Just get on and ride. It'll make you feel better."

Wherever Dr. Robert picked up that dubious piece of medical advice it seemed to work, or maybe it finally got through to Tony that the killer really could have followed us this far. With a good deal of groaning and other vocal suffering he dragged himself to his feet, took possession of his 415 Pro and started to wheel it back out to the road. Robert and I followed, and Liddy, evidently fearful of being left behind, stumbled upright and pulled herself along in the rear.

We started off again, but it soon became clear that Liddy and Tony were barely up to the task. I dropped back to ride alongside Tony and called ahead to Robert. Robert turned in his seat and took in the situation at once. He slowed until Liddy came level with him, and thus we continued toward town, in two pairs and with agonizing slowness. I stole a glance from time to time at Tony. He was not sweating so badly now, although his face was still pale and he still shivered spasmodically.

Overlook Road comes to an end, eventually, at Seminole, where a left turn will take you all the way to the Old Kingsleytown Road. When you get there, turn right and it's a straight shot into town. We took the turn, but within a hundred yards Robert pulled to the side of the road, signaling for the rest of us to stop. We convened in a tight group, handlebars touching.

"OK, so what are we doing?" asked Robert of no-one in particular. I didn't understand the question and waited for someone else to respond, but Liddy and Tony still seemed to be preoccupied with creating new and unusual skin tones on their faces. Getting no response to his question, Robert tried again.

"What are we gonna do, guys? We gonna go home and watch MTV? We gonna tell our folks about this over dinner? Or are we going to the cops?" There was a moment of silence.

"Hell, we have to go to the cops; we have no choice" I said, finally.

Tony was staring hard at the ground. He cleared his throat.

"Couldn't we just... couldn't we just forget about it?" he asked.

"How the hell can we do that, Tony? We just saw someone murdered. There's two dead men back there" I retorted, gesturing vaguely in the direction we had come. There was another silence. When Tony responded it was in a smaller, more hesitant voice than I had ever heard him use.

"We gonna bring 'em back?"

This, then, was Tony's way of dealing with the situation. He had had his fill of horror and wanted no more. He wanted to go home now, go to school tomorrow, go to Little League next Saturday. He just wanted to go on living the life he'd been living up until an hour ago as if, by doing that, he could somehow turn the events of the last hour into fiction; as if he could undo history by looking the other way. And perhaps, so far as he was concerned, he could. Perhaps he could think it all away so completely that he could make himself believe the new reality he had created. If someone asked him about it in a few years' time he might be able to respond in genuine, honest-to-God ignorance of it. But even if he could create a new history for himself, it would be for himself only. Unless all four of us bought into a conspiracy of silence and personal denial, there would always be at least one of us who could not look the others in the eye and live their lies. And even if we could, there would be a reality outside of the one we were creating, in which two men had been murdered and an armed killer was at large in the town where we lived. It wasn't like that old garbage about a tree falling in the forest and not making a sound unless someone actually heard it. Whether we had heard it or not, whether we wanted to admit it, deny it, remember it or forget it in years to come, it had happened. And that was why I could not share Tony's way of dealing with it.

"Of course we're not going to bring them back, Tony" I said at length. "But that guy in black is still out there. You want him to come looking for you? You want him to get away with murder?"

Tony shifted uncomfortably, still concentrating hard on a spot two feet ahead of his front wheel.

"I don't—" he started, but couldn't quite bring himself to finish with the word 'care'.

"We don't even know who that guy was, who he shot" he blurted out.

"Don't matter who he *was*" rejoined Robert. "He *was* alive. Now he's not. You know that much, right enough?"

Tony was evidently beginning to feel under siege. He started looking rapidly from face to face, as if seeking support. It must have been clear to him already where Robert and I stood; only Liddy had not yet ventured his opinion.

"Liddy-?"

Liddy looked nervously from face to face. The defiant air that had governed her behavior in the dump and on Birch Road was utterly missing, beaten out of her, I guessed, by the violence of the last ten or fifteen minutes.

"If we tell the cops they'll know we were in the dump, where we weren't supposed to be!"

I was so taken aback I think my jaw actually dropped. I struggled to find a response.

"Liddy... Liddy—think about what you're saying. What's the worst that can happen to us? We get told to play somewhere else? We get a lecture from the desk sergeant? You think the cops aren't going to want to know about a double murder and a car full of money?"

Liddy was obviously feeling on the defensive herself now. Her face took on a stubborn look.

"Yeah, and they're probably gonna come and close the hole in the fence up. What are you gonna say then?"

It was Robert who answered her, in a voice so quiet and unemotional that it took me a few seconds to realize the full import of what he was saying.

"It's not like we're ever going back there again, is it, Liddy?"

Of course he was right. Whether they came and repaired the hole in the fence or not, we would not be coming back to the dump—ever. How could we? Even if the killer were caught and put away, could we really come back here as if nothing had happened? Could we do wheelies over the spot where Gumboots' life had flickered out? Or race along the ridge where someone had tried to bury a car and a capital crime? With that one remark Robert had pointed out what should have been obvious to us all in the first place. It was the end. It was over. As far as the dump was concerned, we were history. No more could it be our private playground on a Sunday afternoon. From now on, if we even stuck together as a group, we would be reduced to making a nuisance of ourselves on the town green, or fooling around in the skatepark, or just sitting and staring at each other. Something special to us had died today, even before Gumboots had. And it had no better chance of being resurrected than he did.

A DEATH UNDER SAND

SUNDAY, 3:05 PM

Robert and I leaned our machines against the railings flanking the front steps of the Gretchyville Police Headquarters and climbed the steps to the entrance. Just him and me; no Tony, no Liddy. In the end we could not convince them that they should come with us to the police; in the end they accepted that it was the right course, but they simply wanted to rid themselves of the business; and in the end, as they turned off onto Plover Road toward the part of town where they both lived, leaving Robert and me to continue on alone, a fragment of the fragile unity that had existed in our group went with them.

If I really thought about it, it was Robert's attitude that was most surprising. His family's relationships with the Gretchyville Police were, at the very least, strained. His father had done some dumb—and certainly not legal—stuff with cars in the past, and I know there was some kind of connection between him and the auto salvage place on St. Patrick's Road that turned out to be a chop shop. But the police had a habit of paying a visit to Robert's apartment whenever there was any criminal activity in town to do with cars. Robert's dad could be out of town and a hundred miles away and they would still make the call. It was like a checklist item they had to perform before getting down to the real investigation: call in on Freddy Juneau, see if we can pin it on him first. In fact, my friend's father was out of town more often than not, and neither Robert nor his mother seemed to know when he would next turn up. But so far as the unwarranted visits were concerned, they had helped to create in Robert an attitude of resistance to—or lack of respect for—authority, directed principally but not exclusively at the police. And since Robert was honest (or perhaps foolish) enough never to mask his true feelings with fake courtesy, our town's finest soon categorized him in the same way as they did his father, i.e., if he weren't in trouble it wasn't because he hadn't done anything but simply because he hadn't yet been caught.

Yet in no part of the discussion with Tony and Liddy about the action we should now be taking, nor at any time since, had Robert made a single disparaging remark about the police. I had to admire him for being able to put distance between his feelings about the Gretchyville Police and his recognition of them as the only body to whom we could report all that had happened today. And he was never in any doubt that what had happened *did* have to be reported. As we passed through the main entrance of police headquarters our eyes met briefly.

"Ready for this?" he asked.

"Ready or not..." I replied.

A DEATH UNDER SAND

Within the next thirty minutes we told our story three times: first, in abbreviated fashion to the desk sergeant, then to a detective in extremely plain clothes, and finally to another detective and Chief Bonaventura himself. Robert and I sat side by side in the Chief's office telling our story, occasionally interrupting and correcting each other and filling in the blanks in the other's memory until it was all told. But not quite all. Tony and Liddy had made us promise that we would not mention their presence in the dump. As far as the police and the world were to be concerned it was just Robert and I up on Silver Hill that day seeing murder committed. I was a little uneasy about starting off our story with a lie but we had promised, and I was doing my best to keep that promise.

I recognized Chief Bonaventura, both from newspaper photos and from seeing him marching at the head of Gretchyville's Fourth of July parade every year. He was a large man, but not fat. I know a lot of late middle-aged men of that weight who have stacked it all in the same place—around the belt line—but the Chief's weight seemed to be distributed evenly throughout his body. He was tall, with muscular arms, a broad chest and large, expressive hands. 'Big-boned', my mom would have said. His size gave him a natural yet controlled air of authority, which he would have carried even without the dark blue uniform, its glinting buttons and yards of braid. He was quite bald, but had a head so well shaped I couldn't help thinking that a covering of hair would have detracted from his impressive appearance.

The Chief sat on the far side of a large, pale green metal desk, leaning forward with his forearms flat on the desk and listening intently. He held a ball-point pen lightly between the fingers of both hands, occasionally operating the plunger to push the point in and out of its housing. He said little, but regarded each of us in turn through his rimless aviator glasses. He would fix his large brown eyes on my face whether I was speaking or not, locking eyes with me for what seemed like an eternity, then, without moving his head, would give Robert the same treatment. It was as if he were trying to decide whether we were telling the truth not from what we said but from what was in our eyes. The detective, who was wearing even plainer clothes than the first one and was therefore presumably senior to him, asked most of the questions. He stood to one side of the Chief's desk, closer to Robert than to me, and seemed to spend most of the time watching Robert closely. He was a lot younger than the Chief, of medium height and slightly built. There was a nervousness about him, an attitude of not wanting to linger on any one subject for long before moving on to the next, that made me uncomfortable. I had the feeling that if I didn't answer one question completely before he jumped on to the next that I was somehow losing points.

"Now tell me again about this money" he was asking. "You say it was in bags?"

"Kind of," Robert answered. "Like... there was one bag full of something, and the other one was split open and the money had spilled out all over the place."

"And what was in the other bag? Was that full of money too?" Robert and I exchanged glances.

"We don't know," I said. "It was closed up tight. But it was the same kind of bag as the open one, so I guess it had money in it."

"What kind of bags were they? What were they made of?" I mentally scratched my head. Robert really did scratch his.

"Cloth, I think."

"Canvas, maybe."

"What color?" Again Robert and I looked at each other for support.

"Dunno."

"It was kind of dark in the car."

"I think maybe brown, or..."

"...or maybe dark red."

"Any writing on the bags?"

"Writing?" The detective became impatient.

"Printing. Any words printed on the outside?"

Once again I tried to visualize as accurately as I could the inside of that car, and once again found myself staring not at the bags but into a pair of dead eyes. The detective drew breath to ask another question. Guess we lost points on that one.

"Are you sure it was a lot of money? Are you sure it wasn't just a dollar or two lying around?" We started to protest, but the Chief raised his hand to calm us down.

"It's all right, boys. It's sometimes tough to remember all the details."

He leaned even further forward in his chair, his dark-complexioned face moving into a patch of bright sunlight.

"Now, what about this last man—the one that did the shooting—can you remember what he looked like?"

Between us, Robert and I tried to come up with a description of Gumboots' killer. We told them about his clothes, about the kind of hat he was wearing, about how skinny he looked, and about the fact that he was unshaven. But the more questions they asked the more obvious it became that we could never, with complete certainty, identify this man. He had been too far off, and what parts of his face had not been obscured by his hat were hidden behind his heavy stubble. We did not know the color of his eyes, had not seen any distinguishing features or scars, and might have difficulty picking him out of a line-up unless all the other members of it were 250-lb. pregnant women.

Finally the questioning came to an end. Chief Bonaventura leaned back in his chair and addressed the detective.

"In the circumstances, Henry, I think it's worth taking a trip to check this out. The car matches—maybe—and if the money's there, we've really lucked out." He turned back to us.

"That reminds me—did you notice if the money was stained a funny color?" Already puzzled by the Chief's previous remark, I was completely taken aback by the question.

"What kind of color?"

"Kind of dark...maybe purple or maroon."

"I don't think so...but like I said, it was dark in the car. There wasn't much light getting in." The Chief nodded slowly, then focused his attention on a spot in the middle of his blotter. After a while he turned back to the detective and spoke more assertively than he had done up to that point.

"Let's have four uniforms, Henry, and bring Jacobson along for the experience. Have Sergeant Camillo coordinate with State and have them meet us there. Have someone tell Joe Woods at Public Works what we're doing. And make sure Forensic is ready to roll if we need them." Henry rolled his eyes.

"If it turns out to be a big game, Chief—"

"I know, I know" the older man replied, returning his eyes to us. "There's a risk. It's not a game, is it boys?"

It was obvious what he was asking. He wanted to know if we had made the whole story up and were pulling a hoax on the Gretchyville Police Department.

"I swear-"

"Just as we told you." The Chief looked from Robert to me and back again.

"All right, boys. We'll take a look. I want you to go with Detective Sergeant Raleigh here and show him exactly where this all happened. I'll be coming too, and so will several of my officers. I want you to do exactly what Sergeant Raleigh tells you, OK?"

We nodded, and the two men conferred privately again. I looked at Robert, trying to gauge his reaction; his expression, part excitement and part apprehension, as much as said to me "too late to back out now!"

I could not claim to be surprised that the police had not believed us unquestioningly; I would almost certainly have been suspicious in their position. But I was gratified that at no time since we had entered the building had anyone pointed out to us that we were trespassing in the dump, were really very bad children and should find somewhere more suitable to play. At least the cops had their priorities in order, even if Liddy didn't.

Within ten minutes a parade of cars had formed up in the front parking lot, including the Chief's official vehicle and three cruisers, with an unmarked sedan in the middle of the pack. Someone had pulled our bikes into the building and left them beneath a long coat rack opposite the front desk. Finally, Raleigh came back up the steps, stepped inside and announced that they were ready to roll. The Chief put one hand on Robert's shoulder and the other on mine. His touch was gentle and his voice reassuring.

"All right, boys, let's see what this is all about, shall we?" I led the way through the front entrance, but as Robert followed me the detective stopped him with a hand on his shoulder that had none of the gentleness of the Chief's.

"Juneau, is it? Robert Juneau? Is your father Frederick Juneau?" My heart sank as I watched Robert's face harden. Why did the cop have to do that? Why couldn't they just leave well enough alone? What difference did it make, who his father was?

"What's the matter, Henry?" asked the Chief. With his hand still on Robert's shoulder, Raleigh looked up at his boss and spoke in a disparaging tone.

"I thought so. Freddy Juneau's kid."

SUNDAY, 3:50 PM

The parade of police cars cut through the clutter of Gretchyville's Sunday afternoon traffic with barely a pause. With lights flashing from the roof of every car we must have looked like the escort for a presidential visit. Cars ahead of us slid off toward the side well before we reached them, pedestrians fled to the curb and gaped—perhaps wondering about the identity of the master criminal being transported to prison—and even backed-up intersections served to slow us down only temporarily. The lead cruiser would sidle down the line of waiting cars, straddling the road's center line, then with a sudden blast of its siren would nose out into the crossing traffic until it halted; the parade would then sweep grandly through the intersection and continue its progress, leaving awed drivers stranded in mid-maneuver and mid-intersection. It was a high-octane experience, or would have been but for two sobering considerations.

Firstly, the Gretchyville police had shown themselves in their true colors with the reference to Robert's dad; it meant that they would now be looking for reasons to implicate him in whatever crime they uncovered, and at the very least would be less likely to believe anything told them by his son. And while neither of these considerations were likely to prove harmful—Mr. Juneau was, as it happened, on another of his extended absences from home, and it would be difficult for the police to disbelieve Robert when confronted with the back half of a car sticking out of the sand just as we had described it—it still left a bad taste in the mouth to know that my friend was already being considered a second-class citizen.

Secondly, it soon became obvious to Robert and me that the car in which we were traveling was the center of attention in this illuminated convoy. Its identity as the only civilian car in the line and its position at the mid-point gave it some sort of bogus celebrity status. After less than half a mile we found ourselves hunkering down in the back seat to minimize the risk of being recognized by anyone who knew us by sight. Knowing how the grapevine operated at Gretchyville Junior High, we would be likely to walk in on Monday morning to questions about how high our bail had been set.

The reason the Old Kingsleytown Road is called the Old Kingsleytown Road is not because it leads to a place called Old Kingsleytown. It's called the Old Kingsleytown Road because it used to lead to a place called Kingsleytown, and now it doesn't. The reason it doesn't is because they built the dump clear across it. Maybe no-one wanted to go to Kingsleytown any more, or maybe no-one from Kingsleytown wanted to come to Gretchyville. I couldn't blame them. Of course, it could have had something to do with the new highway making it easier to get from one town to the other. Whatever, Old Kingsleytown Road now ends abruptly at the boundary of the dump. A few hundred yards before that the Gretchyville Police Express turned off onto Valley Drive, skirted the southern edge of the dump and came out onto Silver Hill Avenue. Figures that the best-sounding road in town would lead past the gates of the town dump. We came up the hill, turned onto the approach road and slowed down to pass through the main gates. The shambling wonder who presided over the entrance, granting or forbidding access to his domain at whim, watched in amazement as the massed motorized strength of local law enforcement drew up in a cloud of dust at his tollbooth-like 'office'. The lead driver spent about three seconds filling him in, then began to accelerate again. As we passed his seat of authority one by one, he generously waved us all in. Like he had anything to say about it at this point.

As soon as our car gained some running room Raleigh gestured to the driver—Jacobson, the detective who had first interviewed us—to overtake the lead car. While he was performing this maneuver, Raleigh turned to us.

"OK, kids. Tell us where you say you saw this car." Where we *say* we saw it. It had started already.

"It doesn't matter which way around you go" I said. "Left is probably quicker."

Jacobson grunted, turned left off the leveled access track and picked his way over some rough ground until he found the perimeter track. Then he turned right and drove cautiously around the circumference of the dump.

"You boys tell us when you recognize something" he called back. For the moment, the landscape was unfamiliar to us; we had not yet left the more heavily trafficked sector of the dump, which we habitually avoided. It was some time before I began to recognize landmarks but when I did, I leaned forward to tell Jacobson that I thought we were getting close. Raleigh immediately signaled for the cruiser following us to switch positions with us again; they were taking no chances on the killer still being in the area and gunning for the two thirteen-year olds with them. The cruiser bounced its way past us and took up the lead again. Soon afterwards I saw some of the 'dozer tracks that I had first seen while perched on the top of the berm where the car had been buried.

"I think we're there" I called. The driver flashed his headlights several times and the cruiser ahead of us came to a halt, followed by the rest of the column. For the next minute doors opened and closed all the way down the line. Armed and uniformed men emerged and moved past us to the head of the line. Only when this protective screen had been thrown out well ahead of us did Raleigh and Jacobson let us out of the car.

"OK now, follow the line of officers and show us where this car is" instructed Raleigh. If they're walking in front of us, I thought, they won't need us to point it out, but all I said was "OK".

Robert and I closed up on the police screen with the two plain-clothes men in our rear, and the whole arrangement moved off as a single unit. Again it occurred to me that the precautions being taken by the police were somewhat redundant. It hardly seemed likely that the killer would be waiting around for the police to stroll up and arrest him, but if all they were doing was playing safe with our lives it was difficult to fault them.

Suddenly I recognized the area in the tree line where the killer had stood to do his shooting, and pointed at the spot.

"That's where he was—up there! He fired right across the track, so the car and the body are just around this next ridge." The police line continued to move forward, but almost immediately I felt Raleigh's hand on my shoulder.

"Just wait here" he said quietly to both of us. Robert, the two detectives and I stood together while the line moved cautiously on and around the next bend. Soon I could only see the two outermost men on the line, but it was evident that the entire line had come to a halt. The officers we could see should have been staring at the spot on the ground where Gumboots had fallen or the place at the ridge's end where the car was sitting. Instead, they

94

were alternately looking ahead into the middle distance and back toward us. Finally, one of them signaled for us to join them.

"Something's wrong. Isn't this the place?" asked Robert.

"Sure it is. They must be able to see it," I replied, but feeling less certain than I sounded. The four of us moved up to join the advance guard, from which position we had a clear view down the next couple of hundred yards of perimeter track. And nowhere in that space, which had been the scene of so much activity that afternoon, could we see anything resembling either a car or a dead body.

I looked wildly around, checking and rechecking my bearings. There was no doubt about it—this was where it had happened. I could see the bush that had helped to obscure the killer from us and the torn section of fence under which he must have slid to enter the dump. I could even make out the scars in the bluff caused by his rapid descent. But where Gumboots had been lying there was nothing, not even a patch of blood; where the car had stood the sand was scattered around in great heaps, but there was not so much as a hubcap to be seen there.

"Damn..." I heard Robert's frustrated oath and turned my head to look at him. As I did, I caught sight of one of the cops staring hard at us. There was no mistaking the attitude in that look; so far as he was concerned, this had all been a waste of time, a stupid trick being played on the police by two troublesome kids with nothing better to do than invent crime stories. I looked from face to face and read the same message in each one. Even the Chief's formerly sympathetic manner had taken on a hard edge.

"What happened to the car, boys?" he asked, in a tone that suggested we had just one chance to come up with a satisfactory answer. I walked over to where the crescent-shaped ridge came to an end and cast around on the ground for evidence. There was the strip of corrugated iron that Robert had used as a shovel and over on the track, further around, were the remains of BMX tire marks. But what use were they? There was nothing—absolutely nothing—to suggest that our story about buried cars and murdered men had any foundation in truth. I turned back to the ridge and inspected more closely the spot where I knew the car had been. It looked as if a giant hand had descended on the ridge, squashed it and scattered the sand roughly around the whole area. As I stared hopelessly at the mess I heard Robert come up close behind me.

"He drove it away, man. Or someone did." I looked at my friend in astonishment.

"How could he have? How long do you think it would have taken him to dig the whole car out?"

"Maybe he didn't have to dig the whole thing out."

A DEATH UNDER SAND

"Don't be a jerk! He would have had to have dug his way to the driver's door, at least. We'd only dug out the back section; how long would it take him to do the rest, all on his own?" Even before I'd finished, Robert was shaking his head emphatically.

"Think about it, man. It was a hoosiewhatsits—a coupe or a hatchback, whatever they call them. We'd already gotten the tailgate clear; if he had the keys he could've got in through there, crawled forward and started it up. Then he just backed it out and drove off."

My mind was reeling with the improbabilities in Robert's theory. Could the killer have got the car to start, still partially entombed? And could he have freed it by simply putting it into reverse, with all that weight of sand still on it? If he did, that would certainly explain the volume of sand thrown around the immediate area. There was just one problem with the theory, as I pointed out to him.

"So where are the tire marks, Robert?" We both searched the ground again. From where we stood we could clearly see our BMX marks further down the track, but nothing to suggest that a car with a full set of tires had ever been in this part of the dump. As I raised my eyes from the ground I found myself staring into the eyes of the Chief. He was waiting for his answer, and the desperation in our eyes must have been plain to see.

"This is where it was, Chief, honest!" we both tried to say at once.

"It was buried right here, where we're standing."

"Up to the height of this ridge thing."

"We half-uncovered it, you see—"

"—And we think he got in through the back."

"Started it up and just backed it out of here."

"Yeah, look at all the sand thrown around. He must've done that as he came out."

"And where do you suppose he went?" asked the Chief. Again we cast about desperately.

"Well...maybe he hid it somewhere else" I ventured.

"Or maybe he just drove out through the main gate, like everyone else does" put in Robert.

"We could check on that" said Raleigh. "Although there's not much to go on; just the color and maybe the type—coupe or fastback or something."

Chief Bonaventura already had his hand up, silencing Raleigh.

"There's only one thing wrong with all of that, boys. I see no tire tracks, neither coming in nor going out. Now, my car made tracks as we were driving in here. Even your bicycles made tracks; I can see them further up, so I know you were here. But there's not a mark on the ground to show there was ever a car here. Am I right?"

Robert and I were running out of answers. There was nothing in what the Chief had said that we could dispute. The surface between where we were standing and the far side of the perimeter track was, except for our footprints, as smooth as if it had been wiped down with a monster dishcloth. I was still trying to come up with a revised theory when the Chief spoke again.

"Now, where did you say this other fellow was shot?"

We walked the few steps out to the middle of the track and tried to position ourselves on a direct line between where we thought the shots had come from and where the car had been. We both shuffled about a bit in an attempt to gauge the exact spot, but what did it matter? There was nothing there—no scuffmarks, no blood, no Gumboots. He had taken a hike, along with the car. For all we knew he had come back to life, jumped through the roof into the driver's seat, pointed the car straight down and was by now well on his way to Australia. I looked back at the Chief, raised my hands and let them fall in a gesture of hopelessness.

"We're not lying to you, Chief. Every word we said is true." The Chief did not respond immediately. He seemed to be deep in thought, his hands clasped behind his back, his eyes directed at the ground at his feet, and his head bobbing up and down in little nodding movements. Perhaps he was trying to determine just how bad to make it for the two of us, now that we had brought him and a sizable portion of his force all the way out here for nothing. He looked again at the scattered remains of the berm, then cast his eyes up and down the track before refixing them on us.

"Maybe you are telling the truth, boys. But there's nothing here for us to go on, is there?" I was trying to think of something to say when he raised his voice and addressed the uniformed officers, who were all now beginning to regard us with looks of disgust.

"You fellows take a few minutes and search a few hundreds yards more of this track," he instructed. "See if you can find anything to make all this worthwhile." Without any great show of enthusiasm the uniformed cops obeyed their Chief, continuing around the track in the direction of the gap in the fence. The Chief turned to Raleigh and Jacobson.

"Henry, why don't you go do what you suggested before? See if anyone over on the other side saw the car leave." The two detectives departed, glad, I think, not to have to be around us any more. That left us, the Chief, and what was getting to be an unbearable silence. Finally, rather than put up with it I nudged Robert and suggested we take a look at the other side of the ridge. In fact, we climbed several of the ridges and hills, and poked around behind each of them in what proved to be a futile search for any kind of clue. We were still at it when the patrolmen came back from their equally futile search, shaking their heads resignedly at their Chief. At about the same time two more cars pulled up from the other direction, one from the Sanitation Department and the other a State Police cruiser. From each car two men in civilian clothes emerged. The Chief went into a brief conference with the new arrivals, punctuated with further episodes of head-shaking, then turned and called to us up on the ridge.

"Come on down now, boys." Of all the cops there, I had the impression that he most wanted to give us the benefit of the doubt, but at this point there was precious little benefit to give. He was waiting for us as we descended the ridge and walked us back toward the four men, the only one of whom I recognized was the self-important keeper of the gate. I guessed that one of the men from the Sanitation Department car, to judge by the gatekeeper's deferential treatment of him, was his supervisor from the town hall. The other two men were undoubtedly State Police detectives.

Chief Bonaventura asked us to describe Gumboots again for the benefit of the group. For the fourth time that day we strained to remember every detail of Gumboots' appearance: his paunchy cheeks, his curly, untidy black hair, his wide, pock-marked nose, on and on. But at no time during our word-painting exercise did either the gatekeeper or his boss show any sign of recognizing the man we were trying to describe as one of the dump workers. Eventually their combined head-shaking got into a perfect rhythm, and I had to suppress the urge to raise my hands and conduct the two of them. The end result would still have come from the same menu: either Gumboots had radically changed his appearance for our benefit, or the staff of the Sanitation Department could not remember who worked for it, or—as I had suspected for much of the afternoon—he really didn't work there, and was just another trespasser. Join the club.

Finally, the Chief brought the session to a close.

"Well, boys, whoever he was, he evidently didn't work here. And if there was something here in the sand, it's gone now. But if someone did take the car and the body away they did a very good job of covering their tracks. In fact, I don't see how anyone could have done such a good job in such a short space of time."

So that was the verdict. Without coming out and saying it, he had come down on the side of not believing us. And yet he stopped short of calling us liars, at least not to our faces. God only knows what he was going to say to his troops back at police headquarters.

Said troops were now all returning to their cruisers. As we dragged after the Chief I could see that Robert was fighting some sort of internal battle, as if trying simultaneously to expel and retain something disagreeable. The Chief had reached his car and was about to swing himself in when he resolved the battle.

"Look, Chief. Think about this. We weren't supposed to be in here, right enough? We come in every Sunday through a hole in the fence, we fool around on our bikes, and then the guys from the dump see us and yell at us and tell us we're breaking the law, and chase us out of here. Now they're probably gonna close the hole up so we can't do this any more. I mean—we didn't need to do this, am I right? We didn't need to come and tell you about this. We could have kept quiet and not told no-one. Now we're in trouble with you, and probably with our folks, and anyhow we probably won't be able to come back here ever again..."

Robert's voice trailed off. The Chief, one hand on the driver's door and one foot inside the car, was nevertheless giving Robert his full attention. He studied Robert's face closely for several seconds after he finished speaking, but his only visible reaction was a slight nodding of the head, his only audible reaction a single, thoughtfully spoken word.

"Yes..."

The Chief pulled himself into his car. I opened the back door and Robert and I slid onto the back seat. Each car in the line, including the State Police cruiser and the Sanitation Department car, carried out its own awkward 'Y'-turn and started to head back along the perimeter track in the direction they had come. The two of us sat morosely behind the Chief, who gave no further indication that he was considering Robert's speech. It was, in fact, impossible to know how he had received it. Robert had gone out on a limb in reminding the Chief of something that he had not raised or even acknowledged himself—the fact that, every time we came into the dump, we were breaking the law. But his logic was sound, and I only hoped the Chief could see it. But what was the meaning of his single-word response? What was he agreeing to— that we were breaking the law? That he would have to write a memo to the Town Hall to get them to repair the fence? Or that, after all, we had been telling the truth?

Robert nudged me and gestured toward the Chief. He was evidently—and understandably—not satisfied with the Chief's ambiguous response. He wanted resolution, but I felt we had pushed our luck far enough and shook my head. Right now I wanted more than anything to be out of the dump, out of the Chief's car and out of the hands of the police.

We were just about to reach the final turn before heading back out through the gates when Raleigh's car approached from the other direction and halted next to the Chief's. Raleigh put his elbow on the windowsill and leaned out.

"No-one over here has seen a car anything like their description in the last two hours." The Chief nodded again in that slow, thoughtful way of his. As he did so I looked out toward the metal hut that served as Dump HQ Central, lunchroom and smoking lounge for the half-dozen sanitation workers there. The whole workforce was assembled outside, looking quizzically in our direction. Raleigh's cold gaze flickered over to where we were sitting. While still looking at us he spoke again.

"You know what I think, Chief? I think they read about it in the newspaper and decided to put a bit of drama into their lives at our expense. Remember whose kid that one is."

Robert, unmoving as a rock, returned the detective's look with one of equal hostility. I shared my friend's anger but was distracted by what else Raleigh had said. What were we supposed to have read about in the paper? What was it that the police knew that we didn't? I leaned forward.

"What's he talking about, Chief?" The Chief twisted his head and shoulders around so he could face us in the back seat.

"Oh, I think you know, boys," he said. "He's talking about the bank robbery that happened downtown yesterday and was in the papers today. You would have read about it this morning before you came out to the dump, wouldn't you?"

SUNDAY, 4:55 PM

The return journey to police headquarters was as sedate as the outbound journey had been exciting. Without benefit of lights or sirens the parade of officialdom made its way back into town, stopping at intersections and taking its place among the orderly flow of traffic. Nor was there, in the Chief's car at least, any conversation between leaving the dump and arriving at the police building. And the passage of time between the access track and the dump gates had been more than sufficient for us to air and re-air our protests, all of which were ignored by the Chief. On the steps of Police Headquarters Bonaventura addressed us over his shoulder.

"Why don't you boys pick up your bicycles and go home now." Without even looking at us he hurried into Headquarters. By the time we had mounted the steps and pushed our way through the doors he was already in his office on the far side of the building.

Hey Chief—remember us?

Robert and I retrieved our BMXes, bounced them down the steps and pedaled away. No-one else talked to us or even acknowledged our departure. Again we passed down Main Street, again in silence. Robert led, and I followed his hunched shoulders and bobbing head without trying to make conversation.

A DEATH UNDER SAND

To reach South Gretchyville from downtown you normally stay straight on Main until reaching the lights on the east side of the mall, then jog right onto Burnett until it runs into Compass Avenue. I live off Compass on Sachem Street, while Robert lives much further down in one of the units of the Rosario Apartments. It looked to me as if Robert was headed in that general direction, which suited me just fine; I didn't really want to go anywhere else but home right now. So it came as a surprise to see him suddenly peel off onto Shore Street, long before we had even reached the mall. This was the quickest way to the ocean, I knew, but it was certainly no short cut to South Gretchyville. I started to ask Robert where he thought he was going, but he was already accelerating out of earshot and I had to devote my energy to catching up with him again. It was as if he were not aware that I was still with him, or even that he didn't care.

I followed him all the way down Shore Street and into the first of the string of parking lots that ran behind the dunes at the head of South Prospect Beach. This late September Sunday the parking lot was only a third as full as it would have been a month earlier, and we pedaled diagonally across it to the first of the fenced paths running through the dunes to the beach. Robert kept going off the blacktop onto the sand, passing the 'NO BICYCLES' sign and entering the path. I still followed him, and we labored through the soft sand until we emerged on the beach side of the dune. Robert immediately jumped off his Viper, threw it down and climbed easily over a collapsed section of fence onto the nearest dune. He climbed the low feature to the top, then sat facing the ocean, his arms folded on his knees and his chin on the back of his hands. I left my machine next to his and followed to where he was sitting. Once again we were trespassing, since the fence we had crossed was intended to keep people and their tromping feet off the dunes.

Something was working on Robert. I sat beside him and slightly behind, and tried to read what was in his face. His eyes were fixed on the ocean, from whose dancing surface the sun fired back at us a thousand images of itself. Where the sea met the beach some little kids were splashing in and out of the shallows, screaming with delight as the incoming surf broke against their legs and splashed up their uncovered bodies. Further up the beach their parents sprawled on their towels and read heavy-looking hard-cover books or talked together, glancing up every few seconds to reassure themselves of their offsprings' safety. Out beyond the surf zone some sailboards were maneuvering backward and forward as their owners attempted to avoid the darting, dangerous-looking jet skis. And further out still, two or three small powerboats bounced spectacularly through the swell, sending gouts of spray flying upward to catch the sunlight briefly but brilliantly.

Robert's eyes reflected none of the joy of this scene; indeed, I doubted whether any of it even registered on his brain. His eyes seemed to be fixed on a reality that started on the far side of the live, sparkling canvas before him and spread outward and backward much further, peopled throughout with dark-hued and troubling images. My own mind was a cauldron of conflicting emotions, heated to boiling point by the treatment we had received from the police, but Robert... Robert was in a different place, and I knew I had to wait for him to return before I could communicate with him. It took a long time.

At last, in stages, he began to come back from the outland where he had been. He started by shaking his head, forming a fist with his left hand and pounding his right knee repeatedly. Then the flow of curses started, apparently thrown out not so much as a form of obscene word-painting intended to describe the cops or anyone else, but more as a way of ridding his body of the poisons that had been building up inside it. Finally, something coherent emerged.

"You should've gone on your own, Peter; not with me."

"What, because of your fa-"

"Or Tony. Or Liddy. Or all three of you, damn it. Just not me." A small window opened for me into Robert's reality. I began to understand where he was going.

"They'd 've believed you. Could have told 'em the tooth fairy did the shooting. Evidence or no evidence, they'd 've gone with you. Never believe me. Never."

This was not a road I wanted to go down with Robert, but he had already set foot on it and if I counted myself his friend I would have to walk with him. Still, I tried one last time to divert him from it.

"I swear, Robert, it's just because of your dad. You know, sins of the fathers and all that crap. They're just trying to paint you with the same brush."

"They don't need to paint me with no brush. That's the whole point; I'm already painted, remember?"

Robert held his right arm up only inches in front of my face. The part of his arm closest to me bore the small scar he had acquired the time he nipped his arm in the hinge of our screen door. But that was the lightest part of the swath of skin blocking my vision. Robert's skin was as dark as mine was pale, a distinction that, so far as the two of us were concerned, was not only invisible but irrelevant. But every once in a while it would happen, and always around the involvement of some outside party, that this skin-deep distinction would be thrust in our faces. It might be the Shack, that self-appointed brotherhood of African-

A DEATH UNDER SAND

American kids at school, ragging on Robert for hanging with me instead of with them. It might be a passing comment or just a look from some older person who knows me and, like the Shack in their own way, expresses surprise or disapproval at my choice of best friend. Or it might be the whole damn Gretchyville Police Department automatically disbelieving Robert, partly because of his father's reputation but mainly because of the color of his skin. Although Raleigh had made reference only to Robert's parentage in his remark at the dump, if I gave it any thought I would have to admit that his whole attitude toward Robert from the moment we sat down in the Chief's office had been marked with a shade of distrust and suspicion which he had not extended to me. And it didn't take much more thought than that to realize that a similar attitude was responsible for the Department's harassment of Robert's father in the first place.

I wanted to tell Robert that he was imagining things, that it didn't matter which one of us told the story when we had no evidence to support it, but I didn't. I didn't because I didn't believe it myself. I tried to visualize it in the terms that Robert had proposed: me, Peter, nice little blond-haired fresh-faced white boy, spinning my story for the police and looking oh-so heartbroken when the evidence disappeared. I visualized Tony... Liddy... all three of us together. What I didn't have to visualize was Robert being right, because I knew that was true.

Collectively or individually, the three of us would have been spared the automatic filter of disbelief through which people like Raleigh would always force Robert.

I reached up, took hold of Robert's arm and pushed it down by his side. I knew that I would have to choose my next words carefully, having just blown it with my paintbrush comment—only about the most bone-headed metaphor I could have uttered. I took the low road.

"Life sucks, right?"

He snorted.

"What would you know?" he retorted bitterly.

"I know what you go through" I said quietly. "I'm your friend, remember?"

I had deliberately not removed my hand from Robert 's arm, hoping it would somehow serve to reconnect me to him in a way beyond the merely physical. But Robert was not yet ready to let go of his anger, which was radiating enough heat to be scorching everything within range—friend, foe, and inanimate objects alike.

"You don't know the half of it."

"That's probably exactly how much of it I do know. I know I can't ever know the rest." Robert shook his head slowly, his face still drawn tight in a mask of resentment.

"It's the other half that really sucks. When they come around the apartment. Or the time my mom just didn't bother applying for that promotion. Or

112

when you ask a question in Creel's class, and he looks at you like you're wasting his time, like you couldn't possibly understand his stupid Social Sciences anyway, so why even answer the question? Or the look you get when you walk into a store, like they know the only reason you walked in there was to rip them off, so they keep watching you all the time you're in there to see if you're gonna grab something and put it under your sweater and walk out with it. They don't have to say nothing; it's just that look. Same one I got from Raleigh. 'You don't belong here.' 'You're trouble.' 'You're just wasting my time.' That's what it says."

He paused.

"And then there's the Shack. 'What you doin' with the white boy? You should be eatin' at our table. Brothers not good enough for you?'" He looked at me directly.

"Well, what am I, Peter? Am I too good or am I not good enough? All depends who you ask, right enough? Why can't I just be 'OK' for everyone? What did I ever do to..."

He didn't finish the sentence. He didn't need to. I knew there was a ring of truth to everything he had said. I had seen the look myself, heard the accusing tones of the Shack and felt the weight of disapproval that bore down on him, from people who should have known better, whenever he drew attention to himself. I had even shared the anger that propelled him as he tried to fight his way up the face of great waves of ignorance and prejudice.

No, that wasn't true either. I could see, hear and feel as much as was humanly possible, but I could never share. Could sympathize with Robert but never suffer with him. I knew that look well enough, but I also knew how easily it would pass over me and light on him. I knew that when Robert and I separated at the end of the day, each to his own home, I could go to bed and fall asleep, only thinking of the injustice done to him. Robert would go to bed and lie awake, living the injustice. And it really didn't matter how much of a friend I was to him; I could neither protect him from the look and all its implications for his future, nor truly understand what it must be like to set your face against the world and steel yourself for the look from the moment you pass your front door in the morning. Sure, none of this was my fault, but if nothing else, today had served to remind me not to be so free with the phrase 'I know what you go through.'

I had given up nothing to be Robert's friend— nothing that I cared about, anyway—but Robert had given up a lot to be mine. He knew that there was no compromise so far as the Shack was concerned; you couldn't hang with them *and* with someone of your own choosing, and Robert had chosen to hang with me. And whereas he could quite easily hold a friendly conversation with any one of the Shack in isolation, the moment two or more of them got together, drawing strength from each other, their only form of communication with Robert would be to remind him that he was not part of their circle but that he ought to be. And one part of me could understand that, since every member of the Shack had the look to deal with, and solidarity was the way in which they dealt with it. But solidarity has to be complete to be effective, which is why Robert's determination to go his own way so irked them.

However, in going his own way Robert had excluded himself from any support that the Shack could provide. For him there was no group of like-minded people with whom to share experiences and to whom he could turn for strength. In this respect he and the Shack were both losers, but perhaps he was the greater loser, since without the Shack all Robert had was me, and while his choice had been a free one it was never clear to me whether, on balance, I represented a net gain or a net loss.

And what kind of a friend was I, anyway? Had I ever done one thing—one real, concrete, meaningful thing—to improve Robert's lot? Exactly how much use was it to be sympathetic if I couldn't find some way to turn that *look* back in the faces of the jackasses giving it? Because if I couldn't, my friendship may have been worthless to Robert, and I was suddenly desperate to make it worth *something*.

"That Raleigh…" Robert was saying. "I know him; I know what he's like. I've seen him a couple of times when they come to the Apartments. You can tell he thinks he's getting his clothes dirty just by being in our place. What a piece of work. And half the cops around here are the same." He made a sound that was more snort than laugh.

"Can't you just see him riding a horse through the cotton fields, big hat, bullwhip and all? He'd be right at home. Nothing changes for guys like him, Peter. I bet, if you knew what he was really thinking, he'd just as soon put us all on ships back to Africa. I don't know; maybe the kids in the Shack are right—you can't deal with people like that, so you just gotta get together and fight 'em."

"Sure, you've got to fight them" I replied. "We've all got to fight them, not just the Shack. But then you've got to figure out just *how* you fight them. What are you going to do—start an army? Invade their country? Take them out, one at a time? Trouble is, they don't wear pointy white hats any more. You can't tell who they are 'till you scratch them and see what they're like inside."

"Hell, I wanna do more than just scratch him. But you're right; for every one like him you know about, there's a dozen more who think the same way, no matter what they say to your face. Seems like it's been like that forever. I guess there's nothing you can *really* do." Robert's tone had changed; the anger and bitterness that had driven his earlier outburst had given way to a creeping resignation that alarmed me more. But if my friend was preparing to reconcile himself with the way the world worked, I certainly was not.

"I don't know what to tell you, Robert. Maybe the only way you can fight these dumbasses is to make them look stupid and out of touch, but don't ask me how you do that. And I know why the Shack do what they do, but sometimes I think they're their own worst enemies and—you know what?—when they stick it to you they're every bit as dumb as Creel or Raleigh or some of my lousy relatives. They're all just trying to say you're wrong 'cause you're different, or you're not good enough 'cause you're different. But since when did 'different' mean any of that? Different just means different, that's all."

I finally released his arm and held my own arm up in front of his face as he had done to me, completely blocking his vision.

"See?" I said. "Different."

It took Robert a few seconds more, but eventually I sensed that he had come back to the same planet, the same dimension, the same time zone and the same damn sand dune that I was on. He allowed himself a slight grin, then he took my wrist in his left hand and, tightening his grip, pulled me hard in his direction. As I keeled over toward him he wrapped his right arm around my throat and pitched forward off the top of the dune, dragging me down with him.

"Get outta that!" he laughed. I tumbled down with him, trying to use my legs to throw him off balance, tickling him under the arms and punching him in the ribs to make him break his hold on me. We wrestled our way down the face of the sand dune, rolling over each other and laughing until we reached the beach. Then we just lay there on our backs, alternately laughing and poking each other in the ribs. It was over. Nothing had been solved, no wrongs had been righted, and tomorrow morning Robert would still have to set his face against the world at large, but for now at least all the intruders and spoilers had vanished from *our* world, leaving it the way it worked best—with Robert and me as sole inhabitants.

"Well, they can all go play with themselves" he remarked eventually. It was an off-handed dismissal of all those who would demean him or interfere with our friendship, but it was said without rancor. At this moment Robert appeared truly not to care what any of them did or said.

SUNDAY, 5:40 PM

Robert sat up and looked around him. There was no tension now in his face, and for the first time he seemed to be aware of the activity on the beach. We both stood, shook sand out of our clothes and walked together down toward the sea, where three small kids were playing with their father in the surf. In turn they would hurl themselves at him, provoking him to roar like a story-book ogre and pick them up bodily before throwing them, shrieking with laughter, into the onrushing waves. The eldest of the children was a boy of about ten, sufficiently heavier than his younger brother and sister to cause his father to strain to lift him. But he did so uncomplainingly, and if he was not able to achieve much in the way of distance when it came to throwing him, the boy either didn't notice or didn't mind. All four of them were enjoying the game and each other so much that they were quite oblivious to the occasional warnings from Wife and Mother on the beach about the condition of Father's back and the dangers of gulping down too much seawater.

We watched the performance in silence for a few minutes, each of us lost in our own thoughts. Then my brain began to loop back over the day's events and the Family Kodak Moment before us began to appear bizarre, not for what it was but for how it shared space in my mind with all the other images and experiences of the day: the upside-down staring face in the car, the jerking marionette that was Gumboots having the life shot out of him, the murderous look on the black-dressed man's face when he saw the four of us, and the sight of two of my friends heaving their guts out in front of me. I envied the man in the water and his entire brood; they knew nothing of this, had nothing more taxing on their minds than how much fun they could pack in before day's end, and were probably looking at mild sunburn as the most painful reminder of their day's activities. Suddenly the contrast became altogether too violent for me and I turned and started back up the beach toward our bikes.

"Come on. Let's get out of here."

Robert followed, and we trudged back in single file up the beach, retrieved our machines and wheeled them over to the path. The sun was now low enough in the sky to put us in the shadow of the dunes as we trekked along the path and out into the parking lot. Once on the hard surface we mounted up and pedaled unhurriedly, side by side, back up Shore Street. My mind was still back in the dump, and we had rounded the curve where the road starts to point inland before I broke the silence between us.

"So if the guy in black really did get the car out of the dump..." I started. Robert waited for me to finish the thought, but I was still stuck on how the killer could have spirited the damned car away from its sandy garage without a trace. I ended up with a snort and a headshake, which did nothing to advance the argument.

"Maybe he had help getting it out," suggested Robert.

"Yeah, maybe... I mean—he *must* have done. How long was it, do you think, until we got back there?"

"Well, we had to wait for Tony and Liddy to finish puking... Then we had that pow-wow on the side of the road... Then it was about twenty minutes into town... How long at Police Headquarters?"

"Oh... about forty-five minutes, I think."

"All right... Then about fifteen minutes getting back to the dump, I'd say. How long's that?"

"Hour and a half; hour forty-five, maybe."

"He could've done a lot in that time, even on his own."

"Yeah, but-" I felt like banging my head repeatedly on my handlebars out of sheer frustration. "-but what the hell did he do with the friggin' thing? No-one saw it coming out the main gate. There's nowhere else to drive a car out. The hole in the fence isn't big enough, even if he could get it up the slope. I tell you, it has to be somewhere else in the dump. It's *got* to be!"

Even before I had finished speaking Robert was shaking his head.

"Only if he was strong enough to pick it up in his arms, carry it half-way across the dump and bury it again. Peter, you said it yourself. There were *no tire marks*. There were none around where we were looking; did you notice any on the way in?" I shook my head.

"Only 'dozer tracks."

"Right. And the cops went a few hundred yards in the other direction, looking, and still found nothing. He'd 've needed an army to wipe out his tracks for that kind of distance."

"I know, I know," I said, with an edge of exasperation in my voice. We rode on in silence for a minute or two.

"Did you know about the bank robbery?" asked Robert. I looked at him in surprise.

"No, of course I didn't. I told you that."

"No, you told Bonaventura that. But you didn't know about it, right enough?"

"No. How about you?" Robert shook his head.

"We don't get a paper. I know you do, though."

"Yeah, but my mom always stays in bed late on Sundays. She says it's the only day of the week she can, and she's going to take advantage of it. So she takes her tea and a Danish and the paper back up to bed with her, and I swear she reads every page— probably every word. I don't usually get to see it 'till the evening." Robert was chuckling.

"Danish in bed, huh?"

"Yeah, well, it's only her now and a big double bed, so what does she care? Actually, I think she makes a point of doing it, knowing she's not going to get bitched at."

"So I guess the point is, you didn't see the Sunday paper either, right?"

"You got it. But hey—let's go back to my place now and look at it. I want to find that story."

We started cutting through side roads in the direction of South Gretchyville, and after a few minutes came out on Compass Avenue a few blocks down from Sachem Street. Turning left, we pedaled up Compass, alternating between road and sidewalk as it suited us. The first hundred yards of Sachem are downhill, and out of habit we accelerated into the turn, then took our feet off the pedals and let gravity and momentum do the rest. If you get it right you can coast all the way to my house without touching the pedals again, running out of speed and balance just as you hit the gravel of our short driveway. We must have been in form that day, and both got all the way to our garage before having to stick a foot down to stay upright. As we leaned our bikes against the wall of the garage and turned toward the kitchen door, Robert, who had been silent since our conversation on Shore Street, suddenly asked:

"So who do you think he was?"

"Who?"

"The guy in the car."

I stopped with my hand on the latch of the screen door. The sun was striking the screen at a fine angle, picking out the detail of the meshwork and making it opaque. Onto this coarse cinema screen the gut-wrenching scene of Gumboots discovering what was in the car was projected in glorious Gretchycolor, as my mind rewound and played, yet again, a selection of the day's scenes. Once again I saw him clutching the side of the car, as if he could drag it out of its grave with his bare hands; once again I felt the despair in the man's voice and heard him calling a single name over and over again. Jimmy... Jimmy... Did he think that by screaming his name to the heavens he could revive him? And why did it matter so much to him?

"What did you say?" asked Robert. I realized I had been repeating the name aloud myself.

"Jimmy—that was his name, I guess. That was what Gumboots—the guy in the overalls—was yelling when he was at the car."

"Yeah, but what was he doing there? Was he trying to stop the robber getting away and got himself killed? Was he one of the robbers? And if he was, who killed him?"

"Maybe he got shot inside the bank." Robert shook his head.

"Are you kidding? Did you see those holes in his chest? The second he got those, he was out of it, man."

"So maybe he was in the car when he was shot. Maybe someone got him as they were driving away."

"Yeah. Maybe. You see any bullet holes in the windshield?"

"No, but I wasn't exactly looking up there."

"I know what you mean; me neither."

"Hey, listen—whoever he was, this Jimmy, he and Gumboots were either brothers or best buddies or something, the way he was carrying on. Did you ever hear anything like that?" Robert shuddered; I guessed that he too was recalling the harrowing scene of Gumboots at the car.

"Yeah, it's like it just drove him mad. Crazy. And the way he went after the guy in black—like he was out of his mind. Didn't do him any good, though. Poor bastard."

"That's not nice language, Robert."

Startled, Robert and I jumped and yelped at the same time (there has to be a word for that— yumping or jelping or something). For the second time that day, someone had come up behind us and caught us unawares. On this occasion it was my mom, who was standing in the side doorway of the garage; she had been in there all the time we had been talking and must have heard every word. As my heart rate started to recover and as Robert and my mom exchanged apologies, in his case for using the b-word and in hers for giving us such a shock, I frantically reviewed the conversation we had been having. It didn't take me long to compute that what we had said in the brief time we had been standing there would force any mother to jump to all kinds of conclusions, most of them pretty accurate. And in case you were wondering whether we had had any intention of sharing with our families the happy events of the day—trespassing in the dump, seeing people dead and being made that way, getting ourselves shot at and being grilled by the police— you shouldn't spend too much time on it.

In my mom's case, she didn't let us down; she quickly processed what she had heard and asked exactly the kind of question we didn't want to answer.

"What was all that about? What have you two been doing?" I knew that the next time I opened my mouth, a good story had better come out.

"It was a movie. We were just talking about it."

"You went to the movies? What did you do with your bikes?"

Er.

"What movie was it?"

"I didn't say we went to the movies. We went over to Tony's place and watched a video. Some murder mystery. I don't even remember the name. It was pretty lame."

"Seems a shame, then, to waste such a lovely afternoon cooped up inside."

A DEATH UNDER SAND

"Speaking of which, mom," I responded, noticing her appearance for the first time, "what have you been doing?"

My mom was dressed in dirty dungarees and a shapeless sweatsuit top, with her oldest pair of sneakers on her feet and her blonde hair scragged back into a bun. Her hands were covered with grime and oil, much of which had spread to her sweat top as far up as her neck.

"Oh, I thought I'd clean all the old newspapers and coffee cups and *soda cans*" (the emphasis was to indicate my part in the desecration of the family automobile) "and scratch tickets out of the car. Then I noticed how much garbage there was in the garage and decided to clean the whole place up."

"Gee, mom, if only I'd known—I could have helped you." My mom, no dummy, wasn't impressed.

"Well dear," she said with unconvincing sweetness, "as it happens, there's still a lot to do. Perhaps you'd like to sweep the floor in here."

"Well I would, mom, but I think you've got most of it in your hair."

Never fails. My mom turned around and, using the car window as a mirror and muttering to herself, tried to find and remove the reported dirt from her hair. And that gave us ample time to make our escape into the house.

A word about my mom. While she's never exactly been a fashion plate, she's not normally a slob in her personal appearance. Working where she does, as the dental hygienist in Dr. Karstadt's office, she can't really afford to be. I guess the good doctor wants the person who scrapes the food scraps from between his patients' teeth to be at least as well dressed as they are—not too difficult most days. I imagine it must get kind of vanilla to spend day after day flossing other peoples' teeth, but she sticks at the job because it means she can get off in time to pick my nine-year-old sister up from school and get home not too long after I do.

My mom's not exactly a career woman, but her being one had never been part of my parents' master plan. Of course, when my dad upped and left four years ago the job—or at least the income—became a lot more important to her, so it wasn't as if she could just quit because she'd lost interest in it. And on balance, I'd have to say she's handled the change in her situation pretty well. The first couple of years were grim much of the time, and my sister and I took the brunt of a lot of her anger for no good reason. Since then, however, she's shaken herself out and begun to enjoy life again, by which I mean only that she's reconciled herself to the situation. I know that's not quite the same as getting a big charge out of living, but at least now she's more open to the idea of getting to know new people and actually having some kind of life beyond work, the two of us and the tube. Of course, with her being in her mid-thirties, who knows whether any of that will actually happen? Most people I know of that age seem to be past any kind of social life, unless you count polka clubs or bowling.

Once inside the house I ran up to my mom's room, pulled the scattered pieces of the Sunday paper together into a pile, then returned to the head of the stairs and called Robert. He made it to the top of the stairs just as my mom, having satisfied herself that no passing male stranger would overlook her charms on account of grease and wood shavings in her hair, motored in through the kitchen door.

"Peter!"

"Upstairs, mom. We're in my room." Technically not true, but we were most definitely on our way there because I knew that my room represented a safe zone, kind of like the 'Just Visiting' space in 'Monopoly'. Everyone knows you can't get into trouble there, and my mom would assume we were reading comic books or playing games; that meant she would leave us alone, since she knew we would get into less trouble doing that than roaming the town. Not so my sister, who appeared in the doorway of her bedroom clutching a half-naked Barbie and demanding that we help get her ready for the prom.

"Not now, Marla" (not ever if I can get away with it). I quickly got Robert inside my room and managed to get the door shut on her distraught face without shutting it on her fingers.   As I expected, that got the noise generator going.

"MOM! Peter won't let me in his room!"

"Oh... well, leave him alone, sweetheart. He wants to play with Robert, not with you."

"But mommy..."

"Tell you what, sweetie. Why don't you come down here and help me decide what to do for dinner tonight?"   The noise generator instantly changed pitch and Robert, Barbie and I were forgotten as my little sister trundled downstairs, conned yet again into obedience.

SUNDAY, 6:20 PM

I quit leaning against the inside of my door, and Robert and I got down to sorting out the newspaper and searching for the bank robbery article. It didn't take us long. There on the front page of the main section was the entire story, photos and all, threatening to push the school committee's vote of no-confidence in the Superintendent of Schools and a US Senator's explanation of his relationship with a certain Congressional aide off their respective sides of the page. We hunkered down on the floor and began to read.

Maple County Bank robbed at gunpoint

Staff unhurt; robbers escape with estimated $10,000

The Maple County Savings Bank on Main Street was robbed yesterday by two masked, armed men in a daring daylight hold-up. The men escaped with an estimated $10,000 in cash, mostly in small bills. Nobody was hurt during the robbery, which staff members later estimated to have lasted no more than four minutes.

Detective Sergeant Henry Raleigh of the Gretchyville Police said: "From the eyewitness statements we have so far, it appears that two men entered the bank at about 4:15 pm wearing stocking masks and carrying handguns, and ordered the tellers to empty out their cash drawers. When the tellers had filled two bank cash bags with small denomination bills the robbers grabbed the bags and left. No shots were fired during the robbery, and nobody was injured."

Asked if the police were able to obtain a description of the robbers, Sergeant Raleigh said that one was reported to be wearing a green Chipmunk Workshop sweat shirt, jeans and sneakers; the other was described as wearing a Dodgers jacket, jeans and dark-colored boots or shoes. Since both men were masked, no physical description was possible.

"We also have a description of the criminals' getaway car", reported Sergeant Raleigh. It appears to be a late model red Excalibur Coupe."

The police would not comment on whether they had identified the license plate number of the robbers' car.

Maureen Van Damm, manager of the Main Street branch of the Maple County Savings Bank, said: "It was all over very quickly. It is Bank policy that our employees do not stall or try to delay robbers in the event of a situation like this. The tellers did what the robbers instructed them to do, and gave them no excuse to become violent."

The story was continued on an inside page. I waited for Robert to catch up to me, then turned to the conclusion of the article.

Asked whether any bank employee had sounded a secret alarm to summon the police, or whether dye bombs had been inserted in the cash bags, Mrs. Van Damm indicated that it was not Bank policy to comment on such procedures.

As luck would have it, only one customer was in the

bank at the time of the robbery. Millicent Estabrook, 79, was preparing to make a withdrawal when the robbers burst in. "They were very rude" said Mrs. Estabrook. "They were shouting and waving their guns around, and using curse words all the time they were in here. And I still haven't been able to get my money out."

According to tellers Lisa Lupinski and Charmaine LeTourneau, when the robbers exited the bank they ran to their car, which they had left in the bank parking lot, and drove off along Main Street in an easterly direction. "We weren't really very frightened" said Ms. Lupinski. "Our instructions are to do exactly what the intruders order us to do; that's just what we did. It was all over very quickly, and nobody got hurt."

The two men who entered the bank appeared not to have any accomplices. According to several witnesses, there was no driver waiting in the getaway car, which was driven away by one of the robbers.

Asked to comment on whether the police expected to make an early arrest in this case, Gretchyville Chief of Police Tiberio Bonaventura stated that, while he could make no predictions, his department had several leads to follow and were making full use of State Police resources in their hunt for the bank robbers.

The Main Street Gretchyville branch of the Maple County Savings Bank was opened in 1990. It has experienced only one other robbery attempt, an unsuccessful one in 1995. In that incident two young men from Cold Harbor, who were later found to be under the influence of controlled substances, ran into the bank demanding money. An alert customer service representative directed them into the ATM lobby, which the head teller then closed by remote control. The two would-be robbers were taken into custody.

"Well, d-uhhh!" exclaimed Robert.

"What a pair of dickheads!" I remarked, and we both fell to laughing at the thought of the gang who couldn't think straight. Then I closed the paper up again and we looked at the photographs accompanying the story. The main photo showed the building of the Maple County Savings Bank with a road sign in the foreground showing that this was the intersection of Main Street and Custance Road. The caption read:

The Maple County Savings Bank at the corner of Main Street and Custance Road

A smaller photo showed a middle-aged woman sitting behind a desk, upon which was a nameplate that read 'MAUREEN VAN DAMM BRANCH MANAGER'. The caption read:

Maureen Van Damm, branch manager

The third and final photo on the front page showed an Excalibur Coupe of the type used in the robbery. The caption read:

An Excalibur Coupe of the type used in the robbery

For another minute or two neither of us spoke. My brain was trying to come to grips with the connections it was making between what we had read, what we had heard in the Chief's office and what we had seen in the dump. Robert spoke first, tapping the photo of the car with his finger.

"That's it; that's the car we saw in the dump." I nodded.

"Sure looks like it."

"So the bags we saw in the car would have been the ones the tellers filled up."

"Yeah. I wonder why one of them was broken open." We both thought about that one for a while, but came up blank. Suddenly Robert struck me lightly on the shoulder.

"Peter—what is it with us? Why was the damn money still *in* the car? They robbed the bank, they hid the car, why didn't they take the money?" I stared blankly at my friend.

"You got me beat."

We started re-reading the article. After a while I shook my head again.

"You know, Robert, there's a lot of stuff here that's got me beat. I mean, look at this: they didn't even have a driver, for God's sake. They left the car parked outside the bank for everyone to see, went in and robbed the bank, then went back out and drove away up Main Street. Busiest street in town on a Saturday afternoon. Then they hide the car but forget to take the money out." Robert laughed.

"And we thought those two druggies were brain-dead." We laughed again.

"I'll tell you one thing" said Robert. "I bet the police *do* know the license number of the car, right enough. Anyone looking out the window must 've had time to write the thing down twice over." I agreed, but could not understand why they would not have published the number in the paper. Robert flipped back to the inside page and stabbed at the first paragraph with his finger.

"What's this stuff about dye bombs? Do they blow the money up?"

"No, I think they're like paintballs or something. I saw it in a movie once. They put them in the cash bags, then when the robber tries to open them they explode, and all the money gets covered with this weird-colored dye."

"So what good does that do?"

"Well... I guess it means the people who steal the money can't actually use it. You know—try passing a purple dollar bill, and everyone who sees it knows you stole it." Robert still looked confused.

"OK, so you catch the thief and get the money back, right enough, but then the bank can't use the money either, right? What good's that?"

"Well..." I scratched around for an answer, and finding none, settled for swatting Robert's close-cropped curly black hair with the back of my hand.

"What do I look like—a banker? I don't know what they do with it. Maybe they have orphanages full of little barefoot bankerettes, scrubbing the money with their toothbrushes till it's clean, and that earns them a bowl of grease soup. How should I know what they do with it? I'm just telling you what the dye bombs are." Before I had finished speaking, Robert was climbing up onto my bed.

"I bet I know how they get the bombs in the bags. They fly them in in dye-bombers!" And so saying, he dive-bombed me in the style of a Ju87 Stuka from an altitude of two feet.

"You great walking cowflop!" I yelled, as I struggled to free myself from the death-grip of Herr Oberleutnant Juneau of the Gretchyville *Luftwaffe*. "Just 'cause you're dumb as dirt, don't take it out on me!"

In mid-struggle I suddenly remembered something.

"Hey, wait a minute! That's what Bonaventura meant, when he asked us if the money was stained a funny color." Robert instantly lost interest in the fight.

"That's right. But it wasn't, was it?" I shrugged.

"Like I told the Chief, I don't know. It was too dark in there. You know that."

I started reconstructing the robbers' day. First they must have stolen the getaway car; or maybe they had done that the previous day. In the late afternoon they had arrived at the bank, parked, and carried out the robbery. Then they drove to the dump, entering via the main gate, and somehow slipped away from the access road onto the perimeter track unseen. At some point one of them had split open one of the cash bags; was there a dye bomb inside, and did it go off? And if it did, is that why they abandoned the money along with the car? Lastly they picked a spot, parked the car, covered it up and left. The only trouble with all that was that it left as many questions unanswered as answered.

"Must have taken them all night to bury that thing," I murmured.

"What was that?"

"Oh... just thinking out loud."

"Well, keep it down, will you? Or at least let me know what you're talking about?"

"I'm talking about the car. Think how much sand there was on top of it. How long do you think it took the guy—or guys—to do all that?"

"Depends what kind of tools they had, I guess."

"Guess so. What kind of... Oh my God! What kind of tools? Robert, it's so obvious! I just realized how they got the car buried! If it'd been any more friggin' obvious, it would have slapped us in the face!" Robert still wasn't with me.

"Look, you remember when we first got to the top of that slope? We were actually sitting on top of the car, 'though we didn't know it at the time. I remember looking down and seeing a whole mass of 'dozer tracks about ten yards away. Now I know Tony took us way out of our normal space when he laid out that trail, but no way were we anywhere near where they usually run the 'dozer. So that means the 'dozer came over there specially, just to bury the car. The car must have pulled up at the end of the ridge; then the 'dozer kept piling sand on it 'till it looked like it was just part of the ridge. It probably took no more than ten minutes."

"Wow..." Robert stared wide-eyed at me, apparently struck dumb with admiration at my detective prowess. I guess I should have known better.

"Wow..." he repeated. "Peter—you got imagination that just won't quit... but I wish it would. What—you think he just strolled over to the far side of the dump and asked to borrow their machinery? Or did he have his own private 'dozer there?"

I swore and sat back hard against my chest of drawers. Too hard. I banged my head against a drawer handle, swore again, and ended up vigorously rubbing my head, although even that failed to coax any more answers out of my brain.

"The question, Watson," said Robert, puffing on an imaginary pipe, "is not so much *how* they buried it, but *why*?"

"What—why didn't they just dump the car in the street and transfer the money to another car?"

"Yeah. Why go through all that trouble—getting all the way to the dump, somehow getting around to our side of it, and somehow burying it. Why?"

We both pondered this, the latest question that didn't seem to have an answer. Then:

"Oh no..." groaned Robert.

"What?" My friend slapped both hands onto his face.

"We already know they're dumb. You don't think they were dorky enough to use *their own car* for the robbery, d'you?"

My jaw dropped. This was a possibility I had not even considered. Certainly, if the robbers needed to make the car drop out of sight after the bank job, it made sense to bury it. And if we hadn't blundered onto it, that's where it would have remained— literally out of sight. But what kind of jerk uses his own car in a crime, especially when he practically parades his license plate for everyone to see? It was almost as if they wanted to be caught. Robert and I tossed the question around between us for a while longer but still couldn't make it fit.

I pulled the paper toward me and started reading the article for the third time, looking for something—anything—that might make sense to us. Robert was off on a tangent of his own.

"I guess that's why the Chief was in, working on a Sunday."

"Hmm?"

"Him and Raleigh. Didn't you think it was kind of weird, them working on Sunday?"

"I guess so. Kind of inconsiderate of Black Hat, wasn't it?"

"Black Hat—the guy with the gun? You think he was one of the robbers?"

I looked up from the paper, surprised at Robert's question. I had assumed this all along about Black Hat, but nothing else about this whole business made sense, so perhaps it would be just as well if I followed Robert's lead and questioned all my assumptions. After all, what did I really know about Black Hat except that he was a killer, he didn't shave, and he liked wearing black clothes and... My eyes found the words on the page at the same time as the thought entered my head.

...*and dark-colored boots or shoes.*

Dark cowboy boots.

And that damned cinema projector started up again to show Black Hat scrambling down the bluff and crossing the track, his feet shod in what could have been dark cowboy boots. So what? It was the feeblest, most inconclusive of links between the newspaper story and our own experience. And certainly it would not serve to pick a man out of a police line-up, but perhaps it was a strong enough link, added to what little else we knew about Black Hat, to place him in the bank the previous afternoon. I pointed out the connection to Robert, who didn't seem impressed.

"Hell, Peter, I didn't see what he was wearing on his feet. I was kind of busy watching for him to catch sight of us."

"Well, who knows? Maybe just a coincidence anyway. How many pairs of cowboy boots are there walking around Gretchyville right now, I wonder?"

I was not expecting an answer to my question, but Robert appeared not to have even heard it. He was staring out of the window, a worried frown on his face.

"Peter?"

"What?"

"D'you think he'd recognize us if he saw us again?"

"God, I don't know. I hope to hell not."

"How far off was he—a hundred yards or more?"

"About that."

"A hundred yards... broad daylight..." Robert shook his head, then turned to me, still frowning. "We're talking a football field here. Would you recognize someone in the opposite end zone?"

"I... I don't know. If he wasn't wearing a football helmet or a band uniform... I probably would."

"That's what I thought, right enough. That's what I thought."

We were both silent for a couple of minutes. We already knew we could not be certain of identifying Black Hat, but if he could recognize us and decided to come searching, was the town of Gretchyville large enough for us to hide in?

"Well, we can't do nothin' about it," remarked Robert finally. "Just gotta hope he's got crummy eyesight." If that was what we were betting our lives on, I didn't like the odds. But Robert was right. There was nothing to be done about it.

A DEATH UNDER SAND

We had squeezed as much intelligence out of the newspaper story as we could, but it had left us without answers. We could take nothing back to the police to convince them that we had been telling the truth, and the identities of the three men in the dump were as much a mystery to us now as they were three hours ago. If the police really were going to make 'an early arrest in this case', they would not be looking to us for help. Perhaps just as well; I could see my mom attaching me to the house with a bungee cord, if not a steel cable, once she found out about our Sunday afternoon activities.

So where did that leave us? Were we supposed to forget everything that had happened to us? Should we dispose of our experience as if we had witnessed a minor car crash, where metal gets bent, glass gets shattered and names and addresses get exchanged, and which for the casual bystander is full of short-term drama and forgotten by the next day? I knew that could never happen. None of us—not even Tony—could blot this thing out from our consciousness. If the police never made an arrest, never put names to the two corpses that had been added to the list of discarded matter in the Gretchyville Landfill this weekend, those faces would keep bobbing up in our minds' eyes like kids in fright masks at the door on Halloween night. It might take a hypnotist to make those faces surface in Tony's mind one day, but even for him they would never completely disappear. They would be like restless spirits in a ghost story, still walking the Earth until they could understand the nature of their death, still demanding recognition for the fact that they had once lived, then gone to their deaths unseen and unlamented. They would never know peace, and the feeling was growing on me that if they remained anonymous and unfound, neither would we.

A DEATH UNDER SAND

SUNDAY, 7:30 PM

I watched the glow from Robert's taillight become fainter as he pedaled away from me toward Compass Avenue. As the dusk gathered outside, we had talked idly of other matters: of Tony's and Liddy's attitude toward the day's events, of the likelihood of our mothers learning about our forays into the dump (particularly today's), and of whether Chief Bonaventura was basically a good guy or a pain in the Astroturf. Eventually the conversation had drifted off into more pedestrian areas—what homework was due on the following day and how we could best bait the school bus driver—but it was just too bizarre to be discussing such trivial matters at the end of a day like today. We had lapsed into silence, and I ended up reading the comic pages while Robert caught up on some sports scores. When the sound of the dining room table being laid had come chinking and clattering up the stairs, Robert knew it was time to make himself scarce.

As we headed for the kitchen door, Robert and my mom had performed the usual ritual verbal exchange.

"Oh... Can't you stay for dinner, Robert?"

"Sorry, Mrs. McLeod. My mom wants me home." I glanced at the broiling tray in my mom's hand and the three chops it held. Nice one, mom.

Outside, Robert had wished me goodnight as he wheeled his machine out of our driveway and mounted up.

"Don't let Black Hat catch you," I called. Robert twisted around in his seat.

"Not funny, man." And I guess it wasn't.

When he disappeared from view I turned back to the house, stowed my Cozmo in the garage and went in to dinner. I made a conscious effort during dinner to set aside my memories of the day's events, but it simply wasn't possible, no more than it was possible to prevent my mom from noticing my brooding silence.

"You all right, honey?"

"Sure, mom. Why?"

"Well, you're awfully quiet." I shrugged.

"Just tired. We did a lot of riding today."

"I thought you were at Tony's house, watching a video." Oh fine. You'll never make double-0 rank if you can't get your cover story straight.

"This was afterwards. In the skatepark."

"Oh. Well, if you're tired, don't stay up late. Do you have any homework to do?"

"Yeah, a little."

"Better do that right after dinner. You probably should have done it yesterday." Oh rats. She had activated the dwarf.

"Peter's going to be in tro-o-u-u-ble. Homework not done—he'll get suspe-e-ended!"

"Oh, shut your face, Marla!" I retorted, with much more venom than I really felt.

"Peter, you watch your mouth! There's no need to talk to your sister like that. And you can pipe down too, Marla. You deserved that." My mom's exquisite display of illogic brought a welcome silence back to the table. I finished dinner as quickly as I could, retreated to my room and got busy on my English homework.

I had not been lying when I told my mom that I was tired. A great and unnatural fatigue had swept over me in the moments immediately following Robert's departure, as if it had been his company alone that had staved off the mind-sapping effects of our day's experiences. Now, alone in my room and stretched full-length on the floor over my English textbook, I felt overpowered by it all. The homework assignment was not particularly hard—certainly not for someone who genuinely enjoyed English—but I could not focus. I answered the first three questions on the sheet relatively quickly, then stalled and spent ten minutes staring at the fourth question in an uncomprehending daze.

"Peter! What's the matter with you? Are you deaf?" I jerked awake at the sound of my mom's voice. I was still lying face down on my bedroom floor, in which position I had fallen asleep, my head resting on the textbook. Now I pushed myself up into a sitting position, unaccountably cold, shivering and disoriented, and quite unaware of how many minutes or hours I had been asleep.

"What? WHAT?" I called back, half-expecting to hear that the house was on fire.

"That's the third time I've called you, Peter. It's your friend Liddy on the phone." I stumbled down the stairs to where my mom was standing, holding the cordless phone. Judging by the look on my mom's face as I took possession of it I must have looked at least as bad as I felt, and probably several times worse. I retreated to my room with the phone and with mom's laser look burning twin bald patches in the back of my neck.

"Liddy? What do you want?" At first I thought Liddy was out of breath, but soon realized that she was whispering into the phone; she must have hidden herself in some corner of her house out of earshot of her family to make this call.

"What happened, Peter? You go to the cops?" Fighting back the urge to point out to Liddy that had she stayed with us she would not need to ask this question, I gave her a summary of our dealings with the Police Department and advised her to read the newspaper story for herself. My explanation was interrupted several times by excited responses from the other end of the phone, all of the "wow!", "no foolin'!" and "outta sight!" variety. Liddy seemed to be particularly awestruck by the image of Robert and me being escorted by a parade of official cars, but when she started asking about which way the rotating lights on the cruisers' light bars turned, I cut her short.

"Look, Liddy, I'm really beat. We'll fill you in on everything tomorrow at lunch, OK? Gotta go now." I ended the call and checked the time on my alarm clock; even allowing for the duration of the call I must have been asleep for twenty minutes, and felt worse now than before I had conked out. My mouth tasted like a gorilla's armpit, while my eyeballs felt as if they were being sliced open from the inside.

I ran downstairs to hang up the phone, only to encounter my mom in medical attack mode. Before I could reverse out of the kitchen she was feeling my forehead and cheeks with one hand, and fingering the glands in my neck with the other.

"Are you sure you're all right, sweetheart? You look like you're coming down with something."

"I'm OK really, mom. Just tired. I want to finish my homework and get to bed."

"I think that's a good idea. And I'm going to check on you in the morning just to be sure you don't have a temperature." It occurred to me that I might just have created, without trying, a convincing case for a day off from school, but for once I was not interested in goofing off. I had the feeling that the business of the car in the dump was not over, and that if more developments were to bubble up in the days to follow then I did not want to be out of circulation when they surfaced.

Back in my room I slogged through the rest of my homework, then undressed, washed and jumped into bed. Even though it was still early I expected to be asleep within minutes, but my brain perversely refused simply to log off and shut down; like a bug-ridden software program it kept cycling backward and forward through all the material it had received that day in an infinite, nonsensical loop. After nearly an hour of this I began to wish that my brain really *were* a computer so I could disconnect it from the power supply, but knowing this was not an option I could do nothing but lie there while it jabbered away uselessly, asking the same questions over and over again without ever getting an answer. Finally, in a desperate effort to distract my brain, I turned on my radio and listened to a call-in talk show. Thus it was that I finally fell asleep that night to the sound of an angry taxpayer asserting his right to keep loaded firearms in his home to guard against the danger of a sudden takeover of the US Government by the clandestine communist army known to be forming in Canada.

A DEATH UNDER SAND

MONDAY, EARLY

Uncle Cam accompanied me to the car dealership, which was located in what used to be the Food Fair supermarket building. As we entered the parking lot I noticed that he was wearing his Air Steward's uniform, or at least the top half of it. Below his jacket I could see that he was wearing brown corduroy pants, in which he had apparently just been doing some heavy gardening. As we walked up and down the lines of cars Uncle Cam would point to each car and ask me if that was the one. But not one of them was exactly right. They were either the wrong make, the wrong color, the wrong year or the wrong model, or they had wheels or windshields missing.

"Well, if we don't find it here" Uncle Cam pointed out, "we have to check every car in the state alphabetically."

That made no sense to me, and I went to find the manager of the dealership to tell him so. In the manager's office, Chief Bonaventura was sitting on the corner of the desk with his legs crossed, laughing at something that Robert had said. Robert had evidently beaten me to the manager's office, but I couldn't fathom what he could have been saying to put the Chief in such a good mood. Seeing me come in, the Chief stood and announced that we would have to wait outside, as he and my uncle had important business to discuss. I looked around, but Uncle Cam seemed to have disappeared, and before I could locate him we found ourselves ushered out into the parking lot.

"Come on, Peter," said Robert urgently. "Better get out of here before it gets dark."

That was easier said than done. The parking lot was so vast and so full of cars that it was impossible to determine the direction of the exit. We walked for several minutes but only seemed to be plunging deeper and deeper into the jungle of automobiles. Suddenly I saw something bob up quickly and disappear again behind the hood of one of the nearby cars. It was a man's head, topped with a black, long-peaked baseball cap. With a cry of warning I turned and we ran in the opposite direction but had not gone far before we saw, several car-lengths in front of us, a thin figure in black scuttling between two cars. In a panic we turned away at a right angle. On this new course we quickly came to the edge of the parking lot, where it overlooked the steep muddy banks of a swiftly running stream. Half-way down the near bank stood Mr. Canfield, our 5th-grade science teacher, who pointed upstream and advised us that the future lay in that direction. Ignoring him, we tumbled down the bank and continued our flight downstream, but came upon a sight around the first bend that stopped us dead.

A DEATH UNDER SAND

Four car seats were ranged in a row on the opposite bank, facing the stream. In the seat furthest from where we stood, propped grotesquely in a rigid sitting position, was the body of Gumboots. In the seat next to him was the body of the unknown man from the Excalibur. Standing close behind, Robert kept urging me to keep going, but I was loath to pass so close to this macabre display and turned back to Robert to tell him so. There, standing only a few feet behind Robert and a little way up the steep bank so that he towered over both of us, was Black Hat, obscenities and foul threats starting to flow from his ugly, brutal mouth. I screamed in terror and blundered away from him, tripping and splashing clumsily through the muddy stream. As I reached the far bank and tried to pull myself out of the water, I suddenly looked up and found myself staring directly into the face of the unknown dead man. He was kneeling on the bank and reaching down to me with his hand.

"Come on" he growled impatiently. "You know these other two seats are for you, don't you?"

In horror I staggered back into mid-stream, where a large, brawny hand suddenly gripped the back of my neck from behind.

"NO!"

I sprang up, gagging, retching, and frantically tearing the sweat-soaked bed sheets off me. I lurched across the floor of my darkened bedroom, desperately trying to keep my stomach muscles in check until I could reach the bathroom. Somehow I made it and, falling to my knees before the toilet bowl, became the third member of our group to suffer in spectacular fashion the effects of delayed shock. Awash with perspiration, I gripped the upraised seat with both hands and vomited until I could swear I was bringing up parts of my soul along with the more recognizable material decorating the inside of the bowl. Again and again I heaved until, like Tony and Liddy so many hours before, my stomach had nothing left to offer up. And still I heaved. Finally I collapsed into a half-sitting position, wedged between the side of the bowl and the wall.

Drained, trembling, and exhausted, I sat and waited for what I thought was the inevitable: my mom appearing at the bathroom door in her robe, a concerned look on her face and a "you get to take the day off school" look in her eye. Yet as the minutes ground by, and my stomach's convulsions began to peter out, the doorway remained miraculously empty. My mom is known to have woken up and come running into one of her children's bedroom at the sound of a mild fit of coughing. She must have been sleeping exceptionally heavily that night to miss the ralphing performance going on in her bathroom.

After what felt like an hour I carefully levered myself up from my cramped position, flushed the toilet and, fighting the gagging sensation in my throat, cleaned the bowl out as well as I could. I toweled the perspiration off my body and returned quietly to my bedroom. Crossing to the window, I slid the screen all the way up and put my head out into the cool, dry air. A gentle breeze was blowing toward my side of the house, and I remained motionless in the window frame to allow the refreshing night air to play on my face. After only a few minutes Mother Nature had worked wonders with me, almost making me forget my porcelain puking episode, but I was in no hurry to return to bed. Sleep was out of the question for now.

I mentally revisited my nightmare. Normally my dreams make even less sense than this one did, with pink zebras carrying Easter baskets through our living room and well-known politicians dressed in taffeta riding on our school bus. At least this one represented, in standard dream fashion, a collage of many of the images and happenings of the day: cars found and missing, Robert, the police, Black Hat, Gumboots, death and pursuit (and, naturally, our 5th-grade science teacher, whom we had not seen in two years). But now that I had recovered from the shock of being 'caught' by Black Hat, I found myself fixating on the image of a man whom I had only seen in death, now—so far as my dream was concerned—alive, moving and talking.

Was this what he had been like in life, I wondered. Did his voice use to rasp the way it had done in my nightmare, or was that merely a detail invented by whatever mechanism in my brain writes the screenplays for my dreams? And had he been impatient with teenage boys as my dream-figure had been? I had no way of knowing. All I truly knew about this man was that he was dead, and all else was fruitless speculation.

But, for that matter, what did I even know about this death? It was unlike anything I had ever encountered, unlike any description I could have rendered of what death looked like or what sensations it would generate within me. And nothing could have prepared me for what I had seen in the car: no amount of gruesome movie killings, of which I had seen plenty, nor any number of funeral parlor visits, of which I had experienced but one or two. All my worldly knowledge of death, such as it was, felt as unreal and meaningless as a playground game of "bang bang you're dead" compared to the sheer *undeniability* of the death that had been thrust at us. This was no actor dropping picturesquely to the ground on the director's cue, only to stand up again in time for the next take. This was as stark and real and uncompromising as anything I had known.

I rested one shoulder against the window frame and closed my eyes. In the stillness of the night, free of the interruptions and distractions that had marked this day, my mind reproduced the scene in the car with greater clarity than ever before. I could see where the man's bushy eyebrows almost met above the bridge of his nose, and the point where the short, straight scar on his left cheek disappeared into his mustache. Most clearly of all I could see, on the left breast of the dead man's sweatshirt, a well-known clothing line logo. More than anything for me, this logo took the man's death out of the sphere of fiction, of fantasy, of video entertainment. In my closet I had several shirts sporting that logo; I knew where they sold them in town and could remember every word of the TV commercial. So this was a death belonging to the real world, the world in which I woke up every morning, in which I went to school and ate dinner and ragged on my sister. In this world the man in the car, whoever he was, had probably walked the same streets of Gretchyville as I did; we may have passed each other in the mall, even brushed against each other in a crowd. But even if we had done this hundreds of times, no power on Earth could make it happen even once more. I could walk the streets and cruise the mall till I was an old man, and never would I even catch sight of him. From the moment the world disappeared from his eyes for the last time, no plans he may have made would ever be realized, no appointments ever be kept, no promises ever be honored. Everything that he was or may have aspired to be became null at that moment, and would remain so until time ground to a halt.

I don't know how long I stayed in the window that night, turning these thoughts over, backwards and inside-out. I had never had such thoughts about death before, but then, I had never before encountered it the way I had that day. I guess most people never do, and those that do get to wait until they're a lot older than Robert and me. Whatever else this death meant to me, it was making me grow up at an uncomfortable speed.

And there, in the cool silence of the night, one of the day's unanswerable questions was suddenly answered. That damned logo on the man's sweatshirt grew ever larger and ever clearer in my vision, demanding that I identify it. And the moment I did so a line from the newspaper story barged in: *Sergeant Raleigh said that one was reported to be wearing a green Chipmunk Workshop sweatshirt...* The embroidered cartoon of a toothy ground-squirrel wielding a hammer was now the clearest image in my head, picked out against the green material of the dead man's sweatshirt and identifying him as one of the two robbers of the Maple County Savings Bank.

A DEATH UNDER SAND

MONDAY, 7:30 AM

The school bus pulled up at the end of Sachem Street, and the half-dozen waiting Junior High kids shuffled forward unenthusiastically toward the open door. Don't you just love Mondays? I let the rest of them clamber into the bus ahead of me, then put my left foot onto the platform and dragged my right leg stiffly up to join it. I continued up the steps this way, wincing with each one, until I reached the top.

"Sorry" I gasped to the driver, by way of greeting. "New leg. Stitches not out yet."

Celeste, the scatterbrained driver of bus #17, stared at me in pity through her thick pebble lenses.

"Oh no… What happened?"

"Don't make a fuss. I can manage" I responded bravely, and limped determinedly past a dozen or so chattering kids toward the rear of the bus and Robert's widely grinning face.

"Got her," I reported triumphantly, high-fiving my way into the seat beside Robert. As the bus lurched off and continued its agonized progress up Compass Avenue, I turned to Robert to share my revelation of the previous night. I found him inspecting my face closely and suspiciously.

"You OK, man? You look terrible," he observed. Although I was feeling relatively sound I still looked a little green around the gills from my pukefest, a fact I had managed to conceal from my

159

mom at breakfast by limiting my movements to the darker corners of the kitchen. I gave Robert a blow-by-blow account of my evening, up to the throw-by-throw episode in the bathroom.

"It got you too, did it? I thought you looked kinda pale," he said, lightly pinching my cheek. I brushed his hand away.

"More than I can say about you" I laughed, remembering our conversation on the sand dune the day before. We scuffled light-heartedly until I noticed Celeste's disapproving look in the rear-view mirror. Suddenly I grimaced, clutched my right thigh and gave a pained wail.

"The leg! Not the leg! I can't stand the pain!"

"Hey you two! Stop that right now! Do you hear me?" Celeste yelled in a semi-hysterical voice. We relaxed and sat back, grinning. The day was off to a good start.

By the time we turned into the school driveway I had filled Robert in on the significance of the logo on the dead man's breast. The news imposed a thoughtful silence on him that lasted until the bus halted in line before the front steps of the cinderblock palace we knew as the Gabriele M. Ciccone Junior High School.

"I don't even recall what kinda shirt he was wearing," he admitted, as we followed the slowly-moving line of kids toward the door of the bus. We passed the driver's seat and descended the steps, for which maneuver I decided to switch legs, and hobbled painfully to the ground on my right foot while holding my left leg stiffly out, grunting and gasping with each step. Robert was obviously still pondering the meaning of my discovery.

"If he *was* one of the robbers…"

"What?" We paused on the steps.

"…he must have been shot by the other one."

"You think so?"

"Well, who else? There were no cops at the bank; the story in the paper said no-one fired any shots there. He was alive when the car left the bank and dead when the car got buried. They must 've had a fight over the money or something."

"Or maybe someone was waiting for them at the dump and killed him there," I suggested.

"What—an ambush kind of thing?"

"Yeah, I guess. Maybe they killed the other one, too."

"Nah. Why leave one body there and take the other one away?" I couldn't ignore Robert's logic.

"So whether he had help or not, the other guy from the bank was part of it—the killing, I mean."

"Must 've been. And either he was Black Hat, or the person they met—if they *did* meet someone—was Black Hat."

"That's for sure," I agreed. "Remember when he first saw Gumboots? He was really mad; he kept yelling for him to get away from the car. So he knew the car was there, and he could see Gumboots looking into it and seeing the body, which I guess was still meant to be a big secret."

"Right enough. And Gumboots must have known him."

"How do you figure that?"

"Well... if he and the dead guy—Jimmy, whatever—really were brothers or something, he must've wanted to tear whoever killed him to pieces. And the moment he saw Black Hat in the trees, he pitched a total fit. Went beresk, remember?"

"Berserk, Robert."

"That too. Ape-kaka." Once again I saw the tragic figure of Gumboots lurching frenziedly across the track to meet his death. Robert was right; Gumboots had known that Black Hat was somehow implicated in Jimmy's death, perhaps solely responsible for it. He hadn't stopped to question or accuse him, but had thrown himself bodily at a man he probably knew to be a murderer with no thought or care for his own survival, so great was his hatred. And how dearly he himself had paid for it.

"You're right," I said. "He knew Black Hat. And he knew he was involved in the killing."

"And that's why Black Hat had to kill him too, because he'd found out about it."

"Yeah, and don't forget us. We found it, and he tried to kill all four of us." Robert was shaking his head.

"Un-freakin'-believable. Guy's ready to kill six people over a stash of money he didn't even want."

By this time we were alone on the steps. As the last of the buses pulled out into the driveway its driver sounded his horn and shouted something unintelligible out of the window at an old and dirty-looking black Mercedes illegally parked there. Almost at once the offending car started to move slowly away down the driveway, but through the grime of the back window I could see that the driver was twisted around in his seat, staring hard in our direction. All I could see of him was a head of dark, untidy hair, but it was enough to make my mouth become suddenly very dry.

The Mercedes suddenly accelerated noisily away and was gone before I could find my voice. And when I found it I couldn't find Robert; he had already started into the gloom of the building's main entrance. By the time I caught up with him I was already doubting the flimsy evidence of my own eyes. Had Black Hat really succeeded in tracking us down so soon, or were my fears of Sunday afternoon turning into unreasoning panic on Monday morning? The man in the car could have been anyone—a father who had just dropped his kid off, a stranger to town who had taken a wrong turning—and I was not about to infect Robert with my panic over what was probably nothing.

We arrived at our homeroom and prepared for another day of combat with the education establishment. Neither Tony nor Liddy were in our home room or in any of our classes that morning, so until first-wave lunch period dragged itself around there was no reason or opportunity to rehash Sunday's events yet again. But when Robert and I emerged from the cafeteria line, trays loaded with food still warm but not yet identified, Tony and Liddy were frantically signaling for us to join them at a small table in an isolated corner, which they had apparently discouraged all others from sharing with them. We joined them and, over lunch, brought them up to date on all that had happened since we had parted company at Plover Road, including most of the theories we had developed about the affair. They had both read the newspaper story by now, but neither could advance any alternative theories to improve upon what we already knew. Most frustratingly for me, I appeared to be the only one of the group who had actually identified the Chipmunk Workshop logo on the man's sweatshirt.

"I wonder if they found the car yet," said Tony at length, to no-one in particular.

"What—somewhere else in the dump?" I asked.

"In the dump, out of it," he shrugged. "Wherever it got taken to."

"I'm telling you guys, that car *did not get out of the dump!* It's still in there somewhere. It's *got* to be." Suddenly Robert looked up from the chocolate milk carton that he was noisily draining.

"Hey! Did anyone see today's paper?" Apparently none of us had.

"Why?" I asked. "Do you think there's going to be anything new in there?"

"Maybe the cops found some other stuff out since yesterday afternoon," he suggested. Tony snickered.

"Yeah, maybe they found they could get you guys into a honey bucket full of trouble by telling the paper your names and what you did with them yesterday afternoon." Robert and I exchanged concerned glances.

"Would they-?"

"Oh God, I hope not." I was suddenly reminded of my brat sister's hopeful little song from dinner, cheerfully wishing me into trouble, and realized with growing concern that she might just get her wish. But Robert seemed more inclined to action than panic, and stood up abruptly, sweeping his food tray off the table.

"Come on," he said. "Let's find out."

"Where are you going?"

"Library. They have the papers there." And without waiting for approval, disapproval or discussion he set off toward the cafeteria door, the rest of us trailing behind him.

The school did indeed receive copies of the local and national newspapers as part of a tepid attempt to wean its students off a diet of superhero comics, but when we arrived at the library it was to discover that the only available copy of that day's Gretchyville Times had been appropriated by Geoffrey Treedle. Robert was not dismayed. He leaned down close to the Treedle ear and whispered conspiratorially:

"Hey Geoffrey—you know that Heather Palastanga?" Geoffrey's perpetually sleepy-looking eyes lit up.

"Yeah?"

"She just gave me a buck to tell you she's waiting out behind the bleachers."

"So?" On Geoffrey's carcass of a face there was not a twitch of comprehension.

"So, you big jackass, she wants to see *you* out there—right now" said Robert, simultaneously winking, leering and nudging. "What are you waiting for, man?"

"Oh-h..." The gears finally meshed in Geoffrey's head. He hauled himself up from the table and, powered by his internal lust motor, wobbled at warp speed toward the exit.

We gathered around Robert as he sat down, closed the paper up and scanned the front page. There was the article, occupying the bottom half of the page; we quickly read it and found it to be a basic regurgitation of Sunday's story. There was no mention of us (thank God) nor of anything we did not already know, meaning that if the police had made any progress since mid-afternoon they had not disclosed any details to the press. After we had read and digested the story, I pointed out that there was still no reference to the car's license plate number or ownership.

"Is it like when someone gets killed in a car crash, and they won't give out the name until they've found the family and told them?" asked Liddy.

"Could be," I replied. "Although if they knew the plate number from the start—and I bet they did—they would have had the name, address and everything on Saturday night. But there's nothing here to say the car was even stolen."

"So like I said before, maybe it wasn't stolen; maybe it *was* their own car," put in Robert, but without much conviction. Since no-one else had any contribution to make there was a long, unproductive silence. I stared out of the window at a group of seventh-graders playing a pick-up game of football, while Robert simply stared at the opposite wall. Tony and Liddy were lost in their own thoughts. Finally, Tony asked whether we were going to go back to the police and tell them about the sweatshirt logo or our theory concerning Jimmy's killer. I gestured hopelessly.

"Why bother? The Chipmunk Workshop thing was in the original article, and they already think we read that *before* we went to the dump. And they probably figured out who killed the guy the same way we did. I'm not about to have them call us liars twice in two days. Are you, Robert?"

I looked down at Robert, expecting an answer, but he appeared not to have heard me. He was slowly gathering himself up into a standing position, his unblinking gaze fixed on the opposite wall of the library. He reached his full height then leaned forward with his fists on the table, still staring hard. Irresistibly, his position and his silence forced me to turn my eyes in the same direction, where I saw on the wall a framed reproduction of an old map of the local area, covering Gretchyville, most of Cold Harbor and portions of Kingsleytown. I couldn't see what it was about the map that was transfixing Robert, and was about to ask when he turned to me with a light in his eyes unlike any I had seen there before.

"I know how they got the car into the dump," he said simply. While his voice was controlled and even, he seemed to be fighting to keep a sudden uprush of new ideas properly ordered within his head. He turned back to the map then started to push his way around the table, barely waiting for us to shuffle out of his way.

"I know how they got in, and I think they got out the same way," he declared, marching over to the map and inspecting it minutely. The rest of us bumbled stupidly after him and gathered in a semicircle in his rear, attempting to see from a range of three feet what he had apparently seen from across the room. I had never paid much attention to the map before; I knew it hadn't been put there to help present-day Gretchyvillians (villains?) find their way around, since several roads that I knew to exist were not shown on it. Nor was it some ancient document: there was not a single sea monster to be seen off the coast. Finally I found a legend in the bottom-right corner indicating that the original had been drawn up in 1953, when the towns were much smaller and more tightly clustered around their respective Main Streets. Robert was examining at close range the lower-left quadrant of the map, where the center of Gretchyville was located.

"OK, so this is Main Street, and this... this here must be Custance—see, there's a road cutting it on the diagonal further down; that must be Fishkill Road."

"Custance is longer than that; it goes all the way down to Shore Street" put in Liddy, squinting over Robert's shoulder.

"Well, now it does. But I bet you ten bucks it didn't then. Not back in..." He searched the map for a date. I pointed out the mapmaker's legend and finished his sentence.

"Fine, so the bank's right here, on this corner. Now, when the robbers got out of there, they hit Main Street going east, right enough? And that's the last anyone saw of them." The rest of us were lagging some way behind Robert's thought process, but he was only just hitting his stride. With his index finger he traced the line of Main Street, starting from the present location of the bank and moving steadily eastward. Before long he arrived at the point where Main Street and Old Kingsleytown Road meet, merging at such a fine angle that even today no-one has figured out what to do with the wedge-shaped lot bounded by them. I had not appreciated it before, but Main Street actually bends away at that point; as Robert's finger passed from Main to Old K., it was describing more of a straight line than had it remained on Main Street. On he went, tracing the route taken by the police when they drove us back to the dump, except that where the police had turned off onto Valley Drive to circumnavigate the dump the flying Juneau finger continued without deviation on Old K. On this map that was easy: not only did Valley Drive not exist, *but neither did the dump.* Robert continued to follow the road until it crossed into Kingsleytown and came to an abrupt end, meeting the neighboring town's Main Street at a right angle.

"You see?" he exclaimed. "It's a straight shot. Straight as an arrow. Even with the traffic it wouldn't take more than—what? four minutes?—to get from the bank all the way down Old Kingsleytown, plus they were going *away* from Police Headquarters, where any cruisers would be coming from." Tony voiced the objection that must have been on all our minds.

"But you can't get all the way down that road," protested Tony. "It stops dead, just before the dump." Robert, still way ahead of us, waved him into silence with one hand while fishing a pencil out of his pocket with the other.

"Of course it does. Now the dump must be... about *here*, right enough?" He inscribed a large, irregular circle on the map, cutting across the road, while three heads swiveled around like that kid's in *The Exorcist* to see whether any teachers or their pets had witnessed Robert's act of vandalism. None had, although I suspected that even had they done so, Robert would not have throttled back from his present power setting. I moved in closer.

"That's about right," I said. "Look, this must be Seminole leading away to the north, but there's no Overlook or Birch. Not built yet, I guess."

"Not yet," agreed Robert, swiftly penciling in the approximate locations of the two roads and provoking a second round of head-swiveling from his friends.

"Now look, you guys. This must be about where we always cut into the strip of woods to get into the dump. The trail Tony laid out took us way down to the right, down to about—*here*, which is where the car was." He finished his dead reckoning by drawing a small circle at what he considered the most probable position of the car. It fell directly across the line of the Old Kingsleytown Road.

"But it still doesn't make sense," objected Tony. "The road's not there any more. They would have torn it up when they built the dump. Even if these two guys went tanking up Old Kingsleytown before anyone could stop them, they would have come to a dead stop where the road runs out." Robert, uncharacteristically, waited patiently for Tony to finish.

"Anyone know how long the dump has been there? We know it wasn't there in '53, but how long after that did they pull the road up?" No-one knew, but Robert had already jumped to the next car in his train of thought.

"Those trees all around the dump—what are they? Scrub oak? Scrub pine? How long do they take to grow?" Finally a light bulb began to flicker on in the space above my skull.

"Oh hey, you don't think…"

"Anyone ever been in that part of the woods, between where Old Kingsleytown ends and the dump begins? Betcha there's no trees there—just bushes and stuff. Nothing that couldn't be hacked out of the way." Tony looked to be in physical pain. He was thinking.

"Yeah, there's trees there, I think. Or at least, there's no big bare patches."

"I'm not talking about big bare patches" said Robert. "I'm only talking about the width of a car." Now Liddy was on board; only Tony was still groping to understand, looking uncertainly from face to face. For the benefit of us all, Robert summarized his idea.

A DEATH UNDER SAND

"The way I figure it, these guys spent some time in the woods before Saturday making sure they had a clear path. Comes time to bail out of the bank, they head right up Main Street into Old K., get to the end in less than five minutes *and keep going*. They go right through the damn woods into the dump without coming anywhere near the main gate. Six minutes, tops. No-one sees them go in, and no-one sees the car get buried. Then Black Hat, plus anyone else who was helping him, leaves on foot the same way he came in, covering up any tracks he left in the woods." I took up his theme.

"And when they needed to get it out of there in a hurry-"

"-they did the same thing in reverse. Literally in reverse, maybe. Straight out of the sandpile, across the track and through the woods to grandma's house."

"Whose grandma?" asked Tony.

Liddy and I were too busy trying to take Robert's theory on board to answer Tony. While there was still a barrelful of questions yet to be answered, if Robert were right about the robbers' escape route then it did at least explain why none of the landfill workers saw the car enter or leave, and how it was that the car was nowhere to be found inside the dump when the police made their search. I could visualize—I think we all could—the red Excalibur accelerating like a bat out of hell off Main Street into Old Kingsleytown Road, rocketing down it to the end, then disappearing like the Batmobile into the woods at about the same time the first cruiser rolled up outside the bank. As Robert had said, it was a straight shot.

The silence was broken, finally, by the shrill sound of the bell announcing the start of period 6. Like robots we started to shuffle toward the library door, although I knew that we still had unfinished business. So, evidently, did Liddy.

"How you gonna prove all that, man?" The look Robert gave her in response said, in effect, that he had already determined how to prove his theory, had already transmitted his intentions to us, and fully expected us all to be a part of the process.

"What's the matter with you? You know what we've all got to do, right enough. We've got to go back to the dump today—as soon as school's over—and find the evidence in the woods."

A DEATH UNDER SAND

MONDAY, 3:30 PM

So, of course, it was just Robert and I who ended up going back to the dump. Robert finally succeeded in explaining his theory to Tony, whose face briefly took on a look of wide-eyed enlightenment. That lasted until his brain was attacked by the realization that he was expected to return to the place where he had been shot at, in order to scrabble around on the ground looking for clues. And when he finished voicing his fear that Black Hat would be lying in wait there, ready to murder us and bury us in the woods, he and Liddy got into a routine of synchronized mental underwear-whizzing and sudden recollection of homework demanding instant attention. Of all of us, Robert had the least concern about returning to the crime scene. My enthusiasm was a little muted by my experience on the school steps that morning, and while I knew I would support Robert I could not help wondering whether Tony and Liddy had good reasons for their fears.

When I arrived home I hastily scrawled a note advising my mom that I was visiting Robert, headed out on my BMX and reached Compass Avenue at about the same time he was penning the same kind of note to his own mom. When he joined up with me we rode together across town as fast as we could, arriving at the end of Old Kingsleytown

Road at about three-thirty. The road comes to an end in a way that anyone who did not know how the dump came to be built would consider unusual. Almost all the dead-end streets in town end in some kind of turn-around mandated by the Fire Department: either a circular patch of blacktop, a paved loop enclosing a small area of brush and trees where the local homeowners take their dogs after dark for a clandestine piddle, or—in the tonier parts of town—a larger loop containing one or two upscale houses enthroned on their own private island. Old K. fits none of these descriptions. As you approach the dump from the direction of town, you pass the last house on the road two or three hundred yards before reaching the end of the road itself. That makes sense; from the moment the creation of the Silver Hill Landfill was announced, there must have been very little incentive for builders to put up properties closer than the closest existing one—as in: 2 bths., 3 brms., 2-car grge., oil heat & putrid smell. And where the road ends, there is no turn-around of any kind; the pavement ends abruptly where the scrubby woodland starts. Nor is the dump itself visible from this point, since the hundred-yard-wide buffer zone of vegetation surrounding it inclines upward from the road's end to the edge of the dump proper. All we could see from our position on the last foot of this lonely stretch of road was a tangled belt of overgrown bushes and skinny trees, growing out of a carpet of rotting leaves and fallen, decomposing tree trunks.

I could see one other thing at once: Robert had been right about the condition of the ground along the line of the vanished road. When the Town started to create the landfill, they must have torn up the road within its boundaries and left the ground beneath exactly as it was: almost pure sand. Over the years some topsoil from the area where we were standing must have blown over and down into this slightly lower strip of land, but not enough to support vegetation of any significant size. In this narrow leaf-clogged path was growing nothing more substantial than a scattering of unhealthy-looking bushes (I should probably have known what they were called, but they wouldn't have looked any healthier if I had, believe me).

"No trees," I remarked. "How did you know?"

"Just a guess. Only a guess."

"Damn good guess, Robert. Even so, these bushes... they're still too big for a car to get over."

"I know. Let's take a look."

Dropping our machines on the blacktop we started toward the tree line, but had not covered five paces before a sudden thought checked me.

"Hey, Robert... let's put the bikes out of sight while we're doing this." Robert gave me a questioning look, then scanned the woodland around us. I wondered if he thought I was being overly cautious, particularly as I had still not told him about the beat-up Mercedes outside the school, but presently he nodded in agreement.

"Yeah… just in case." Wheeling our machines off the pavement, we stowed them behind some thick shrubbery off to the side. Although fall had, by the calendar, already started, the woods in and around Gretchyville still held such color as they had managed to produce at the height of summer. Admittedly, this only amounted to the green of the leaves and some scraggly yellow blooms on the bushes, but it was enough to make me notice that the bushes on the line of the old road were a little dingier and more tired-looking than anything else growing around them. I had assumed this to be due simply to the different soil type on the road line, so was surprised when Robert, walking a few steps ahead of me, suddenly dropped to his knees and stared hard at something at the base of the nearest bush. After a few seconds he let out a cackling laugh, which turned into a whoop of triumph as he pounded his fist into the ground. Jumping up, he grabbed the bush with both hands and gave an almighty heave.

Now I know that Robert is no more capable of pulling a full-grown bush out of the ground than I am, so my second surprise in less than a minute came when it flew through the air and landed six feet away. Robert was after it at once, turning it upside-down so we could both see clearly where the trunk had been sawn off flush with the ground.

Discarding the bush, Robert ran to its nearest neighbor and repeated the operation. I followed him and joined him in pulling away the mutilated undergrowth up and down the road line. Every one of the bushes had been severed from its roots but left in position on the ground, in such a way that nothing less than a close examination, of the sort Robert had performed, could have uncovered the deception. It was also quite obvious that, with the bushes cleared away to the side, there was nothing to prevent a car from being driven clean through the woods between the dump and the road. I stopped in my work and looked up at Robert.

"You're the man" I said quietly. Robert smiled, regarding the naked stumps half-covered by leaves and dirt, and nodded with obvious satisfaction. Then, suddenly, his expression became serious and he dropped to his knees again to examine the ground. Most of the surface along the road line, like all the ground in the woods, was thickly carpeted with leaves. But in one or two places, where the ground was particularly uneven, the sandy soil was only lightly covered or completely uncovered. Robert had directed his attention to one of these spots and was carefully brushing away the few leaves that interrupted his view of it. There, unmistakably, were what we had not been able to find twenty-four hours earlier. I joined Robert on the ground and looked in awe at the bare patch of ground with its overlapping tire tracks, which told us one of two things: either two cars with identical tires had passed this way, or the same car had entered and left the dump by the same route. Our eyes met, and in Robert's I saw the light of pure triumph, a light that burst out from within him and illuminated his whole face with a joy that I saw only infrequently. I understood, and was glad to be there to witness it. He must have been experiencing a crowning sense of satisfaction to see his theory proved so dramatically; it meant that he could return to Police Headquarters, throw that *look* right back in their faces, and demand the respect that they had owed him in the first place. And when he did, I wanted to be there to witness that, too.

"Come on" he said, springing up and turning toward the dump. "Let's go all the way in."

We followed the line of the road in, casting aside the remaining bushes as we passed them. When we reached the inner edge of the woods, most of the remaining parts of the mystery of the car's movements fell into place with a damn-near audible *click*. Firstly, where the ghost of Old Kingsleytown Road crossed into the dump proper, the edge of the worked area was marked not by the usual twenty-foot-high near-vertical scarp but by a relatively low feature that a car could easily negotiate without burying its nose in the ground. As we approached the fence we could see how the sheer cliff edge gradually tapered down on our left until it reached its minimum height in front of us, then began to climb again to its normal height, which it reached a couple of hundred yards away to our right. We had actually passed this point on our way in with the police but had not paid it any attention, probably because the line of the cliff edge actually pulled away from the perimeter track here to a distance of some fifty yards; all we could see from Raleigh's car was what we expected to see—a continuous fence line. And about that fence...

That was the clincher. Until we arrived at it, neither of us could explain how the car could have tunneled under, vaulted over, or threaded its way through the fabric of the fence. But, of course, the answer was right there for us to find. I reached the fence first and, intent on following the tire marks on the ground, leaned unthinkingly against it close to one of the high metal stakes. Perhaps Robert, whose brainwave in the library had led to our discoveries, deserved to be a witness to the piece of slapstick that followed, rather than a participant in it. With pinging and scraping noises, the fence gradually leaned inward under my weight, then sprang open, depositing me on the sand in a squall of arms, legs, torn clothing and obscenities.

"Why, thank you, sir" said Robert, curtseying and mincing his way, unimpeded, through the huge gap that I had created. He reached me and pulled me upright, and we both stood and stared at the fence. I recall that one of us was shaking his head in wonder, but it wasn't Robert; he seemed to have been expecting it, and perhaps if the gray matter between my ears were not lint I would have expected it too.   When we examined the fence closely we could see that the links had been carefully clipped from top to bottom near one of the stakes. Since the stakes were some eight feet apart, the entire section of fence that traversed the road line could be swung back like a drape, leaving ample room for the Excalibur to pass through. And when it had, it must have been as easy as peeing on a tree to hook the severed ends back on to the stake to make the fence appear whole. It had certainly fooled us, not to mention the stumbling sleuths of the Gretchyville Police Department.

"And that's how," was all Robert had to say.

We moved to the perimeter track and immediately picked up the scars left on the surface by the police convoy carrying out its turning maneuver; at the point where we intercepted the track we were no more than fifty yards from the burial spot. Robert continued toward the spot, minutely inspecting the ground, but I hung back. I was suddenly overcome by the feeling that, having discovered as much as we had in the last few minutes, we were beginning to push our luck. As closely as Robert was examining the ground, so was I scanning the tree line, half-expecting to see a bush rustle and shake as an armed and menacing adult brushed past it with murder in his eyes.

"Let's wrap it up, Robert" I called. Robert did not appear to have heard; his business at the burial spot was consuming all his attention. At long last he turned and faced me, squinting into the sun, and I saw his arms rise and fall in a gesture of frustration. He said just two words.

"Tire marks!"

"What about them?"

"Ain't none!" I started to turn and point to the road line we had just been following, but realized almost at once what Robert was talking about: regardless of what we had found in the woods, there were still no marks leading out of the berm where we had found the car. And without them, nothing else made sense.

We stood in our respective spots, looking around for inspiration, illumination or just plain salvation. Nothing came. The sun took a brief header behind a fragment of wispy cloud dawdling its way in from the sea, then reappeared. I was growing more and more anxious to be away, without quite knowing why. We had not seen another human being since we passed the last house on Old K., and beyond each other there was certainly no-one to see here. Nor could I hear any sound of human activity beyond the uneven buzz and rumble of an unseen dump vehicle. It did not sound like the big 'dozer, more like a smaller, lighter and swifter version of it, and its sound kept surging and fading as it traversed the confusing topography of the dump. I could not guess at its location from the engine noise, which died down to a kind of low purr even as I listened to it. I tried Robert one more time.

"Come on, Robert, we've done all we can here. Let's—"

The yellow dump vehicle burst into sight from behind a ridge no more than one hundred yards away to our right, turning sharply onto the perimeter track in our direction. It was a front-end loader, running not on treads but on wheels, and seriously speedy. As he completed the turn the driver caught sight of us, slowed for a moment then rammed his foot down on the gas pedal, a gout of sand flying up from the vehicle's huge rear wheels to announce its acceleration.

I kicked up a piece of sand myself as I turned and took off for the fence, thinking as I did so that the dump guys finally got to score one. Now we would get treated to a lecture about private property and acting our age, with a dash of how lucky we were that our parents would not be informed. Or at least Robert would. I had not advanced far enough into the dump to be cut off from the escape route, and it quickly became clear to me that I would beat the vehicle to the fence, although it meant missing out on the driver's speechmaking. Halfway to the fence I snatched a look over my shoulder and saw that the driver was, in fact, ignoring me; he had not deviated from the perimeter track and was heading at high speed straight for Robert.

In another half-second Robert was no longer in my field of vision, cut off by an outcrop of the boundary scarp, but I knew he was still directly in the path of the front-end loader. The driver, a heavy-jowled middle-aged man dressed in landfill orange and a grubby white hard hat, had not slowed for a moment. I watched in mounting horror as the vehicle disappeared behind the outcrop, still driving hard, and winced as I heard the high-pitched squeal of brakes and juddering of heavy wheels.

"Robert..." I gasped. My mind was filled with the vision of my friend's body crushed under the weight of the loader's front bucket. The driver must have been a lunatic; was this his idea of cutting down on the crime of juvenile dump-trespass? Did he just ride a fifteen-year-old boy down to his death because he was standing some place he wasn't meant to be?

As the noise of the brakes died away I could hear the driver's voice raised in anger. I hovered irresolutely a few yards from the fence, not wanting to abandon Robert, but fearing that if I reversed my course I would be caught in the open at the very moment the front-end loader rounded the corner and began to bear down on me. In the end the driver took the decision for me. The sound of his angry tirade died away, to be replaced by the noise of the loader's engine revving loudly. I backed away, still keeping my eyes on the edge of the scarp where I expected to see the vehicle emerge, then after a few steps turned and ran for the fence as fast as I could. I crossed into the woodland and followed the road line back until the dump was hidden from view, then swung off to one side and threw myself down behind a tangle of shrubbery.

This, I suppose, is as suitable a place as any to clarify a couple of notions for you. First, understand that it would have been easy to write a heroic part for myself in this story. I never did read an autobiography—still haven't—in which the author ever admitted to being frightened enough to drop a donation, even if, in the actual incident he was describing, he instantly filled both pants legs from the inside. Nor can I remember a single comic book story in which the hero didn't face up to every adversity with cool determination and a jutting jaw. Given all this, it would probably have been perfectly natural for me to portray myself as master of every situation, unfazed by uncertainties and setbacks, and neither shaken nor stirred at the prospect of danger.

Second, you should know that pretty much everything you've read so far is accurate. I haven't made anything up, turned any heroes into villains (or vice-versa), or created any characters that didn't exist. OK, so I've taken a few liberties with our vocabulary. It may shock you to know that fifteen-year-olds actually know and use some language that's pretty extreme while not being extremely pretty, but we do, and our conversations are generally built on a sturdy framework of obscenities. Well, it's one thing to talk that way and quite another to put it down in writing, where adults could read it and fret about our moral decline and the potential for corrupting other teenagers who for some mysterious reason have never learned such language. So the language has been diluted in order to head off a parental lecture series, but with that exception noted, what I'm writing here is the truth.

Now when you put those two notions together, you have to figure that if I wanted to make myself look good without abandoning notion #2, I'd have to behave at all times like Superman, or at the very least Spiderman. But if I'm serious about #2—and I am—then I have to tell you exactly what kind of a hero I was as I lay in the leaves on the outskirts of the dump.

I had not been running long enough to wind myself, but as I lay hidden behind the shrubbery I was aware of my breath coming in great panting sobs. I was weeping, crying out in near-hysteria at the thought of my best friend lying dead a couple of hundred yards away, at the thought that I had turned my ass toward danger and left him there to die, and at the thought that the driver was even now preparing to hunt me down and give me the same treatment. I didn't even have the guts to get up and try to reach my bike in case he spotted and pursued me. I was incapable of movement—unless you count the violent trembling that was running through most of my body—and I think, to judge by the condition of my clothes when I later examined them, I was trying to press myself into the soil through multiple layers of leaves. That, to the best of my recollection, was the way I demonstrated my loyalty and valor that Monday afternoon at the edge of the Gretchyville Landfill. So imagine how I reacted when I first heard the footsteps crashing through the woods from the direction of the fence.

The owner of the feet was coming down the slope in a hurry. Suddenly not daring to breathe, I lifted my head and tried to squint through the undergrowth to locate and identify him, but the tangle was too thick. I wanted to roll forward until I was part of the tangle and therefore (I hoped) invisible but feared that, if I did so, I would be trapped there if discovered. And the moment quickly arrived when rolling forward, backward, or up my own butt would have achieved nothing; the footsteps were close enough that any movement on my part would have given my position away. No, I didn't pee my pants, but I think that was only because that fluid was, like me, too scared to come out of its hiding place.

The runner suddenly burst into view twenty yards to my left. It was Robert, and in marked contrast to me he did not appear to be in fear for his life. As I scrambled to my feet I heard a wordless utterance of relief spring from my own lips; catching sight of the movement Robert turned abruptly toward me, signaling me to keep my head down. He had almost reached me when, with a sudden look of surprise, he became airborne and flew the last five or six feet, coming in for a landing that looked as inelegant as it must have been painful. Robert grunted as his touchdown knocked the breath out of him, but still managed to wriggle in to my hiding place behind the shrubbery, where he lay panting. Happy as I was to see him alive and uninjured, I was impatient to learn how he had escaped the front-end loader driver. I started to question him, but he silenced me with a gesture and a single word.

"Listen!" I listened, holding my breath, but could hear nothing over the continuing sound of Robert's panting. Eventually, Robert worked his way up until he could see over the thick green screen before us.

"OK" he said at length. "I didn't think so. He's not following us."

"What happened in there?" Robert dropped back into the leaves and started to rub his left ankle.

"Oh, he just wanted to ream us out for being in the dump, the way they always do."

"God, I thought he'd run you down." Robert snorted.

"Nah, he was just trying to catch me. Probably wanted to hand me over to the Supreme Court of the Landfill. But he never got anywhere near me."

"How did you get out?" Robert looked at me, a broad grin on his face.

"Remember when Black Hat came into the dump, where there's a gap between the bottom of the fence and the cliff edge?"

"Yeah?"

"I used the same gap—only going the other way. By the time the guy stopped I was already half-way up. I was clear through the fence before he started yelling. He's lost interest in us by now, right enough."

"Nice work, dude."

"Yeah, well... like you said, we'd seen everything we came to see. I just wonder—what the hell *was* that?" All this time Robert had been rubbing his ankle as if it were injured, and now he sat up and looked back at the point where he had started his aerial ballet.

"What was what?"

"What I tripped over. Back there a few feet—I put my foot in something and did a world-class pratfall."

"I dunno. Probably a tree root or something."

"No, it wasn't that." Robert squirmed around and started to retrace the course of his recent flight to its launching point. I couldn't understand why it mattered, but I did understand that Robert seemed to have a need to figure things out for himself before he was satisfied; a 'probable' tree root wasn't going to cut it.

"Here it is," I heard him mutter. He was on both knees with his back to me, pulling up at something half-buried in a shallow layer of leaves. Standing to give himself more leverage, he heaved with both hands and came up with something less like a tree root than I could have imagined. I joined him and stared at his find in wonder. At first glance it looked like a thick, industrial-size welcome mat, measuring about six feet by four feet and made of some sort of coconut matting. But it was the object's attachments that made me realize it had a very different function: strongly anchored to one of the long sides of the mat were two curved lengths of thick rubber, which could act as handles for anyone wanting to carry or manhandle the thing. It was one of these rubber handholds, which Robert was now using to hold the heavy mat, that he had snagged with his foot as he came running toward me.

And now Robert got really weird. Taking a handle in each hand he first tested the weight of the mat, then performed a series of sweeping motions with it, brushing the surface layer of leaves aside as he did so. Finally he looked back at me, and broke into a laugh at the sight of what must have been a look of utter bewilderment on my face.

"Last piece of the puzzle, my man," he announced. "This is how they got rid of the tire marks."

By way of demonstration he repeated his extravagant sweeping actions with the mat, and suddenly it was as if a pair of double doors had been banged open in my head, exposing my dim brain to the light of day. All at once I could see Black Hat backing away from the buried car with the mat in his hands, dragging it over the sandy surface until his arrival route was quite buried. And I could see him hurrying through the unplanned repeat performance twenty-four hours later, wiping away all incriminating evidence—footprints, tire marks, blood stains, and everything else that had marked his activity in the dump. On both occasions he must have hidden the mat here in the woods before escaping down Old Kingsleytown Road.

It was only now, as it finally lifted from me, that I felt the full weight of the misery that I had been carrying around with me since we stood on the vacant site of the car's burial chamber the day before. It was there that we had experienced the collective disapproval of the whole posse of authority figures for having apparently lied to them and wasted their time; it was there that we had found we had no answers either for them or for ourselves. I knew that Robert had felt it more than I, and with good reason, but those looks of impatience and disgust had affected me too. They had been a major factor in shaping my actions since we left the beach—dissecting the newspaper story, identifying the dead man as one of the robbers and supporting Robert in his theory of the car's disappearance. And now, with that theory indisputably proven and with our frustration and shame banished, I felt a surge of elation that made me want to scream and holler like a demented football fan. We had done it. *Robert* had done it. He had figured out the whole answer back there in the library, and nothing we had discovered since then had come as a surprise to him.

"You are A-number-1-bloody 'mazing" I laughed. I took a couple of steps forward, winding myself up for a high-five maneuver, and fell flat on my face. Robert, still standing with the mat in his hands, made an observation I could have used a few seconds earlier.

"Well look at that, will you—there are two mats." There sure were. The second mat, like the first, had been hastily concealed with a layer of leaves; unlike Robert, I had not put my foot into one of the handles but had slipped on the leaves where they overlay the main surface of the mat.

"What—everything I do, you gotta copy?" Still sprawled at Robert's feet, I recovered enough of my breath to respond.

"You are an A-number-1-bloody hole."

"That's not nice language, Peter." Ignoring his dig at my mom, I struggled to my feet and considered the significance of the second mat.

"*Two* mats. Why would he need two, unless…" Our eyes met, and we each read the answer in the other's face.

"One for him…"

"…and one for the guy who met them here!" Now Black Hat's accomplice, like everything else, was more than mere theory; he was as real as the chunks of coconut matting we had just discovered. This time our hands rose together into a spontaneous high-five, which resounded through the woods like a clash of cymbals.

MONDAY, 4:30 PM

I don't think we could have made it back down Old K. and Main Street any faster if we had been in NASCAR vehicles. Our newfound exhilaration propelled us along at absurd speeds, each of us trying to outdo the other in radical maneuvers and outlandish war cries. At one point we actually overtook an old dear plodding along Old K. in a fifteen-year-old Chevy. At the time I was making a sound like a police siren, and as Robert passed her he sternly advised her to pull over, ma'am. You'll never believe this: she did.

We rampaged into the front parking lot of Police Headquarters at the end of a highly dangerous passage of Main Street, which included a transit of the Berkeley Avenue intersection against the lights, in line abreast, in perfect wheely configuration, and with rebel yell accompaniment. Oh yes, and with gestures. We raced each other up the front steps and banged through the doors. Five minutes later we were back in the Chief's office, spilling our guts about the butchered bushes, the tire marks in the woods, the surgically altered fence and the mats we had found. I even remembered to throw in my recollection of the Chipmunk Workshop logo, although it seemed somewhat anticlimactic after all the other information we had given them. Bonaventura, having recovered from what I took to be a disinclination to listen to any more of our stories, became more interested in us as we added detail to this, our latest and best story. He started with his slow, deliberate nodding routine, accompanied this time with a smile of encouragement that had been missing on previous occasions. I had the impression that he had been rethinking his earlier treatment of us, or that something significant had happened since our last meeting to soften his attitude. Finally he gave a brief chuckle, as if in response to some secret joke, and clasped his hands together on his desk.

"You know, boys, if I'd known you were intending to go back into the dump I would have had your parents ground you straight away. You see, I really did think you were telling me the truth yesterday; I couldn't act on your story because… well, let's face it, there was no evidence. But I still thought it was dangerous for you to be poking around there in case this gunman came back. Now, however…" He stood, walked around to the front of his desk and perched on the corner nearest me.

"Now, if the car is definitely out of the dump, there's no reason for him to go back there. Of course, you shouldn't have been there either and I think you know why, don't you, boys?" He looked from Robert to me and back again, waiting to hear the answer he already knew. It was Robert who finally broke the silence.

A DEATH UNDER SAND

"Er... because we should have been at home, doing our homework?" he suggested, with the kind of unconvincing yet endearing innocence that no-one else I know can pull off. The Chief regarded him in silence for the space of a couple of heartbeats, one eyebrow raised like half of a McDonald's sign. Then, unexpectedly, he burst into laughter, the non-judgmental laughter of one who is genuinely amused and thoroughly enjoying the joke. Robert, who could not have come out with a line like that had he not sensed that the Chief's attitude was more relaxed today, laughed with him. I would have done so too, but my brain was suddenly swamped with the knowledge that a scene from my dream of the previous night had just replayed itself before my eyes. There was Bonaventura, sitting cross-legged on a corner of his desk and laughing at Robert's remark, so closely mimicking the snatch of my dream that had taken place in the car dealership office that it sent an unnatural shiver—déjà vu, cordon blue, whatever you call it — through my mind *and* body.

"No no no," said the Chief, firmly but good-humoredly. "You know the dump was always off-limits to you. You even said so yourself yesterday. But I don't want to get into that; I understand why you went back there. You brought us all the way out there yesterday and had nothing to show for it. And you wanted to be able to prove to me that you really had seen something. Of course I understand.

And it sounds like you did a very good job. I'll send a couple of detectives and some crime scene investigators up there to confirm what you've found. Who knows—perhaps they can find some more evidence, although I have to say that the two of you have been pretty thorough."

Suddenly, his brow furrowed.

"I was just thinking: the handles of those mats you found—what did you say they were made of?"

"Some kind of hard rubber, I think," I replied. Robert nodded his agreement.

"Hmm. We just might be able to lift some fingerprints from them" the Chief explained. Robert's eyes met mine, and I could see what was in his face.

"Sorry about this, Chief," he said hesitantly. "We kind of… gave them a pretty good handling when we found them." The Chief sighed with evident regret.

"Shame. Still, you weren't to know," he added charitably. "By the way, which one of you thought all of this out—about the escape route and what they did in the woods—or did you work on it together?"

"Robert figured most of it out. Come to think of it, he figured it all out, all by himself."

"Is that so?" The Chief gave Robert a look different from any I had yet seen on his face, one that I swear bordered on admiration. Robert, looking thoroughly embarrassed, countered by pointing out my part in the investigation.

"You found the gap in the fence and the second mat, Peter."

"Oh, sure I did! First I fell on my ass, then I fell on my face. That was my whole contribution!" The Chief was laughing again.

"Well now, don't get into a fight over it, boys. Frankly, I think you both did very well. Worthy of professional detectives." He drew a deep breath before continuing.

"But..."

With this one emphatically pronounced syllable the Chief had changed the whole tone and mood of the interview, had cast a pall over it as surely as if he had dropped a silent killer fart into the air.

"...for all your efforts, what you found may be irrelevant. We still don't know why they took the car to the dump, nor why they took it out a day later, unless perhaps it wasn't meant to be found and you ruined their plan when you stumbled on it. But that doesn't help us to know what their plan was in the first place."

This interview was no longer going the way I had expected. Had we been wasting our time? Was the information of no use to the police after all? I started to protest, but the Chief suddenly held his hand up for silence and cocked his head to one side as if listening for something. From the yard outside came the sound of a heavy vehicle slowing down and changing into low gear. The Chief stood, walked over to the window and looked out for a moment. Then he turned back to us.

"As I said a moment ago, boys, it's not because I think the gunman might come back to the dump that I don't want you in there. I'm quite sure he won't come back—more sure than you are, in fact." We must have looked suitably puzzled, causing Bonaventura to grin as he started toward his office door.

"Come with me, boys. I want to show you something." He led the way out of his office to a flight of stone steps, and down them to the floor below. At the bottom was a single door, bearing the legend *Security Garage* in plain white-painted letters. Opening the door, the Chief ushered us into a windowless space that must have taken up the whole of the ground floor of the police building. Apart from the door by which we had just entered, the only other entrances were three roll-up garage doors in the rear wall of the building, one of which was in the act of closing after having admitted a vehicle. The garage was lit, unnecessarily brightly as it seemed to me, by a large number of powerful fluorescent lights. A pick-up truck and a couple of motorcycles occupied parking spaces against the far wall, but the vehicle that had just entered and that now stood alone in the very center of the garage was the one that commanded our attention. It was a flat-bed wrecker carrying a single car: a red, late-model Excalibur coupe, with the few grains of sand still clinging to its bodywork being picked out and highlighted by a battery of bright overhead lights.

Our reactions must have told the Chief what he wanted to know.

"Omigod, that's it, right enough!"

"Where was it?"

"So that's the car you two found in the dump, is it?"

"Well, it looks like it—and it's got bits of sand still on it," I replied. "Where did you find it?"

"It was found abandoned on Herring Run Lane about three hours ago. We've had the Crime Services Section from the State Police going over it—you know, for obvious evidence. But we always prefer to do something like that inside, in controlled conditions. That's why we have this facility." As he was speaking, the Chief had taken us both by the shoulders and was walking us closer to the wrecker and its cargo. A terrible thought struck me and I stopped suddenly, unwilling to go even one step further.

"Chief... is he still in there?"

"The man you saw? No, that was the first thing we did. We had the Medical Examiner's van come and take away both bodies for autopsy."

"Both bodies?" I repeated.

"Yes. And I think you can guess which the second one was" said the Chief, looking at each of us in turn. "He was wearing orange overalls and rubber boots, and he died of multiple gunshot wounds to the chest. Anyone you know?"

"Gumboots!" I exclaimed.

"He must have stuffed his body into the car before he drove it out," said Robert. The Chief nodded.

"I'm sure he did. But you see my point, don't you, boys? What you did such a good job of uncovering this afternoon only tells us that the car *was* there for sure and then was taken out of there yesterday. And now we've gone and found it— bodies, money and everything; that's why I'm so ready to believe you now, even before I send anyone up there. But now our investigation has to start over again with *this*..." With a sweep of his hand he indicated the car, which was now being winched slowly down from the bed of the wrecker. "...and it simply may not matter that it was ever in the dump." I could see the disappointment in Robert's eyes, and was sure he could see it in mine. Evidently, the Chief could see it in both our faces.

"Hey, don't get so down. We still don't know who the fellow in the black hat is, remember, and maybe there are some other clues in and around the dump. The next step—*one* of the next steps—is for us to go back there in force and search every square inch of ground between the end of the road and the spot where you found the car. You never know what we might turn up. Don't forget, this investigation has just ramped up from a minor bank robbery to homicide—double homicide at that—and we want to find that man just as much as you want us to!" A sudden frown passed over the Chief's face.

"While we're on that subject, boys…" He paused, and we waited expectantly for what else he had to say on 'that subject.'

"I don't want you boys to get too alarmed at what I'm about to say, but if I were you I would be a little careful in your movements over the next few days. Don't go anywhere where you can't be easily seen by people, and keep your eyes open for anything in the least bit… well, unusual."

Like an unusually grubby-looking Mercedes, Chief? This would have been the perfect time to spill the beans about that morning's incident, but as the day progressed it had seemed more and more to be a non-incident that I should just forget. Accordingly, I kept my peace.

The garage was now filling up with men, some uniformed and others in plain clothes. I recognized Raleigh, the two State Police detectives we had met at the dump and one or two of the Gretchyville patrolmen. The State detectives seemed to be in charge and were directing a couple of other plain-clothes types in their minute examination of the car.

"State Police Crime Services," the Chief explained as he maneuvered us nearer. "They can find a hair on the floor of a barber's that doesn't belong there and use it to catch a bad guy." I snuck a glance at Robert to see whether I was the only one not buying this, and saw at once that I wasn't. But I let the Chief have his moment. He led us right up to the car and invited us to look inside, while admonishing us not to touch the bodywork. There, pretty much as we had seen them the day before, were the bank's money bags. In the garage's bright artificial light we could see clearly that the bags were indeed printed with some sort of legend—the name of the bank, I guessed—and that those bills that had spilled out of the open bag were spattered with a bright purplish stain. I wondered whether the dye bomb had exploded while the bag was still closed, or whether the act of opening the bag had triggered it.

"Are you the kids who found this in the dump?" asked one of the Crime Services guys as he pulled on a pair of latex gloves. We acknowledged that we had that honor, but it turned out he was not working himself up to congratulate us.

"Did you touch it anywhere?" he asked sharply.

"Well—yes... Right around here," I replied, indicating the left rear window.

"Don't touch it again!" he snapped. He turned and addressed one of his colleagues.

"Marty! Get a full set from these two kids." Marty grunted his assent and beckoned us over impatiently. It was left to the Chief to explain to us that they would need a record of our fingerprints so they could be separated from all the other sets that would be lifted from the car.

"Don't forget, Gumboots touched it about here too," Robert pointed out.

"What—the man you saw shot? Are you sure?" asked the Chief, with sudden interest.

"Sure I am. We all saw it... Er... all two of us." Nice save, Robert. We described to the Chief and the State cop, as accurately as we could remember, how Gumboots had gripped the side of the vehicle when he looked into it and approximately where he had placed his hands.

"Very observant of you, boys," murmured Bonaventura. "Why don't you start right there, Hammond."

Evidently irritated at having his routine disrupted, the Statie put on a peevish expression, but dutifully moved to the area of the left rear window and started lightly sweeping the surface with a powder-laden brush. Marty was setting up his fingerprinting equipment on a table against the near wall and called for us to join him. We started in his direction, then on an impulse I reversed direction; it had just occurred to me that one of the remaining 'unanswerables' that had plagued me since Sunday evening could be laid to rest within a few seconds. Both the Chief and the Statie called after me, but could not prevent me from rounding the back end of the car and taking a close look at the license plate. What I saw confirmed the fleeting impression I had had at the moment we witnessed Gumboots uncovering the plate in the dump: there *were* two plates, the original and a fake crudely fixed over it. So even if anyone in the bank *had* seen and remembered the number it would not have helped the police identify the owner on Saturday afternoon. And if the false plate *was* showing on Saturday, Robert's theory may have been dead on— the car could belong to one of the robbers.

The Chief called me again, a little impatiently this time, but I had seen all I needed to see now and rejoined him without argument. In the ten minutes that followed, Robert and I had our fingerprints recorded and were then directed upstairs to wash the elongated circles of black ink off our fingertips. As Chief Bonaventura led the two of us back to the door it was suddenly opened from the far side and Jacobson, Raleigh's junior partner, burst in.

"Oh there you are, Chief," he exclaimed breathlessly. "Henry is coming back from Bass Point now. The car does belong to O'Sullivan. They're bringing him -" Jacobson suddenly broke off in mid-sentence, his eyes shifting nervously from the Chief to the two of us. I looked quickly at the Chief and caught the tail end of the stern expression he had fired at the junior detective to silence him. Evidently, what Jacobson was about to say was not for our ears. The detective's own ears turned a fleshy shade of crimson, which spread decorously to his cheeks and neck as he realized his blunder. Emitting a sound that was part sigh, part growl, and shaking his head sadly, the Chief propelled us out of the garage and into the stairwell. As the door closed behind us we heard a muted "sorry, Chief" from the crestfallen Jacobson on the other side.

"Now don't you pay any attention to that, boys" the Chief said, in a tone obviously intended to minimize the importance of what we had heard. "It's just police business. Nothing you need to worry about."

If the Chief's intention was to defuse our interest in things dumpish and car-related, he had chosen exactly the wrong thing to say. So far as I was concerned, his clumsy attempt to distract our attention from Jacobson's blurted information had only served to magnify its importance. And as we turned on the landing half-way up the stairs and I briefly caught Robert's eye, the quick wink and grin that he gave me showed me that it had had the same effect on him. For the remainder of the climb to the main floor of the building I concentrated on committing to memory every word of Jacobson's ill-timed announcement, so that we could make sense of it later.

In the washroom, Robert and I took it in turns to scrub the ink stains off our fingers. As I dried my hands on a couple of paper towels I glanced at my watch.

"What's the time, man?" asked Robert, noticing my movement. My reply was automatic.

"When Mickey's hand is on his pants leg, it must be -"

"Yeah I know, much too late. No, come on, what is it? We better get home soon before someone's mom calls someone else's mom and blows our story." Before I could answer, the Chief cleared his throat.

"Yes," he said slowly. "I was just thinking about your mothers." His tone was ominous enough to make me pause in mid-wipe.

"You know, boys, I made a serious mistake yesterday when we went to the dump. Police regulations demand that, if we're taking evidence from kids as young as you are—certainly if we're taking you to a crime scene the way we did yesterday—we have to inform your parents. And a parent has to be present when we do that sort of thing." A prickly feeling of dread generated itself in the pit of my stomach and began a slow crawl toward my throat as the Chief continued.

"Now, there's an outside chance that we won't need to talk to you again, in which case it could just remain our secret, OK?" We nodded vigorously.

"But..." There was that word again. "...I fully expect that we will, sooner or later, arrest this man you call Black Hat *and* any accomplices he may have. And when we do that, the two of you may be very important witnesses. You do understand that, don't you?"

"Only if we can identify him, Chief" Robert replied quickly.

"Don't you think you'll be able to?" Robert shrugged.

"We told you before, Chief—we never really saw him close up. I mean, we'd try right enough, but we can't promise anything."

"Hmm. Well, we can only hope, I guess. But so long as there's a chance, I really think I'm going to have to tell your folks what's happened. That way, if we do need to bring you back here in a hurry for any reason, they'll know what it's all about."

I started to protest, but Robert shut me up with a jab in the ribs. I guessed he could see it was useless to argue and to tell you the truth, so could I. As the Chief held the door open for us and we filed gloomily out into the corridor, my mind was already previewing the range of expressions I could expect to see on my mom's face before the day was over: concern at the sight of her son in the arms of the Law, shame at the news that her son was a hardened criminal, horror at the thought of our brush with death, and finally anger over everything that was my fault and most of what wasn't. I could also expect to see not only my Nintendo under lock and key for a month—standard punishment—but also my BMX embargoed *ad infinitum*. It was beginning to look as if my early-morning barfing episode was not, after all, destined to be the low point of the day.

In the corridor the Chief encountered one of the senior Staties and explained to him what we had found during our return visit to the dump. Unlike his colleagues working one floor below us the State cop actually seemed to find our contribution useful, and immediately set about organizing a party to inspect our finds. As we continued toward the main doors they suddenly swung open to admit Raleigh and a gaggle of uniformed officers. They were escorting—by which I mean holding firmly by each arm—a sandy-haired man in his mid-thirties who looked as if he had slept in his clothes and would much rather have been somewhere else. His eyes, set in a broad and unnaturally pale face, shifted nervously around as he came into the hallway. As the group approached I could see that his face had not been visited by a razor for several days, while Raleigh's was radiating a glow of self-satisfied smugness. The Chief tightened his grip on our shoulders as the man was steered past us into an interview room, the door of which was slammed shut by Raleigh with what seemed like unnecessary violence. Bonaventura let out a humorless chuckle.

"Seeing it all today, aren't you, boys?" he muttered.

In the front parking lot we loaded our BMXes into the trunk of the Chief's official car and climbed into the back seat together. It was not lost on me that the last time we had done this, after our unsuccessful return to the dump with the police, our mood was as dark as it was now, although for different reasons. As I settled into my seat, however, I noticed Robert stretching his neck around to squint through the rear windshield at the frosted glass window of the interview room. Catching my eye, he whispered urgently—for the Chief was in the process of lowering himself into the driver's seat—a single name.

"O'Sullivan."

I nodded. Robert and I were on the same track: the man being hustled roughly into Police Headquarters had to be the car's owner, whose name Jacobson had carelessly let slip downstairs. If the police had found the car three hours ago, as the Chief had told us, they had had ample time to identify the owner, locate him and bring him in for questioning. And while I knew we could not positively pick Black Hat out of a crowd, I also knew that *this* man, with his short, sandy hair and round face, could not be him.

"All right, boys," the Chief was saying, "who's nearest? Where should we go first?"

"I guess I'm nearest," I replied. "Sachem Street, off Compass."

"Will your dad be there at this time of day?" The question took me by surprise, and I stumbled over the answer.

"Well... no. I mean, he's... he's not ever there. He doesn't live there... any more, that is." The Chief paused with the key half-way into the ignition, then removed his glasses and turned in his seat to stare closely at me.

"Your mom and dad don't live together anymore, Peter?" he asked. I shook my head.

"I'm sorry to hear that," he said, and sounded as if he meant it. I had come to realize over the last two days that the Chief was not an unsympathetic man, but now I saw a new look in his eyes, one not of pity but sorrow, not of pain but an understanding of pain.

"How long has it been?"

"About three years."

"Has it been rough?"

"No... Well, yes... I mean—things were bad between him and my mom for a long time... really bad toward the end; it was a kind of relief when he left. No, I don't mean that. It *was* rough on us. Especially my mom. She's pretty much over it now, though; so's my little sister. I'd still like to see him more, I guess."

"Of course you would. Nothing wrong with that."

There was an awkward pause. I began to wish Bonaventura would turn back and start the car, but he kept his eyes on my face.

"Do you sometimes look up and expect to see him walking into the room?" he asked quietly.

"What—I never said… Well, yes, sometimes. How did you know?"

Slowly and carefully, the Chief put his glasses back on.

"Lucky guess, that's all."

He turned forward and started the motor, then drove slowly toward the parking lot exit. Before turning onto Main Street he stopped and turned back to Robert.

"What about you, Robert? I know your dad's often not home."

Robert, understanding exactly what the Chief meant and how he knew about his father's absences, snorted.

"No, but he's not gone for good" he retorted. In the next moment he dropped his forehead on the seat back with a groan and reached across to grip my shoulder.

"Sorry, Peter," he whispered. He had spoken two words only, but they were the greatest gift any friend had given me. I don't care who you are, you don't get better friends than this.

MONDAY, 5:30 PM

Ten minutes later, as we made the turn from Compass Avenue onto Sachem Street, the Chief half-turned his head and asked me to identify my house for him. I leaned forward and looked up the road ahead of us.

"You see the one on the right about four or five houses up? The light blue one with dark blue shutters?"

"Yes."

"That's not it."

The Chief exhaled loudly.

"OK, Peter, which one *is* it?"

"It's the next one up. You can just about see the garage from here." Robert leaned forward until his face was level with mine.

"It's the one with my mom's car in the driveway" he said expressionlessly.

"Oh bother," I said. No, that wasn't what I said, but I already covered the stuff about what language I'm putting down in writing here. This was just fine; Robert's mom and mine were already busy putting their heads together, were probably already heating the cauldron into which we were to be lowered as a prize for lie #1. Wait till they got a load of what the Chief had to say.

"Well, in the scheme of things it probably won't make no difference, right enough," Robert muttered, and on reflection I thought he was probably right.

"What—are your mothers visiting?" asked the Chief.

"Sure looks like it," I replied.

"They do that often?"

"No—only when we really don't want them to."

"Well, I really wouldn't worry about it, boys. It just means I only have to explain everything once."

"Oh good," I said, unenthusiastically.

"Yes," agreed Robert in a like tone. "That makes it so much better for us." The Chief made no other sound on the run up to our driveway, but I was distinctly aware of a gentle vibration running through his shoulders the whole way.

The Chief led us from his car to the house. I had expected him to make his entrance at our front door, in keeping with the formal nature of this visit, but it was at this point that he pulled the first of several surprises. Holding his peaked cap lightly between the fingers of his left hand he made straight for the kitchen door, whistling jauntily. When my mom came to the door in response to the light tattoo that he beat on it with his knuckle, the Chief greeted her like a veteran door-to-door salesman trying to make a good impression.

"Mrs. McLeod?" he opened, with a winning smile on his face. "Chief Bonaventura, Gretchyville Police. How are you today?"

My mom, as I had anticipated, favored him with a look of dread which waxed and waned as her eyes darted between her guilty-looking son and his friend and the smiling, reassuring countenance of the town's top law enforcement official.

"Is Mrs. Juneau there? May I come in and talk to the two of you? It really won't take very long," continued the Chief, still smiling. Temporarily disarmed, my mom twitched the screen door open to admit the three of us. As I entered the kitchen I could see Robert's mom standing in the archway leading to the dining room. As she caught sight of the Chief her normally cheerful face took on a harder and more hostile expression, in all probability a habit resulting from the number of such visits she had unwillingly hosted in her own home. When Robert came into view, traipsing in behind me, her expression changed to one that tried to combine parental relief with parental anger. Well, now we *knew* they had been comparing notes on the fairy tales we had told them earlier this afternoon.

Robert's mom was a small, trim woman in her mid-thirties, a couple of years younger than my own mom. Her complexion and the attractive roundness of her facial features suggested her Jamaican ancestry; the musical lilt of her accent confirmed it. Robert had told me that she was, in fact, half-Jamaican, making him one-quarter Jamaican and three-quarters American. Although Robert seemed to have taken after his father in build and in looks, it was the other one-quarter part of his heritage that held an unflagging fascination for him. He was, by his own account, forever bugging his parents to take him there for a visit, although he knew very well that they were never likely to be able to afford it. But for his mother, it was almost certainly the worries associated with her husband's waywardness rather than the irritation of her son's nagging that accounted for the premature pattern of lines on her otherwise youthful and—in a mom-like way—quite pretty face.

"Can we go in and sit down?" asked the Chief. We all shuffled through to the living room and arranged ourselves as if we were hosting visiting relatives on a Sunday afternoon. Evidently sensing a situation in which she could enjoy my unease, Marla sidled in and tried to camouflage herself on the far side of the breakfront. Detected by my mom's early warning radar, however, she was in the process of being repulsed with heavy losses when the Chief threw his arm out and welcomed her to the party.

The Chief's performance over the next fifteen minutes was nothing short of amazing. He started by describing our weekly visits to the dump in terms that made it sound as if we had accidentally jaywalked while helping old ladies across the street. Then, after reminding our mothers about the weekend's bank robbery, he described in admiring tones how we had located the criminals' getaway car when the combined forces of State and local police could not, and how thoroughly we had discharged our civic duty by reporting our discovery immediately to his office. He concluded by congratulating the two awestruck women on having produced such sharp-witted and observant offspring, who might well think of law enforcement as a possible career choice in a few years' time. At no time did he make any mention of dead bodies, murdered men, or bullets whistling past their sons' ears. And to complete his masterwork, he explained by way of an afterthought why it had been necessary for us to practice a little deception that afternoon in order to prove Robert's theory.

As the Chief's explanation progressed, our mothers' expressions miraculously softened from apprehension to cautious relief. They never quite made it to outright admiration, which was perhaps more than we could expect. My sister, seeing her opportunity for a touchdown with two-point conversion fading away, looked positively pissed. Throughout, I hardly dared make eye contact with Robert for fear we would break the spell, and for the same reason had to fight the impulse to leap across the room and hug the Chief of the Town of Gretchyville Police Department.

The first reaction came from my mom.

"Well you know, Peter, I do wish you could have been a little more honest with me. Why couldn't you have told me this yesterday?"

"I would have, mom, but I didn't want to worry you." It was a standard response, usually a fairly reliable way of deflecting an incoming salvo, and while it didn't quite fit the circumstances of this case it appeared to work well enough. It certainly worked well enough to nudge Mrs. Juneau into line; if we had been able to script her next question ourselves we could not have done a better job.

"Is that why you didn't tell me, Robert?" she asked. Robert nodded tenderly and came out with the coup de grâce.

"You've got enough to worry about, mom."

Bonaventura must have sensed that his work was done. He slapped the knees of his uniform pants and levered himself upright.

"Well, I should be getting back to Headquarters" he announced. "Thank you for your time, Mrs. McLeod and Mrs. Juneau. I hope you won't be too hard on the boys; they really have done us a service. Besides, I *know* they won't be going back to the dump again... will you, boys?" As he said this he turned toward us and, with his back to our moms, indulged in a deliberate and very conspiratorial wink. Resisting the urge to break into a grin I responded with an appropriately solemn shake of the head. Robert, standing next to me, picked up the cadence and we shook solemnly together.

At the kitchen door the Chief suddenly remembered—or appeared to remember (I was still in awe of his recent performance and was not ready to take anything at face value)—the main purpose of his visit. He smoothly explained to our moms that there was a remote possibility of our being needed to furnish more information as the investigation progressed, and that he would be sure to contact them directly should that become necessary. He handed a business card to each of them, instructing them to call his private line should they need to… and that was that. The Chief had descended on our house on a broomstick of officialdom, sprinkled some magic dust to make us out to be local heroes, then disappeared in a cloud of exhaust fumes. As his car accelerated out of sight Robert leaned over to me and whispered:

"Now we know how he got to be Chief of Police. What a performance!" We turned back to find two pairs of maternal eyeballs fixed on us.

"Well, you two seem to have made a favorable impression on the police" said my mom, and although she was smiling for the first time since our arrival she still had a suspicious look in her eye. Mrs. Juneau, by contrast, threw back her head and laughed out loud.

"I think it's a jolly good thing that *one* of the men of my family has done that!" she exclaimed.

This seemed, finally, to break the tension in the house and we all managed a laugh, Robert and I forcing an artificial level of heartiness into our contribution—anything to keep the focus on our good deeds and off the less savory aspects of our behavior.

For the next forty-five minutes we were quizzed in detail about every aspect of our recent escapade, and somehow managed to get through the session without contradicting either each other's stories or the Chief's. I was thankful that the questions weren't multiple choice, and pleasantly surprised that we managed to keep our hero status intact throughout.

Finally Mrs. Juneau decided it was time for Robert and herself to leave. As she was gathering her personal debris—pocketbook, car keys, etc.— and exchanging pleasantries with my mom, Robert caught my eye and signaled silently for a private conference. We stepped outside and slipped out of sight around the corner of the garage. As soon as we were hidden from the house Robert spoke in a low but urgent tone.

"O'Sullivan, right enough? That's what Jacobson said. It's his car and he lives somewhere in Bass Point. And that was him they were bringing in as we were leaving, I bet." I nodded.

"Yeah — I heard the same. I'll tell you something else: he's not Black Hat."

"No way; wrong height, wrong hair color, not skinny enough."

"But he could still be the other guy — the one they met at the dump."

"Could be. But I dunno... Did you see the look on his face when they brought him in?" I conjured up a mental image of O'Sullivan's anxiety-ridden face.

"Yeah... He looked pretty unhappy about the whole deal." Robert was shaking his head. Again he was ahead of me in his understanding of the situation.

"He wasn't just unhappy; he was totally..." He waved his hands about expressively. "...discombobulated. You could tell by his face, he didn't know why he'd been picked up, he didn't expect to be in trouble with the cops. He just *didn't know what was going on.* If he'd been Black Hat's #2, he'd 've looked... I dunno, different, you know? Like he'd expected this to happen, almost." A familiar phrase bubbled up in my mind.

"You mean he wouldn't have looked so much like a deer caught in the headlights?" Robert smiled, repeating the phrase to himself.

"Yeah... That's pretty accurate, I guess."

At that point the kitchen door opened and Mrs. Juneau appeared.

"Break it up, junior detectives," she called when she saw us in conference. Her tone was brisk, but there was a broad smile on her lips and a

222

definite twinkle in her eye; she seemed to be well pleased with the outcome of the visit. Juneaus senior and junior climbed into their car and disappeared in the direction of home.

Dinner that night, so far as I was concerned, was a livelier event than it had been the previous night. I had well and truly recovered from the trauma that had blighted my appetite then, and was actually quite fired up by the thought of making a crucial contribution to the outcome of the case. I was not ignoring, either, the possibility that the relationship between the Juneaus and the Police Department might well improve as a result of Robert's involvement, and that couldn't help but make me happy. My mom did make me repeat my solemn promise never to return to the dump, but apart from that and Poison Face's smoldering silence the meal went remarkably well.

Later, as I might have expected, Liddy again called with a barrage of questions about what we had found at the dump. I was frankly even less inclined to bring her up to date than I had been twenty-four hours earlier; her and Tony's unwillingness to grow up and do what, in my opinion, was the right thing was driving a definite wedge between us. I sketched in most of the details for her, then cut short her questions by promising to tell her everything the following day. By ten o'clock I was in bed, plowing through an assigned chapter in our Social Studies textbook about the destruction of slave family units prior to the Civil War.

As I turned the pages of the schoolbook, each photograph of bleak African faces staring out of their grainy misery into the lens and out of their time across a century and a half into my life reminded me only of Robert. This was not for the obvious reason, although I knew very well that I was staring at a portion of his heritage, and that scraps of that heritage still clung to him despite the passage of generations. It was because I knew from the title of the chapter that I was looking at real families torn apart, as was Robert's; families whose mothers had been forced into the task of explaining to their children that their fathers were no longer a part of their daily existence, as Robert's mom must have had to do. Was it any easier for Mrs. Juneau to explain than for these women, simply because the father of the family was not dragged off in irons, or did the fact that Mr. Juneau could have chosen a whole lifestyle but chose instead a fractured one make the explanation all the more difficult to give and to understand?

But even as I realized that I could never answer that particular question, I found myself distracted by a more personal one: how was it that I could see my own face in the sepia groups squatting outside slave cabins and around the trunks of willow trees? Well, the answer to that one is easier than it sounds but a lot more painful, and Robert and the Chief had both, in their own way, exposed its rawness in the car that afternoon. Robert's blurted response to the Chief's comment about his dad not often being at home, although not given with that intent, had served to emphasize the difference between his situation and mine. For whereas his parents were still married, and his father would actually live for extended periods at the family home when he was not off making an uncertain living somewhere else, the same could not be said for me. I had never really dwelt on the comparison before but in doing so now I realized that, while no one could accurately describe Robert's home life as whole, it was measurably less broken than mine.

My father had not left so much as a toothbrush behind when he departed, leaving us with scant physical evidence of his part in our lives over the previous eleven years. And although he still makes the eight-hour journey to Gretchyville to see us every couple of months, the weekend visits are curiously formal, almost scripted episodes. He will ask us what we're doing in school, how we liked the something-or-other he had sent us from whatever part of the country he's currently working in, whether we're doing any sports, all that kind of stuff. But after a couple of years of this it began to occur to me that there was something automatic about his questions, as if he were duty-bound to ask them and could make no sense or use of the answers we gave him. It didn't take me long to figure out why, either. Our lives have diverged so completely in the years since he walked away from us that we're like strangers to each other, with no intimate knowledge of each others' lives either on a grand scale or in the day-to-day details. I think he means well when he inquires into our activities but can't weave what we tell him together with any of the other threads of our lives, since he never sees those threads—has no notion, even, of what those threads are. And the same is true, I guess, about *his* current life, of which we know only the bare outlines.

So it was not entirely surprising to find, as I flipped through the pages of my textbook, that I could connect those bewildered and raggedy black children with myself better than with Robert. Mr. Juneau, despite his long absences, had never completely lost sight of the threads that wound together to make up his son's life. With him it was like taking a walk along Salt Works Beach during an incoming tide. For much of the way you're walking on dry sand, and the many tidal pools in your path never do more than get you wet up to the knees; hell, you can even get across the mouth of Lady's Slipper Creek at high tide and stay dry above the waist. At no point do you ever have to swim, since the sand is always comfortingly there between your toes. You never quite lose touch with the surface. With my father it felt more like traveling along a chain of islands, each tiny land mass separated from the next by a deep ocean trench. None of the islands bears any resemblance to any other, and there is no continuity of language, culture, geology or vegetation between them. And no-one has ever thought to build a causeway to connect the islands.

At this point, probably no-one will.

TUESDAY, 6:45 AM

I woke early the next morning, washed and dressed in double-quick time, then hurtled downstairs and outside to the newspaper tube at the end of our front walk. I extracted the Gretchyville Times, unrolled it and scanned the front page on my way back to the house. The world was apparently full of news that morning: a couple of unpronounceable countries in Africa were competing with each other for the moral high ground by means of mutual genocide; the President of the United States was predicting a rosy economic future as soon as the current eighteen-month recession was over; and in a general election in Britain, the Prime Minister had actually lost his seat. Ow. There were a couple of other odds and ends on the front page concerned with town sewage and beach committee issues, not exactly world-class news but prominent obsessions of the town fathers. But concerning the weekend's big news, the bank robbery and associated murders, there was precisely nothing. No photo, no banner headline about the newly-discovered bodies, not a single column-inch of type. I stopped on the front stoop and went over the page again more carefully, unable to believe that the only piece of news with which I had ever been closely connected had become so old so fast. But there was no mistake. The robbery was, quite literally, no longer front-page news. Nor was it page two news, page three news, or page—

"Peter? What on Earth are you doing?" It was mom, reacting to what was perhaps the only time she had seen me taking an interest in any part of the paper other than the comics and the sports pages. I stared stupidly back up at her through the screen door.

"Just — I was just —"

"Looking for your name in the paper?" she laughed.

"Well, no, I — I just wanted to see if they'd written anything else about it; about finding the car and all. And if they'd arrested anyone or found out who the dead guys were —"

"— or put your names in the paper." Mom was still enjoying my embarrassment. "No, the police wouldn't give your names out, Peter, even if you did want them to. Now come back in and get your breakfast."

I re-entered the house and dumped the newspaper on the sofa on my way to the kitchen. No, I really hadn't expected us to be famous as a result of our involvement in the case, but I was genuinely disappointed that the paper had found nothing new to write about on the subject in the last twenty-four hours. Mom must have sensed my frustration, and when she had finished trying to break the toaster continued in a more sympathetic tone.

"You know, it's entirely possible they're deliberately holding the news back from the papers."

"Why would they do that?"

"Well, maybe they don't want the criminals—assuming they haven't caught them yet—to know they have the car. Or maybe they just haven't found enough evidence in the car to make it worthwhile reporting."

I was about to respond that a car full of dead bodies ought to have been worth a couple of paragraphs somewhere below the High School volleyball scores but, remembering just in time that the Chief, Robert, and I had succeeded in keeping corpses out of the discussion the day before, managed to swallow the remark before it passed my tonsils.

"Hmm, yeah, well... I guess... maybe," I managed instead. What my mom had said made sense, although it still left me with a sense of anticlimax after a day of discoveries. So much had happened to us in such a short space of time that I found myself not wanting the pace to slacken, even for a day.

I said as much to Robert half an hour later as Celeste swung the door of the school bus closed and resumed her torturing of its transmission. Robert sympathized but seemed less surprised than I was; he, apparently, was not expecting to hear of any further developments until some arrests were made.

"That's when they'll come and pull us out of class and take us to ID Black Hat," he said. "Assuming we can..."

At Robert's remark we both lapsed into silence. I guessed that he was—and I knew that I was—trying to conjure up once more a visual memory of Black Hat's murderous face as it turned toward us. I don't know how Robert fared, but I do know I was unable to add even one more distinguishing feature to my mental record of the killer.

The day dragged on as Tuesdays are wont to do at Gabriele M. Ciccone Junior High, with their special treat of double Physics sandwiched between two periods of math à la Bamberg. Even the weather seemed to have a sulk on; the unbroken blue of Sunday and fair-weather cloudiness of Monday had given way to a day of featureless gray overcast. Predictably, Tony and Liddy snagged us at lunchtime and demanded a detailed report on our sleuthing expedition. I think Robert must have getting as impatient as I was with their selective enthusiasm for this affair, since neither of us offered more than a summary report. But under their intense interrogation, most of the details eventually leaked out.

"Holy Stromboli," breathed Liddy at last. "So they got the car *and* the bodies *and* the money. They gotta catch these guys soon."

"That must have been really cool, getting your fingerprints taken," put in Tony. "I wish I'd been there."

It was not a remark for which Robert or I were in the mood, but instead of responding we both gave him a look that told him -- and Liddy -- that they could easily have been there had they so chosen. It didn't seem to faze Liddy.

"So, you find out whose car it is?" she asked.

Neither of us had happened to mention the incident of O'Sullivan's heavily guarded arrival at Police Headquarters but now, as Robert drew breath to answer the question, I swiftly moved my foot beneath the table and brought it firmly into contact with his ankle. OK, I kicked him. Robert lost his composure for barely a second before recovering and offering some harmless remark, at the same time favoring me with a glance that bluntly asked "what's with you?"

Later, as we were straining to close our locker doors on our collections of schoolbooks, comics and contraband, Robert asked the same question less bluntly but more audibly. At the moment when I had bruised his ankle, I did not have a perfect understanding of why I placed so much importance on keeping O'Sullivan's existence secret, just a vague feeling that Liddy and Tony had not earned the right to share the information. Now, having had a few minutes to consider the question, I realized why I had reacted as I did.

"OK" I said. "Pop quiz. Do you think O'Sullivan's innocent, yes or no?"

"You mean, did he know what his car was being used for?"

"Right." Robert looked thoughtful as he brought his shoulder to bear on his bulging locker door. With a metallic groaning sound the door steadily inched its way closed, but it was only when the latch clicked noisily into place that he answered my question.

"If I had to guess, I'd say no. It's like I said last night, he just didn't seem to know what the hell was going on. He probably reported his car stolen and got dragged in and given the third degree for his pains."

"I think you're right; I don't think he had anything to do with the robbery *or* the murders. Which is why I was playing footsie with you just now. If he was as much a victim as… well, not as much as Gumboots, that would be tough… but if his worst mistake was leaving his car where it could get boosted and used by Black Hat and his friends, it's not fair for any of us to go spreading his name around like he's already been arrested and charged." I emphasized my point by backing up and delivering a karate kick to my locker door, the only proven way of closing it. Robert was already nodding his agreement.

"Yeah, I thought it was something like that. That's fine with me; I won't go blabbing his name to no-one." We were alone in the corridor by now, which meant that we were probably going to be late for Spanish and would have to employ the act in which one of us limped into the room while the other carried his books and helped him into his seat. As we hurried along the back corridor with me trying to remember which one of us routinely played the invalid for Mr. Furtada's benefit, Robert voiced a thought that had been on my mind most of the day.

"I don't much give a monkey's if the cops arrest O'Sullivan; I just want to know when they're going to get Black Hat. And the sooner the better."

Spanish came and went in a blur of impenetrable verb endings, and Tuesday dragged its tail through English and Social Sciences before we were finally released back into the world. As I stepped off the school bus Celeste advised me to have my mom take a look at my left arm, which I was rubbing tenderly as if it were badly bruised. I crossed Compass Avenue, trotted down my road, and when I heard the bus finally start to move away turned to wave to Robert. To this day I don't remember whether he waved back, since all my attention was suddenly taken up by what was happening in Dabney Street, which leads out of Compass on the other side from Sachem. About three hundred yards down the street an ancient and dirty black Mercedes was completing a three-point turn, to come to a halt pointing right at me.

A DEATH UNDER SAND

With my heart starting to batter my rib cage and a familiar dryness rising in my throat, I backed unsteadily away. For several seconds I could not even move my eyes away from the car. It was only when I tripped over a crack in the sidewalk that I recovered enough of my wits to turn and run. And run. Panting hard, I burst through our kitchen door, slammed and bolted it, then ran around downstairs locking doors and windows as fast as my legs and fingers would work. When I was done I ran up to my mom's room, where the bay window gave me a view clear down to the end of the road.

Nothing. No black Mercedes. No thin man in cowboy boots. Nothing but the Greenwood kids tossing their frisbee from sidewalk to sidewalk. And the hundred-yard-long rise at the end of the road effectively hid anything that might have been sitting—or just starting to move—in Dabney Street.

I ran downstairs again and went quickly from window to window, searching frantically for any signs of life in the back yard, the front yard, or even the damn garage roof. Nothing. As I returned to the living room, my eyes fell on the telephone and Bonaventura's card lying next to it. This time I knew what I had to do.

"Chief Bonaventura? This is Peter McLeod. You remember what you told us yesterday about seeing anything unusual?"

"Yes?"

"Well, I have. Twice. Yesterday morning and just now. A dirty old Mercedes. I couldn't see the driver properly but it was waiting outside our school yesterday and he was looking at us—at Robert and me. Then when I got off the bus just now the same car—I think it was the same car—was in Dabney Street right across from our street. I mean—it may be nothing, but I don't think anyone in Dabney owns a car like that. Of course, it could just be someone visiting, but—"

"Peter, Peter, calm down now. Listen to me. Where are you now?"

"At home. I'm on the phone. Well, of course, you know that, but—"

"Listen to me, Peter. I'm going to send a car over right now to check it out. Stay where you are, keep away from the windows, and don't open the door to anyone but a police officer. Do you understand?"

"Yes, Chief."

"Good. Now make sure you do what I say. The car will be there in five minutes."

And so it was. Peering out of my mom's window while standing in the middle of the room did not give me the best view of the proceedings but I was able to see the cruiser, lights flashing and siren wailing, make a fast turn into Dabney before it disappeared from sight. Two minutes later it reappeared and approached our house somewhat more sedately. The cop stayed in the car talking on his radio for a further couple of minutes, then got out and knocked on our front door.

"Are you Peter McLeod?"

"Yes."

"Officer Cronin. Everything all right here?"

"Sure. Did you see the car?"

The officer looked about the same age as Sergeant Raleigh but had a much calmer air about him, which I found reassuring. Almost at once I realized I had seen him at a number of sporting events and school concerts, which probably meant he was the father of Ronnie Cronin, a seventh-grader.

"No, there was no Mercedes there. But that doesn't mean it wasn't there five minutes ago. Now listen: Chief Bonaventura is going to make sure you and your friend Robert don't have to worry about this sort of thing. We won't be breathing down your necks, but you'll see a lot more patrol cars around here in the next few days. It's what we call 'establishing a presence.' If someone *is* following you, he'll know he can't put a foot wrong without us catching him. The Chief wanted to be sure I told you that."

"Well, thanks. Thanks a million. Look, for all I know it could be nothing, but the Chief did say to watch for anything like this—" The officer held up his hand.

"He told me all about it, Peter, and you were right to report what you saw, no matter what the outcome. And he said you should still keep your eyes open, OK?"

"OK." Cronin allowed himself a smile, which reached all the way to his eyes.

"That shouldn't be too difficult for you. I understand you're quite the detective." Now I had lost enough of my fear to find room for embarrassment, which I guess was a step in the right direction. Cronin smiled again and departed.

Within twenty seconds I was on the phone to Robert and filling him in on everything, including the planned increase in police presence around the Rosario Apartments. He seemed less concerned than I was about being targeted by the killer, but a little pissed that I had not shared my sighting of the Mercedes the previous day with him until now. I was still trying to get him to reshuffle his priorities when I heard my mom struggling to enter the house through the still-bolted kitchen door; hanging up quickly, I went to help her before she scattered groceries from her one free hand all over the step.

"What's going on, Peter? Why was the door bolted?"

"It wasn't bolted, mom. It sticks sometimes; didn't you know that?" My mom didn't know that, nor did she know why I was looking unusually pale. I managed to think quickly enough to throw the blame onto my school lunch, an explanation that she readily accepted. And by the time she was halfway through preparing dinner my normal color had returned, which made further interrogation unnecessary.

Later that evening I lay on my bed and tried to sort out my thoughts; now that my second scare in as many days had settled down to the status of non-incident, how did I *really* want to see this whole affair resolved? First and most importantly, I guess, I wanted Black Hat *not* to find any of us and give us another demonstration of his skill-at-arms. That much was a no-brainer, but I was having greater difficulty arranging in some sort of satisfactory order all the other possible outcomes that had presented themselves. I knew that, out of a general sense of right and wrong, I wanted to see the crimes solved, the guilty punished, etc., etc; I wanted to maintain a net positive reputation with my mom; I wanted the police to continue to believe us, and I wanted them to start treating Robert the same way they were treating me. Of all these items on my wish list, it was relatively easy to find places in the top slots for those concerned with self-preservation, but—perversely—my wish to see the case solved and closed kept jumping up into their place.

Why was it so important to me? Did I really care enough about the case to want to see it settled more than I wanted to stay out of trouble with my mom? What difference would it make in my life if they never found Black Hat and his pals so long as Black Hat and his pals never found me? Well, whether it made sense or not, it obviously did make a difference to me, and not just because it put me on the side of the angels. I remember one time when my Dad was on a crew somewhere down in Mexico there was a big earthquake, measuring 100% on the Myhousejustfellonme scale. Anyway, my dad and all the guys with him just stopped everything for three days and helped dig people out of what used to be their homes. After that, whenever anything came up in the newspaper or on TV about that part of the country he would always pay a lot of attention to it.

"I can't help it," he would say. "If it hadn't been for the earthquake and what we did I wouldn't care about the place, but I'm involved now. It's an important part of my life. I'll probably always take an interest in it and wonder how the people are managing."

I guess that's how it was with me, admittedly on a smaller scale: I was inescapably involved. Like my dad I had both seen and escaped death. Unlike him I had gone on to question, investigate and theorize; I had discovered perplexing aspects of the affair, some of which had been settled while others were still playing with my head; and I had shared all of this with my best friend in the world. If it were destined to end in its present state—unresolved and full of mystery—I would be still wondering about Black Hat, Gumboots and O'Sullivan when I was a doddering old fart in a Florida condo. And if it were to be solved tomorrow with film at eleven of the Gretchyville Gang in handcuffs, I would want to know every last detail. I was involved. It was part of my life, and I couldn't let it go—or perhaps *it* wouldn't let *me* go.

And that, I guess, is why it kept finding its way up there to the top of my wish list as a favorite outcome, along with simply wanting to live through the whole situation. When you're involved, as Robert and I were, it's just not possible to get *un*involved. I had invested time, energy, sweat, emotions, brain cells and stomach contents in this business; I *had* to know how it was going to end. The only problem with that, now that I had promised mom and the Chief that my sleuthing days were over, and now that the media seemed to have lost interest altogether, was just how the heck I was going to find out *anything*.

WEDNESDAY, 7:00 AM

Ask, and it shall be delivered—in this case, to our newspaper tube twelve hours later. On Wednesday morning the Gretchyville Times and the Gretchyville Police Department made up for their silence of the day before in spectacular fashion. The robbery at the Maple County Savings Bank was once again front-page news, as I discovered when my mom dropped our copy of the paper next to my cereal bowl, without comment, on her way to the coffee pot. About one sixth of the space on the page had been given over to a pair of photographs of men's faces. They were faces that had been totally unknown to me until three days before; more to the point, they were faces I knew I would never see in the flesh again. After studying them for a long moment, I let my eyes fall to the caption beneath the photographs.

James Cardeiro, 44 (left) and Steven Cardeiro, 42 (right), whose violent deaths are believed by police to be linked to last Saturday's robbery of the Maple County Savings Bank

So I had been right when, moments before my mom snuck up behind us on the kitchen step on Sunday, I had surmised that the two victims were brothers. And now, for the little good it would do them, Gumboots and his brother had names. What we had heard that day as he clung to the side of the car in the dump and repeatedly screamed the name of Jimmy were the agonized outpourings of one suddenly confronted with the death of his older brother. Not being anyone's younger brother myself, only the older brother of a brat sister, I could barely guess at the sheer depth of grief that was swallowing him up at that moment. But it would probably be no exaggeration to describe what we had witnessed as the desolation of a man who had lost something greater than himself. How close had they been in life, I wondered. Did Gumboots— Steven—hero-worship his older brother as a mentor, protector and confidant, the way I know some kids at school do with their brothers? In seeing Jimmy's dead eyes returning his gaze, had the younger man also witnessed the abrupt end of whatever security he had enjoyed in life from a close bond with his older brother? I would never know, and could only try to gauge the truth from the mad violence of his response to Black Hat's arrival in the midst of his grief.

I studied the pictures again. The face of James Cardeiro stared out of the page at me with a sullen expression, yet in a curiously formal pose. His head and shoulders were directly squared to the camera, and behind him a completely neutral background gave no hint of the setting of the photograph. By contrast, Steven Cardeiro's picture appeared to have a closer connection with the real world. Gumboots' pudgy face, three-quarters turned toward the camera, wore a relaxed look and seemed to be in the process of breaking into a quick and natural grin. It looked as if he was holding a glass of beer in his left hand, and such background details as were identifiable suggested a domestic setting—someone's family room or den, perhaps. The photograph might have been taken during a party or family get-together, at some undoubtedly happier time in Gumboots' past. A good deal fuzzier than the other picture, it had the appearance of a group shot from which all the other figures had been cropped out, before it was enlarged to match the size of James' photo. United in life, the Cardeiros had been briefly separated by death, and with this neatly symmetrical pair of newspaper photos had been, if only superficially, reunited.

Mom had returned to the table and started to read the story over my shoulder. It suddenly occurred to me that it could contain information that contradicted the carefully constructed untruths that the Chief, Robert and I had presented on Monday afternoon, and that I had better crank up my speed-reading to minimize the chance of her reaching any contentious passages before I did.

Bank Heist Turns Into Murder
Victims' bodies found in getaway car

A DEATH UNDER SAND

Investigation of Saturday afternoon's robbery of the Maple County Savings Bank, Main Street branch took a gruesome turn on Monday as Gretchyville police located the vehicle believed to have been used in the daring crime, and discovered two homicide victims inside it.

The victims were identified by police yesterday as brothers James Cardeiro, 44, and Steven Cardeiro, 42, both of Blueberry Way, Gretchyville. Both men had died of multiple gunshot wounds.

A spokesman from the State Police Crime Services Laboratory, speaking on condition of anonymity, stated that James Cardeiro appeared to have been dead for at least 48 hours at time of examination, while his brother had been killed some time later. It was also possible, according to the State Police source, that Steven Cardeiro had not been in the vehicle at the time of his death.

Asked about the victims' possible connection with Saturday's robbery, Detective Sergeant Henry Raleigh of the Gretchyville Police Department said that there was a strong likelihood that James Cardeiro was involved in the crime, but that this had not yet been confirmed. Raleigh would not speculate on whether the shooting of one or both of the brothers had been the result of a falling-out among the perpetrators of the robbery, nor would he confirm or deny that the money stolen from the bank had been recovered.

The vehicle in which the bodies were found, a red late model Excalibur Coupe, was located by police on a routine patrol early Monday afternoon on Herring Run Lane. According to Gretchyville Chief of Police Tiberio Bonaventura, the police are satisfied that the car is the one used in the bank robbery. Chief Bonaventura said: "We know that the car was stolen specifically for use in the crime, and having located the car's owner we are also now satisfied that, apart from having been a victim of auto theft, he was not involved in any way."

The Chief of Police refused to identify the owner of the car, except to confirm that he lived in Gretchyville and had no knowledge of the use to which his car had been put. As far as the murder weapons were concerned, he stated that the same firearm—probably a medium-caliber handgun—may have been used in both killings, but that this could not be confirmed until ballistics tests had been completed by the State Police.

According to neighbors, Steven and James Cardeiro had always lived in the house originally owned by their parents on Blueberry Way. James had served ten years in the U.S. Navy, but some two years after the death of his mother in 1986 had returned to Gretchyville to live in the family home with his brother. He worked as a driver for the Samuelson Fuel Company. Some neighbors, who did not wish to be identified, thought that he might have had a police record. Chief Bonaventura would not confirm this opinion, however.

Steven Cardeiro had apparently lived and worked in Gretchyville since leaving high school, and at the time of his death was working in the Facilities Maintenance department of the Maple County General Hospital. The brothers' only known relatives, cousins on their father's side, live in Lambourn and have been informed of their deaths, according to the Gretchyville Police Department.

"Oh my God," commented my mom when she had finished reading. "This is awful. They were brothers—why would anyone want to kill the two of them?"

I could have answered her question but was already absorbed with the new information contained in the article—information over whose absence I had fretted for most of the previous day. But the article was more interesting for what it did *not* say. For reasons that were unclear to me the police had not gone public with the information that they had indeed recovered the stolen money, nor had they made mention of the fact that the car, with James Cardeiro in it, had spent time in the dump before being moved to Herring Run Lane (thank you, Chief). The only omission that made sense to me was O'Sullivan's name; I guess they had decided, as I had when I got intimate with Robert's ankle, that if the man was truly innocent then his name shouldn't be broadcast around town.

But at least there was nothing in the article that was going to cause our own story to unravel, unless my mom managed to put two and two together and—

"Peter..."

—and made four. Rats, she can count.

"Peter: if they found the car on Monday afternoon, and this man had been killed in it forty-eight hours earlier, he must have been in the car when you found it." I managed to time the injection of a spoonful of corn flakes, raisins and milk into my mouth at just the right moment, gaining several seconds of valuable prevaricating time while I crunched, slurped and swallowed.

"Mmf... glmm... I guess so. Unless they took him out on Saturday and put him back in on Sunday night." Was that the best I could come up with? It certainly didn't impress Mom.

"That's ridiculous. Why would anyone do that?"

"Well, maybe they didn't. Don't forget, we never got to see much of the inside of the car. If he was in the front, you know, down on the floor, we would have missed him altogether. Did miss him altogether, I mean." Oops.

"I just hate the thought of you being so close to a dead body, that's all" said my mom, shuddering involuntarily. Since her hand was on my shoulder at the time, the shudder transmitted itself right through me and into the milk in my cereal bowl.

"What's wrong with that? When grandpa McLeod died, you made me go right up and look into his coffin. You don't think that was gross?"

"Well, that's different. Grandpa Harold was old, and died of emphysema. No-one killed him." Not unless you count Grandpa Harold and his forty-a-day habit, I thought. But here was a perfect opportunity to re-route the conversation out of danger: I asked Mom what emphysema really was, which got her started on a ten-minute amateur medical lecture. By the time she had finished, it was past time for me to be out of the house. There was a short but impressive flurry of tooth-brushing, sneaker-tying and backpack-grabbing, and I was on my way to the door with no more questions asked. Passing through the kitchen I glanced down at the paper one more time and suddenly thought of Robert.

"Mom, can I take the front page of the paper to show Robert?" My mom was in the bathroom.

"What did you say, Peter?"

"Thanks, Mom." I scarfed the front page and was still folding it as I accelerated through the door.

Five minutes later I was sitting next to Robert on the school bus as he read carefully through the article. The pandemonium in the bus was at its usual morning level, with greetings, taunts, tall stories, betrayed confidences, paper airplanes and personal effects being passed or thrown around continuously. Robert seemed oblivious to it all. When he finished reading he looked back at the photographs, as I had done, and rubbed his chin thoughtfully.

"So that's Jimmy Cardeiro," he said softly. I was surprised by his tone.

"What—you knew him?"

"I know the name. When my dad got into trouble over the chop shop, it was Jimmy Cardeiro got him involved in that, right enough."

"No kidding." So the Cardeiros' neighbors were right about the elder brother being on more than nodding terms with the Gretchyville Police; then why was the Chief so coy about it? My eye fell on the photograph once again and I suddenly realized that I was staring at Jimmy Cardeiro's police mugshot.

"What about Gumboots?" I asked. "Did you ever hear of Steven Cardeiro before?" Robert shook his head emphatically.

"No; far as I know, Jimmy was the only one who did that kind of stuff."

Robert relapsed into a thoughtful silence. I thought he might have been wondering, like me, about the gaps in the story that only we understood, but his mind was evidently working on a different track. I found out what that track was as Celeste was hauling the bus round into Baggett Lane.

"You know, O'Sullivan must 've had one hell of an alibi," he remarked.

"What do you mean?"

"Well, look at this. The cops went to the trouble of telling the world they'd found the car, found the owner, investigated him and cleared him—cleared him so completely they kept his name secret. If there'd been any doubt at all, they 'd 've said something like 'still under investigation' or 'inquiries are continuing.'"

"So maybe he did have an alibi; hadn't we pretty much figured he was innocent?"

"Yeah, but that's what makes no sense. I mean... if he reported his car stolen, or even if he didn't and they just went to his house when they ID'd the car, why'd they need to bring him to Headquarters to question him? If he had such a good alibi, why didn't they check it out at his place? You don't frogmarch people downtown unless you've got a damn' good reason, and you think you're going to invite them to stay a night or ten. That much I know." Knowing Robert's familiarity with police procedures I could believe him, but I couldn't understand why O'Sullivan's treatment was causing him so much heartache.

Whatever the reason for Robert's doubts, they must have been plaguing him all that morning. He seemed to be in a dream, only giving a quarter of his attention to classes, i.e., about half of his usual contribution. This almost led to disaster in math. when Dumberg fired a simple question, concerning plus signs magically turning into minus signs on the other sides of equations, at him. As it happened, Robert had a 50-50 chance of spouting the right answer, so he gambled and spouted with a dangerous excess of confidence. His luck held, although I don't think Dumberg was impressed.

At lunch Tony and Liddy were all over us again, having read the story for themselves that morning. They both seemed genuinely upset that the dump had not featured in the article, but as I pointed out, since they were not in the dump that day it should not be of concern to them. There was some consolation for Liddy: apparently she has a cousin who works at the same fuel company where Jimmy Cardeiro worked, which restored to her a glow of involvement in the affair. Tony was pissed that the police had still not named the Excalibur's owner, to whom, he informed us, he would otherwise have made an offer for the car from the seven hundred dollars he had saved up.

Robert was taking even less interest in the conversation than I had expected, and it came as no surprise to me when he stood up before it was over and headed with his tray to the trash barrel. What did come as a surprise was the way that, as soon as he was out of Tony's and Liddy's field of vision, he turned back to me and canted his head sideways in a deliberate beckoning movement.

Two minutes later Robert and I were secreted in a corner of the library devoted to the lower numerical reaches of the Dewey decimal system— philosophy and psychology, I think—and thus almost always bare of Gabriele M. Ciccone Junior High School students. Robert had led the way from the cafeteria without discussion or explanation and had brought me to a spot so deserted that we could probably have swapped nuclear missile launch codes without compromising national security. Once we were hidden behind the stacks, whatever had been working on Robert throughout the morning came out with the speed and effect of a mortar shell.

"We gotta go talk to O'Sullivan."

"What!?"

"It's the only way we're gonna find out what's really going on. We won't find it in the paper and the cops aren't about to keep us in the loop. And I swear to you, Peter, O'Sullivan knows something— something the cops can't make sense of, but maybe we can."

"I thought we agreed he was innocent."

"He *is* innocent—officially, now. But I still think he's more involved than a guy who just had his car boosted. Something doesn't make sense."

"And you think he knows what it is?" Robert paused, apparently marshaling his thoughts, before continuing.

"Look: you saw Raleigh's face when they were bringing him in for questioning. As far as he was concerned, he'd got his master criminal. Fair description?" The image of Henry Raleigh's face as he hustled the disoriented O'Sullivan into Police Headquarters flashed into my mind. Robert was right: the detective was already congratulating himself on having wrapped up the case. I nodded my agreement and Robert continued.

"So that means they found something at his place, or maybe he said something, that told them he was their go-to guy. And on the strength of that, they dragged him all the way in for questioning. And yet, twenty-four hours later he's free as a bird. See what I mean?"

"Yeah, I know; you're right. It doesn't make sense. But do you really think he knows something he hasn't told the cops?"

"Not for sure, no. But it can't do us any harm to find out. Maybe you put what he knows together with what we know and it makes a difference."

"Yeah, I guess that's possible. It's just that—"

"Just what?"

I sighed uncomfortably.

"It's just that we promised our moms *and* the Chief that we weren't going to get involved in this any more. Well, didn't we?" Robert appeared to be concentrating on a spot on some distant part of the library ceiling. After a few seconds he looked back at me.

"Well... technically we didn't. What we promised was we wouldn't go back to the dump again, remember?"

I groaned.

"Don't do this to me, Robert. Just don't. This means going somewhere and lying to our moms about it again, and I don't know about you, but if I do it and get caught I wouldn't get away with it this time. She'd nail my shoes to the ground with my feet in 'em."

"Why, for God's sake? It's not like we're trying to track Black Hat down in his home, is it? OK, now that *would* be dumb. We're just going to go and... you know... commensurate with this poor individual who, like us, suffered as a result of this shocking crime." The wideness of Robert's eyes and the altitude of his eyebrows told me that he was having fun with me right now, but I wasn't ready to match his mood with mine.

"It's 'commiserate', dickhead, not 'commensurate'," I retorted. Robert shrugged.

"So are you actually going to go to your mom before we pay this social call and tell her what you intend to do?" I asked. Robert thought about it for a moment, waggling his head from side to side.

"If she's in the house at the time… within earshot… in the same room," he answered.

"Aaarrgghh!" I turned away from Robert and stepped over to the nearest stack. When I reached it I beat my head slowly and rhythmically against one of the vertical members, then after five or six direct hits just stood there and let the pain subside.

The worst part of this, of course, was knowing that Robert was right. Unless we really and truly wanted this business to end with neither a bang nor a whimper but more of a silent fart, we would have to find out what O'Sullivan knew. Maybe we were wrong about Raleigh's contented look as he passed us in Police Headquarters; for all we knew, they might just have stopped off at the doughnut shop on their way back from Bass Point. But if there was any meaning at all to whatever was bugging Robert there was some aspect of this business that had not yet been uncovered, that neither the police nor we had deduced, and for which O'Sullivan was the key. How could we admit that to ourselves and *not* try to ferret it out?

"OK, let's get it over with," I said finally. "We'll go see him today, we'll find out what he knows and get out of there fast. Satisfied?"

"That's all we need, my man."

"Good. Now what do I tell my mom?"

"Ohhh… I dunno. Tell her…" Robert paused, spreading his hands as if to catch a plausible excuse as it flew by him. Suddenly his eyes brightened.

"…Tell her the truth!"

"Oh sure. What do I do—drug her first?"

"No—just tell her we're going riding together. You don't need to tell her where."

"As in, half a truth is better than none, right?"

"Right enough!"

"OK, OK, we'll do it. But when? Right after school?"

"Sure. Why wait?" Robert led the way out of the stacks into the main body of the library, but instead of continuing to the door made straight for the bank of telephone directories in front of the librarian's desk.

"What are you doing?"

"Don't you think we should find out where O'Sullivan lives before paying him a visit?"

"Ah." Now why didn't I think of that?

It seems there are over a dozen men in Gretchyville rejoicing under the name of O'Sullivan, and the only basis we had for narrowing the field were their addresses as shown in the phone book. We got lucky; just one of the candidates lived in the part of town known as Bass Point. Robert shut the directory with a snap, returned it to its place on the shelf and turned to me.

"That's it, then," he announced, as if there had not been the slightest doubt that we would find our

A DEATH UNDER SAND

man on the first shot. "Next stop: Michael
O'Sullivan, 23 Eelgrass Avenue, Bass Point."

WEDNESDAY, 3:45 PM

We leaned our BMXes against a tree in the vacant lot opposite Number 23, Eelgrass Avenue and surveyed Michael O'Sullivan's property. There was certainly nothing about it to suggest the headquarters of a criminal mastermind, unless he were one who was suffering an extended run of failed crimes. The front of the single-story ranch house was faced with clapboard that had once been painted a cheerful shade of blue, but the paint had long since dulled and started to peel, matching O'Sullivan's home more closely with its neighbors in this downwardly mobile part of Gretchyville. At some point the windows had been decorated with fake plastic shutters but most of these had long since broken and been removed, or perhaps they had taken a hike of their own accord rather than spend eternity gazing out at the neglected yard. This, too, must have been in decent condition at some time in the past but now seemed to feature crabgrass, moss and weeds in more or less equal portions. On one side of the house a short, decaying driveway led up to the garage, while on the other side two parallel, ragged strips of bare earth in the grass told us that the garage was not the only place O'Sullivan regularly parked his car.

We sidewaysed until we could see around the non-garage corner of the house. At the far end of the bare strips of earth was parked not the red Excalibur (still providing entertainment for the police, I assumed) but an old, dirty, yet powerful-looking pick-up truck. Behind the truck stood a four-wheel trailer, on which sat a boat measurably more functional than attractive. Although a motorboat, it was hardly the type to be seen planing at high speed across Sakesset Bay carrying an equal complement of chest hair (front seats) and bikini hangers (rear). It was a basic clinker hull, about twenty feet in length and fairly wide in the beam, and sporting a large cockpit behind a full-height open-backed wheelhouse. A hatch about three feet behind the bow suggested the existence of usable space below deck, perhaps for storage or sleeping. The overall impression was of a no-frills working vessel used by someone who took his fishing, or clamming, or lobstering seriously.

We returned to our bikes, and for nearly ten minutes scoped out O'Sullivan's house without seeing or hearing any movement from inside. For all we knew, the man could have been at work—probably was, in mid-afternoon on a weekday. I wondered aloud whether we should give it up and try again at the weekend, but Robert had got the bit between his teeth and wanted nothing to do with leaving before he had the answers to all our questions.

"Why don't we knock on his door, at least?" he asked. "If he's not there, won't do any harm; if he is, we can get on with it."

As if in response, a door slammed on the garage side of the house. We took a few steps in that direction and were in time to see O'Sullivan dump something into his trashcan before returning to the house through the kitchen door. It was all Robert needed.

"OK—he's in there; let's just do it!" He was on his way across the road as he spoke, and I had to hurry to catch up with him. We walked together up the short flagstone path leading to O'Sullivan's front door, and stood side-by-side on his stoop as Robert rang the doorbell. A few seconds later we could hear footsteps approaching the door from the other side; it opened and we found ourselves staring through the screen door at the unsmiling face of Michael O'Sullivan.

"Mr. O'Sullivan?" asked Robert.

"Yes," he replied, with a tone of wariness that should not have surprised me, considering the upheavals of his last couple of days. I began to realize that we were going to have to treat this conversation a little more delicately than we had anticipated.

"Are you—er... do you own—er... a red Excalibur?" I asked, with the delicacy of a jackhammer. O'Sullivan's expression shifted from apprehensive to hostile.

"What about it?" Silence from Robert. Silence from me. Why the hell hadn't we worked this out ahead of time? Finally Robert broke the silence and cut to the chase.

"We're the ones who found it."

"So? What do you want—a reward? Anyway, how did you know it was mine?" Robert seemed to have dried up temporarily. That meant it was my turn to screw it up.

"We were in Police Headquarters when they brought you in on Monday night, and we heard—" O'Sullivan had not removed his hand from the door all this time, and now started to close it in our faces. We had 99% blown it.

"We found it in the dump, not in Herring Run Lane," Robert blurted out as O'Sullivan's face began to disappear. "And we saw who killed Steven Cardeiro!"

The door came to within six inches of closing before its forward movement was abruptly stopped; then it reopened to reveal O'Sullivan's face wearing a less hostile but still suspicious expression. He shifted his eyes from Robert to me and back again.

"In the dump?" he queried. "*You* found it in the dump?" We nodded vigorously.

"It was buried. We uncovered it and found James Cardeiro in it and then Steven Cardeiro found us and then Black Hat found him and shot him and he would've shot us only we got away from him" explained Robert without pausing for breath. A sudden look of understanding passed over O'Sullivan's face.

"Wait a minute. Are you the kids the police told me about? The ones who reported it to them on Sunday?"

"That's right," I replied, relieved that we had finally made some sort of impression on him. "And they didn't believe us—not at first. Then when they did believe us they said it didn't matter because the car was already out of the dump by that time. But we saw the guy who shot Steven, and we know it wasn't you, so we figured he or one of his buddies had stolen your car to do the bank job. Then the paper came out this morning and said the same thing—about your car being stolen. And we thought, from the way the cops dragged you in— even if they did let you go right away—that maybe you know why it was your car they stole—"

"—Or who Black Hat is, at least," added Robert. O'Sullivan held up his hand quickly.

"This Black Hat you keep talking about... where did you see him?"

"In the dump, of course. We told you; he shot Steven, he probably shot Jimmy, and he tried to shoot us. Didn't the cops tell you about him?" O'Sullivan shook his head slowly.

"They... they told me the killer had used the same gun on both men—and he'd probably done it in the dump—but that's about all. But then, they barely mentioned you kids either." I wondered how much other information the police had withheld that might have helped identify the car thieves/bank robbers/killers. O'Sullivan might have been thinking the same, because at that moment his attitude changed again and became, for the first time, actually welcoming.

"Listen, why don't you two come in? I'd like to hear what you know about this whole thing."

I opened the screen door and we entered O'Sullivan's house. As we did so the thought struck me that, if we had made a miscalculation about his innocence, then we were walking straight into the worst kind of danger—a couple of gullible flies power diving into a spider's web. It was only then that it occurred to me how simple a matter it would have been to alert Liddy or Tony about our plans and have them sound the alarm if we did not check in with them by a certain time. But even as O'Sullivan closed the door behind us the momentary fear passed from me, to be replaced by the feeling that had driven me ever since we had left the library. It was the feeling that this was something we absolutely needed to do for our own peace of mind—whether or not Robert was right about the guy having some piece of the jigsaw that would fit with one of ours to produce a recognizable picture.

In the few seconds it took O'Sullivan to lead us through the house to his kitchen I learned a lot more about him. First, the guy was unmarried; either that, or his wife was as big a slob as he was (not usually the case in my experience). Basically, the place was a pit. There were so many clothes strewn around the living room that I figured his bedroom must have come without closets. Also, the guy was either extremely fond of beer or had been going around the neighborhood collecting all the empties he could find and decorating every flat surface of the room with them. And I think he had as many styles of furniture in the house as he had actual pieces—as if he had inherited it all from a number of deceased members of several different families. Or maybe his budget didn't reach beyond yard sales and swap shops, which seemed odd for someone whose own yard usually sported a newish car, a powerful pick-up truck and a boat. Finally, there could not be any doubt about the man's principal leisure-time activity; no matter where we looked there were stacks of fishing magazines—*Atlantic Seaboard Fishing, Offshore Fisherman, Rod and Reel*—and framed photos on the walls of groups of smiling men standing on docks and holding up very large, very dead fish.

O'Sullivan motioned for us to sit at the kitchen table, then drew out a chair for himself; we sat opposite him and stared at him over a collection of boating and fishing paraphernalia and engine parts. It was my first opportunity to really examine the man. He certainly looked less harassed than he had done two days earlier, but not noticeably happier. I could understand that. He had been involved against his will in a violent crime and its subsequent investigation; his property was still in the custody of the Police Department and was likely to remain so until the investigation was successfully resolved—*if* it were successfully resolved.

There was nothing remarkable about O'Sullivan; he was of medium height, slightly stocky, with short sandy hair. I had the impression, from the nondescript way that he dressed, that he chose his clothes every day from a large pile in a darkened room. It was not that he was dirty, more that his appearance—like that of his house—was about the last thing he cared about. He was clean-shaven now, and the color that had returned to his cheeks at least made him look more human than when we had seen him on Monday. But it was still difficult to recognize him as the smiling, gregarious man we had just seen in several wall photos. Some dimension of his character, some vital spirit that had shone out through his eyes strongly enough to be captured in the lens of a camera had disappeared; it no longer seemed to be present in the eyes of the living person sharing this small room with us. Comparing those photographs with this reality was like watching a colorful landscape darkening suddenly as thick, fast-moving clouds obscured the sun. Was this really the result, I wondered, of the events of the last forty-eight hours?

"Okay kids," O'Sullivan began. "Who are you, first? I can't just call you 'kids'." We told him our names and, for no reason I could subsequently recall, the part of town where we lived.

"So how did all of this start? You saw my car parked at the dump, is that right?"

I glanced over at Robert, for some reason expecting him to take on the role of spokesperson for the Juneau-McLeod faction, but his attention was elsewhere. He was transfixed by something in the pile of detritus on the table in front of him. Following his gaze, I saw that it rested on a framed photo that must have been taken down from the wall and that now lay nestled in the folds of a particularly foul-smelling foul weather jacket. It showed a group of men perched on the transom of a boat—almost certainly the one we had observed in the yard—and grinning happily back at the camera. Of the three faces in the photo I recognized two; one belonged to the man sitting across the table from us, the other to the man whose police mugshot I had seen that morning: Jimmy Cardeiro.

I looked up at O'Sullivan, my mind racing. He knew Jimmy? So despite everything, how much did he know about the robbery, and how safe were we to be sitting in the man's kitchen? I suddenly found it difficult to swallow, which was unfortunate, since I wanted to swallow really badly just at that moment. But then a fleeting expression of impatience on O'Sullivan's face brought me back to reality, reminding me that he was still waiting for someone—anyone—to answer his question, and the silence was beginning to hang heavily in the room.

"Well, we didn't exactly *see* it," I said, then drew a deep breath and started from the beginning. And with the obvious exception of Tony's and Liddy's involvement I told him everything, from seeing Steven Cardeiro standing with his back to us in the middle of the dump on Sunday afternoon to reading the latest newspaper article on the crimes that morning. O'Sullivan listened intently, expectantly, perhaps hoping to hear some nugget of information from me that would help him make some sense of the whole mess. But by the time I had finished his face had become somber, his gaze fixed on some indeterminate point between Robert's shoulder and mine. Finally he shook his head and exhaled noisily.

"So that's what happened to Jimmy—poor damn fool," he said in a subdued growl that seemed to be part sympathy, part anger.

"You knew Jimmy?" asked Robert. The question was unnecessary, given the evidence of the photograph, but I guessed that Robert was on a fishing expedition of his own.

"Yeah, I knew him. Not really well; enough to know about some of the dumb things he'd done in the past, maybe. He'd been in trouble with the police a few times, but he wasn't really a bad guy, you know. Kind of stupid, maybe. I mean, he kept getting caught and all. But we'd been fishing a few times together—maybe three times in all, so I knew a little about him. I never met his brother, but Jimmy would talk about him a lot. I guess they were close."

"Yeah, I guess you could say that, right enough," said Robert quietly.

"But was it him who stole your car to do the bank job?" I asked.

"Stole it? Who told you that?"

"It was in the paper this morning."

"Was it? I haven't read it yet; it's still outside in the tube. I... well, I don't get to read the paper 'till late in the day. Anyway, it's not true. No-one stole my car; Jimmy asked if he could borrow it for the weekend. He said he had a hot date over Eddeysport way and didn't want to turn up in his old wreck. I told him so long as he took care of it and made sure he was out of it before he started to party, he could keep it 'till Monday afternoon. I was going fishing the whole weekend, you see."

"Didn't you need the car yourself on Monday?" asked Robert.

"Well sure, but not until late. I work nights, you see, at the town hall; I run the computers and the town's data systems. Most of the back office work gets done at night—backing up, running reports and queries, fixing problems with the hardware, all that sort of thing. So I work from midnight until eight in the morning, and my workweek doesn't start until Monday night. I usually sleep until about four in the afternoon, then I do what most people do during the day—you know, shopping, paying bills, cleaning up…" He must have noticed our eyes roaming the kitchen in response to his last comment and chuckled. It was the first time I had seen anything other than fear, suspicion, hostility or melancholy on his face, and it came as a welcome surprise.

"Yeah, I know," he said, still smiling. "The cleaning up takes pretty much a back seat around here. You don't have to tell me."

We all laughed a little at that, but in the next moment O'Sullivan's expression passed into one of distant wistfulness that made me wonder whether other forces, more profound than those generated by the events of the last week, were at work on him.

"Truth is, I don't worry too much about this place. I'm on my own here—now, anyway—and I've never been much of a Better Homes & Gardens type. I like to get out and fish—well, you can see that, I guess—and I probably put more money into my car than my house. Just my luck, right? If I do ever get it back from the cops, it'll probably be wrecked. Hell, even that doesn't matter now; I'll sell the damn thing. How could I drive it again, knowing… well, you know."

Of course we knew; was it not Robert who had pointed out to Liddy and the rest of us that we could never resume our activities in the dump after all we had experienced on Sunday? Why should we expect O'Sullivan to keep tooling around in a car whose most recent passengers had been the corpses of the Cardeiro brothers? I waited for the man sitting opposite me to continue, but it was Robert who spoke next.

"Is that why you don't read the paper until late in the day—'cause you're sleeping for the first part of it?"

"You're quick, Robert. And you're right, too. Life is kind of weird when you work a night shift; your whole day is bass ackward, not to mention your weekend. I probably watch the same TV shows you do, except I'm having breakfast when I do it." We laughed again. The more O'Sullivan spoke, the easier I felt in his company; he still wasn't exactly a bundle of laughs, but he did sound more like a regular guy who had had a bad break than a sinister gang member waiting his chance to slit our throats. Robert continued on the same tack as before.

"So you work 'till eight Saturday morning, then you have through Monday night off?"

"That's right."

"So, on Saturday afternoon—" O'Sullivan suddenly raised his hands and interrupted Robert.

"Hey—I already went through all this with the cops. I was at sea on Saturday, Sunday *and* Monday. *And* I have an alibi." His tone, defensive enough to be verging on hostile, soured the atmosphere, but in the silence that followed he relaxed again, passed a hand wearily over his eyes and muttered an apology. After another short silence he continued, speaking as if reciting his weekend schedule for the eighteenth time (which he probably was).

"Most weekends in summer, and a few in the spring and fall, I spend as much time on the water as I can. Last weekend was pretty typical. I left work a few minutes after eight, bought what I needed at the supermarket and got home about nine. It took me about an hour to get myself and the boat ready, and Jimmy turned up to collect the car while I was loading the boat. I talked with him for a few minutes, just to remind him not to junk the car up, then he was off. I got down to the town ramp next to McAllister's Marina at about ten-thirty, maybe a little later, gassed up and launched, parked the truck and trailer, and got out on the water around about eleven. I headed out for about two hours about twenty degrees east of south; that puts me on top of Magdalene Shoal, close to where I can usually find a pretty good number of bass, plus the usual cod and hake, you know. Anyway, I anchored on the shoal as usual, set some lines and went below and turned in."

"You went to bed?"

"Sure. Remember, I'd been up for over twenty hours at that point. But if I'm on my own I'd just as soon get on the water and sleep aboard than crash out at home; it'd be getting dark by the time I got to the shoal otherwise. And I don't usually do more than nap for two or three hours, then I start up again and head south of the shoal to do some serious fishing. Back when I used to take friends out with me I'd do without sleep altogether until Saturday night, but this weekend I was on my own, so I did what I pleased. Anyway, around about five I got far enough south and put my lines out again. Nothing much happened for over an hour, and I was about to shift into deeper water when I got a bite, then two at once, and all of a sudden I was busy. In fact, I was so busy I didn't notice Sherm Graveney come up from downwind until he blasted me on his air horn."

"Sherm who?"

"Graveney. You wouldn't know him; he's come out with me once or twice in the past when his boat's been out of commission, which is most of the time, I think. But last weekend he was out on it… thank God."

"What do you mean?" I asked.

"Well, think about it. Most times I go out, especially this time of year, I don't see anyone for two whole days closer than half a mile. If Sherm hadn't been trolling that particular piece of ground at that time—" Robert jumped in and finished O'Sullivan's sentence.

"—You wouldn't have had an alibi, right?"

"Right! I'd still be entertaining that Raleigh character at Police Headquarters. God knows, they

272

had enough cause." My ears pricked up; whatever O'Sullivan meant by that, it explained the look on Raleigh's face that Robert and I had been agonizing over for two days. But before I could probe him, O'Sullivan was back at sea off the Magdalene Shoal.

"I chewed the fat with Sherm for a few minutes, then he started back in. The rest of the trip was pretty normal; I went all the way down to Magister Island, made a good catch and came back mid-afternoon Monday. I usually sell most of my catch to the Domingos fish market Monday evening, and that was what I was planning this time. I had no idea of what had been going on in town while I was at sea until twenty minutes after I got home, when the police arrived in force. I'll never forget it; they had a warrant all ready and went through my place like a dose of salts. They said one of the robbers had been wearing a Dodgers jacket; of course, don't I have a Dodgers jacket? And didn't they find it in my garage right where I'd left it last week, and didn't they find a spot of blood on it that turned out to be Jimmy's? Not to mention the wad of cash from the bank job they found hidden in my toolbox. I just didn't know what to say; I was knocked sideways by the whole thing. They bundled me into a cruiser and had me downtown for over two hours before anyone could get hold of Sherm and hear his story. They didn't want to believe me even then, but finally must have figured I'd been set up."

"Set up—who by?" I asked. O'Sullivan gave a short, mirthless laugh.

"That's what I've been trying to work out for two days. It would have been one thing if my car had been stolen just for the robbery, but it was more than that. Someone took my jacket from the garage before the bank job, then stashed it back there afterwards, along with some of the money. I wish I knew who—and why."

"How about Jimmy?" asked Robert. "He's the obvious one."

"I know, I know," replied O'Sullivan, nodding. "Believe me, I thought long and hard about that. And as I told you, Jimmy had a police record, 'though not for anything like this. But he had no reason to get me into trouble with the law. Besides, if he was behind the whole thing... hell, it sure didn't turn out the way he planned, did it? No, if I had to guess I'd say someone else used my car for the bank job and thought they'd throw the scent off on to me. It was probably carjacked with Jimmy in it... Poor guy was just in the wrong place at the wrong time..."

The whirring and clanking sound from our side of the table was coming from inside my head; O'Sullivan's interpretation of events was grinding up against ours like two ill-fitting cog wheels that had not been given a shot of oil for a year or two.

Could Jimmy have been as much a victim as Steven? Did Black Hat kill him and keep his body in the car during the robbery? That seemed ridiculous, but it wasn't the reason I couldn't swallow O'Sullivan's version whole. What was it, for God's sake? All of a sudden the image of Jimmy's body swam back into my head, and there was the answer. That absurd, dopey-looking chipmunk sewn into the breast of his sweat top— that was what had placed Jimmy in the bank, and unless Black Hat and his partner had dressed his body in the sweat top after the robbery and shot two holes in it—how's that for ridiculous?—then O'Sullivan was wrong. Jimmy had been part of the plan from the beginning and must have 'borrowed' the car with the bank job in mind. At some point after the actual robbery there must have been, as Raleigh had put it, a 'falling-out' between thieves. Perhaps Black Hat had calculated that he would net more of the proceeds if Jimmy received nothing, and used his handgun to explain the point to him.

I explained to O'Sullivan about the logo and its implications and watched his expression change, as I did so, from pity for his sometime friend to anger at the deception he had played on him. When I finished he abruptly and noisily pushed his chair back, rose and walked to the kitchen window. Although the late afternoon sun was lighting up his face as it streamed at a fine angle through the window, the expression it picked out on it was blacker and more brutal than any I had yet seen. He stood with his back to us for a few seconds, his hands in his pockets, then spoke in a hollow, barely controlled voice.

"Well then, he deserved what he got, the bloody lying thief! What had I ever done to him except taken him out fishing a few times like a friend? I was supposed to take the rap for that bank job, was I? Serves him right, then. He lost the money *and* his life. Apart from the little they stashed in my garage, his partner must have made off with all of it." Robert and I exchanged a quick glance as we realized just how much more we knew than the man at the window did. Robert put it into words first.

"Mr. O'Sullivan—didn't the cops tell you *anything?*"

"What do you mean?"

"The money. I don't know how much they put in your garage, but I promise you—just about all the rest stayed in the car!"

"What!"

"That's right," I chimed in. "When we first looked into the car, it was all over the back seat. We were thinking, maybe the dye bombs went off and that's why they left the money in there. We can't figure out any other reason; of course, we can't figure out why Black Hat put the car in the dump in the first place, either. It just... just doesn't make sense. We thought maybe you would have some idea about it."

O'Sullivan's face took on a thoughtful look. He came back to the table slowly and rested his hands on the back of his chair, shifting his eyes from me to Robert and back again.

"Black Hat," he said quietly. "The police told me about a man who shot at you in the dump, and who killed Steven. That's him, right?"

"That's him." I gave a short chuckle. "We've always called him Black Hat. I guess I started it 'cause... well, 'cause he was wearing a black hat, and because that's what you call bad guys, right? Didn't the cops describe him to you?"

"In no more detail than you just did. Why don't you tell me as much as you can about him?"

Robert and I dredged up the description of Black Hat that we had given so many times to the police, but it seemed no more adequate then than it did before. Eventually I remembered the cowboy boots and mentioned those, too. I looked over at Robert to see if he had anything to add; he hadn't. As for O'Sullivan, the silence from his side of the table continued long enough for me to wonder if he had fallen asleep on us. I looked up at him and realized that we had finally struck a nerve. His hands were now not just resting on the chair back but gripping it tightly, and while his eyes were directed at the point on the table where my hand lay, he looked as if he were focusing on something a little further away: New Zealand, perhaps.

"Cowboy boots. Oh no. Oh God, I don't believe it." His hands were trembling as he released the chair, and as he turned back to the window I could see that his face had lost several shades of color. He stood with his back to us and stared out at his unkempt yard in a silence that would have been complete but for the sound of his heavy and ragged breathing. When he finally spoke again, there was a strange heaviness in his voice.

"Yes, I do believe it; of course I believe it. Now it all makes sense. I just don't know why he waited this long."

"Who, Mr. O'Sullivan?" asked Robert. "Do you know who this guy is?" O'Sullivan turned and looked at us as if he were seeing us for the first time. He exhaled noisily then returned to the table, sat down and told us what we had come to hear.

"Your Black Hat? Yes, I know who he is. And I know why he did all this. I know why he left the money behind. And I know why the Cardeiro brothers are dead."

WEDNESDAY, 4:30 PM

"I thought he sounded familiar when you described him, but it was the cowboy boots that clinched it. He wears them more often than not; I don't know why—kind of stupid habit for a New Englander, huh? Still, I guess it's right up there with the crummy country music he always plays. Enough to drive you bananas. Anyway, it goes without saying the cops didn't tell me as much about him as you've done. If they had—hell, he'd be in the third-degree room right now, sweating it out. You see, I know more about this guy than I want to know. And what I know is—he's bad news from the moment he wakes up in the morning.

"His name is Gaudett—Gene Gaudett. I got to know him eighteen months, maybe two years ago. Actually, I got to know his sister first, then the rest of her family, including him. Hell, if you ask me, the whole family's a few bricks short of a load... you know, kinda loopy. Even Katie, poor thing... well, I don't want to speak ill of the... Oh God, poor Katie. What chance did you have with a family like that? It didn't have to be that way...

"OK, OK, I'm rambling. Let me start from the beginning.

"I met Katie Gaudett a couple of years ago; she worked in the back office at Domingos, where I sell most of my catch. She was the one who would cut the check for me. She was about thirty, kind of quiet and timid, sweet when you got to know her, nice to look at, single, still lived at home. Anyway, one day her computer was giving her trouble and I helped her with it; we got talking, and over my next few visits got to know each other a little. I asked her out a couple of times before she said yes—like I say, she was quiet and kind of shy—but after that we really hit it off. A couple of months later she moved in with me—here. It was the first time I'd lived with a woman, you know, and it was really great. She made this place look terrific in no time; woman's touch and all that. Made me realize just how much of a schlep I was! Katie loved me and I loved her, though—as it turned out—not enough, I guess.

"I got to know her family during that time. They were OK at first, but none of them seemed to have any real ambition or idea of where they were going in their lives. And Gene... Well, he just got on my nerves in a big way. Always seemed to be asking me things that were none of his business, like how much I made, or when he could use the boat for some deal of his own. Once or twice he bugged me to join in some scheme of his that didn't sound too much above board, and I really took a dislike to him.

"You have to know this guy—or better yet, just steer clear of him. About my age, never had a real job for long as far as I know. I kind of remember him from Gretchyville High, twenty years back. Bad piece of work, even then. There were kids terrified of him. He'd get money out of them somehow—probably in exchange for not pounding their brains out around back of the school. Nearly got expelled for it a couple of times, I heard. And when we all graduated high school, he just graduated to the real stuff. Every so often you'll read the Police Log in the local paper and there he'll be, getting fined, or cautioned, or put on Community Service or something. He even served time for a couple of jobs, if I remember right. Nothing spectacular, you know—receiving stolen goods, burglary, stealing cars... real penny-ante stuff. Guy seemed to have a chip on his shoulder— thought the world owed him a living, and if it didn't deliver then he'd just take it. I don't know where he got his attitude from, although knowing how the rest of the family is, I doubt any one of them ever thought to set him straight. Except Katie, maybe, but he wouldn't have listened to her.

"Anyway, after we'd been together a few months it got worse. Her parents and one of her other brothers started touching me up for money— not that I'm rich or anything—and I swear, stuff started to go missing around here. Katie knew I was unhappy about it, but wouldn't—or couldn't—say anything against her family.

"Then I came home from work one morning to find Gene sacked out in the spare bedroom. Seems someone was looking for him, and it wasn't to give him a Publishers' Clearing House check, either. He said he had to make himself scarce for a couple of weeks and just turned up on my doorstep, like he owned the place. Well, that was the beginning of the end. I told Katie I wasn't putting up with it, and the rest of her family could just damn well back off, too. We got into a big fight; no, that's not true— Katie wasn't the sort to fight, and I guess I did a lot of the fighting and all of the shouting. I went too far; told her she had to choose between her deadbeat family and me. Hell, if I'd really known what Katie was like I wouldn't have put her on the spot like that. I'll never forgive myself for... well, for pushing her so far. *Too* far.

"Gene finally cleared out after a few days, but the family was still making my life miserable. Her parents started ordering stuff—stupid, mail-order stuff—and expecting me to front them money to cover it, money I knew I'd never see again if I was dumb enough to do what they wanted. I guess they were putting pressure on Katie to get me to do it, too. Well... I don't remember what the final straw was... Yes I do, too: Gene came in one day while I was asleep and 'borrowed' the pick-up for some typically shady job. When he brought it back I was waiting for him and told him he could get the hell out of my life—and the same went for his family, too. We nearly got into a fistfight right out there in the yard. Right in the middle of it Katie came back from work; I really had my blood up by this time and told her she could pack her stuff and get out. I didn't mean it; hell, Katie was the first good thing in my life for... I don't know, forever maybe. But she wasn't the sort to fight back. She just went inside as her lousy brother took off, and five minutes later she just... walked out of my life. Didn't even take all her stuff. The last I saw of her, she was walking down the front path with a small suitcase, crying like a kid. Goddammit, I should have gone right after her, but I was just too mad over the whole business. Plus I thought she'd calm down after a day or two, and we could sort it out. If I'd known... if I'd known, I would have...

"Two days later I got a call from the Gaudett's house. It was Katie's father. God, do I remember that call. There was all sorts of noise going on in the background— women crying, men yelling, doors slamming, I don't know what else. And then her father told me. He told me... he told me Katie had taken a bottle of sleeping pills, and they'd just found her dead in her room. He started to ask me why I'd dumped her, why I'd broken up with her, told me it was all my fault; then Gene took the phone from him and told me he was going to get me for what I'd done, called me every name he could think of, said I was a dead man, that he was coming around to do it to me right then... I couldn't take it any more; I hung up on him. I was dying with grief myself and I didn't need this lunatic screaming at me. I stayed in the house. I don't think I cared, frankly, if he did come around and kill me; I was just too... oh, Katie, why? Why? What did I do to you? We would've been fine without them, just you and me. We could have gone on... forever. Forever, dammit."

O'Sullivan covered his face with his hands and leaned heavily on his elbows, gently and silently shaking his head. The silence enveloped us too; it was hardly a time for jokes or smart remarks. O'Sullivan had exposed the unhealed, untreated flesh of an old wound to the elements, and was feeling again in full measure the searing pain of that injury. In setting the scene for us he had brought this tragic history to life so well that it had struck us dumb, motionless and horrified. I could think of nothing to say in response and neither, apparently, could Robert. Hell, what could a person say to a story like that? Again we were staring at grief, but not the same pure, uncontrolled grief of Steven Cardeiro encountering his dead brother. Instead of raging against unknown and vindictive forces as Gumboots had done, O'Sullivan was expressing a grief that was burdened with the weight of his own guilt.

In that moment I felt as if I had taken a great leap in my understanding of the man. Here was someone who blamed himself for the death of someone he deeply loved, and was so tortured by his loss that he was somehow able to discount the accusations of the Gaudett men against him while leveling the same accusations at himself and—at some dimly lit level of his conscience—believing them. I was not often brought face-to-face with such raw and complex emotions nor did I pretend, certainly not at my age, to a deep understanding of human nature; nevertheless, as if catching the indistinct movement of plants through layers of murky water I could now see, vaguely, something of what went on below the surface of this man. I was almost certain that Katie Gaudett had been the great love—perhaps the one love—of his life, that her impact on it was akin to someone suddenly opening all the drapes in a darkened room and letting in the noonday light, and that in losing her, O'Sullivan had also lost interest in almost any activity that involved human contact. From one who had once enjoyed taking groups of friends on weekend fishing trips and—to judge by the photographic evidence on his walls—delighted in the companionship they provided, he now undertook these outings in solitude for days at a time. And I had to believe that this house rarely saw visitors, unless they were the sort to phone ahead and request that their host junk it up in honor of their arrival.

O'Sullivan ran his hands through his sandy hair and, taking a deep breath, continued.

"Well, anyway... For all his talk, Gene didn't come to the house and kill me." The remark was enough to break the awful tension of the previous couple of minutes and make the two of us break into a laugh, which we immediately tried to stifle. But O'Sullivan, realizing what he had said, relaxed a little and allowed himself about three millimeters-worth of smile.

"That's right, I really am alive. And I haven't seen Gene, or any of the Gaudett clan, from that day to this. In the circumstances I didn't feel I could go to Katie's funeral, although I often go to the cemetery—every week, I guess. Don't know why... It helps—sometimes. Sometimes it makes it worse." There was another brooding silence, which continued until Robert cleared his throat and zeroed in on what was, for us, the salient point of our visit.

"So you're saying Black Hat is this guy Gene? 'Cause of the cowboy boots? And he just needed your car to do a robbery? Is that all?" O'Sullivan was shaking his head even before Robert had finished.

"Don't I wish it were as simple as that! No, the money was the least of it. That's why he left it in the car, I bet—because he wasn't interested in it. You know what the point of his day's work was? Me!"

"You?"

"That's right. I don't know what happened in the Gaudett house that day, but someone must have calmed him down—stopped him from rushing out and doing what he'd threatened. But Gene... Well,

A DEATH UNDER SAND

I always thought he was a psycho, and this proves it. As far as he was concerned, I'd killed his sister and he was going to get me for it one way or another, no matter how long it took. I'm willing to bet he spent over a year after Katie's death trying to figure out how to get me into the worst trouble of my life, and last weekend was the result of all that. He knew I spent weekends out fishing on my own, and he must have known I knew Jimmy Cardeiro— probably saw him in this photo. He probably knew Jimmy too—considering what the two of them were like, I expect they'd done some shady stuff together. I'm betting Gene got around him to borrow my car last weekend for the bank job, but I wonder how much Jimmy really knew? Did Gene tell him they were just going to use the car and return it, without me being any the wiser, or did he somehow persuade him that they should put me in the frame for the robbery? Maybe he offered him a bigger cut if he went along with that. I know one thing: Jimmy didn't know the whole plan. Gene was holding back one little detail that would have made Jimmy lose interest in the whole affair, if he'd known it up front."

"What was that?" asked Robert. O'Sullivan leaned forward and looked closely into Robert's eyes for a long moment. Then he smiled, without humor or pleasure or kindness, and continued.

"I said you were quick just now, didn't I? So how come you can't figure it out? Even if Jimmy did think the idea was to pin the bank job on me, that was never Gene's plan. That wasn't nearly enough for him. Do you understand what I'm saying? Gene Gaudett's whole idea from the start was to get me arrested for murder, and the one thing he never told Jimmy was that *he* was going to be the victim."

A DEATH UNDER SAND

WEDNESDAY, 5:00 PM

My eyes fell again on the framed photo on the table, on James Cardeiro's untroubled face and relaxed pose, as I struggled to take in the full meaning of O'Sullivan's conclusions. Staggered as I was by the extent of Gene Gaudett's capacity for evil, I was even more affected by the images associated with his partner-in-crime's last minutes of life. True, I had never known him, and what little I knew of him I did not like, but in my mind's eye was a clear series of scenes that provoked genuine pity for this man marked for death. I could see him in the passenger seat of the Excalibur as Gaudett gunned it up Old Kingsleytown Road, alternately checking behind them for signs of pursuit and wildly celebrating the success of their crime. When the car bumped to a halt at the end of the berm he would have seen with surprise the driver's real partner waiting for them and might have stared dumbly out at him, then turned back to Gaudett with a question on his lips and found himself staring down the barrel of his murderer's gun. Was his mind clear enough at the instant the bullets crashed into his chest to comprehend anything of his true role in the day's events or, as seemed more likely, did he die without any understanding, as an animal is killed instantly by a car as it crosses a highway at night? I did indeed feel sorrow for this man whom I had never met, perhaps deepened by the knowledge of how pathetically unaware he must have been of the reasons for his death.

And in viewing Jimmy Cardeiro's part as a dumb instrument of Gene Gaudett's scheme in the light of all the other information O'Sullivan had given us, I could not help but agree with his interpretation. It made complete sense. What would a man who was prepared to kill four teenaged boys *not* do to achieve his fantastic and obsessive ends? Gaudett's bullets may have found the Cardeiro brothers and missed us, but I felt certain that O'Sullivan was the real target.

"Wow..." The only sound from our side of the table came from Robert, at a level barely above a whisper. I glanced over to find him looking at me and nodding; apparently, he too was convinced by O'Sullivan's story.

"You see the kind of man we're dealing with?" asked O'Sullivan, and I nodded along with Robert as our host continued with his interpretation of events.

"When he'd killed Jimmy, he probably opened one of the cash bags—that's probably when the dye bomb went off—and took out a good handful of stained money to plant in my garage. He made sure Jimmy's blood was on my Dodgers jacket, then they left him in the car and buried it, swept away their tire tracks and footprints and got out the way they came in. Gene had probably left his own car on Old Kingsleytown Road, and he would have swung by my place to leave the jacket and the money in the garage."

"How come nobody heard the shots?" asked Robert. O'Sullivan thought for a moment, then broke into a grin before replying.

"Well, I'm not going to ask you if you've ever actually heard a gun being fired; I know you have, and you were lucky it wasn't the last thing you heard. But don't forget: those shots were fired in a closed car that was shielded by acres of sand, not to mention the fact that no-one would have been around to hear them. *The dump closes at three o'clock on weekends!"*

O'Sullivan's explanation was meant as a response to Robert's question, but it also served to set off a buzzer in my brain that was like an alarm clock ringing in some inaccessible corner of the room: I couldn't silence it even if it were serving no purpose. It had not occurred to me that the dump would have been unoccupied at the time of the car's arrival—we were always out of there before three on Sundays—but I could not put my finger on its significance. Why did this matter? What piece of the jigsaw was still dangling over the puzzle, waiting for understanding to dawn before it dropped neatly into place?

"So you would have been on the hook for murder," Robert was saying, "if you hadn't seen

your friend while you were fishing on Saturday?"
O'Sullivan nodded vigorously.

"I'll have to buy Sherm a case of beer for that!"
he said, standing up and walking over to a coat rack
by the kitchen door. He pulled a windbreaker off
the rack and opened the door, then stood looking
back at us expectantly.

"Are you coming?"

"Coming where?" Robert asked.

"The police, of course. We've done their job
for them and ID'd the killer; don't you think we
should tell them what we know?"

"You want us to come with you?" I queried.

"Well, of course I do. We did this together,
remember?"

"Sure we did. But... Well, I guess the police
aren't exactly expecting to see us again. The Chief
made it pretty clear on Monday, he expects us to
butt out until they're ready to talk to us."

"You don't think they'll be interested to see
you with what we've got to tell them now?"

Robert's face lit up with his famous lopsided
grin. "Well... Now you mention it, it would be
kinda cool to go in and tell them we cracked the
case."

"Yeah, you could describe it that way. Kinda
cool. So are you coming?" Robert was out of his
seat and half-way around the table before I could
get within arm-grabbing range.

A DEATH UNDER SAND

"Hold on two seconds, Robert," I said urgently. "Look: time's getting on. We couldn't get to the cops, tell them all this stuff and get back home without our moms figuring out we've been telling them fairy stories again; they're both pretty twitchy as it is. And mine is going to crucify me, I'm not kidding you, if she even gets a whiff of that. We've got to start back home right *now* if we don't want them comparing notes again."

"Aw, come on man," retorted Robert, who seemed to have got the bit forward of his teeth and clear out of his mouth in the last few seconds. "Think about it. We get to walk in on Raleigh and give him his #1 Suspect's name, address, phone number and favorite girl band. We get to see Black Hat—Gaudett—taken down, and we make Raleigh admit we knew what we were talking about in the first place. Don't you want to do that, Peter? Don't you want to do that *right now?*"

I didn't answer at once. Slowing Robert back down to a trot was going to be a problem. I understood exactly why this was so important to him and why he had specifically mentioned Raleigh by name; it was Raleigh who had first implied that Robert was not to be trusted on account of what he knew of his father, but we both knew the reason to be Raleigh's own broader prejudices. And I hoped Robert knew that it was as important to me as it was to him to stuff those prejudices right back down

Raleigh's throat. But Robert was being his usual impetuous self.

"Look… I know why you want to do this," I said, moving around the table until I stood directly in front of him. "And before this is all over you'll be able to, I promise. But right now we've got to wind our necks in and take care of business at home, 'cause if we don't, life's not going to be worth living. Now, you and I have to have the same story, and if you're downtown while I'm at home it's not going to work. And believe me, even you couldn't talk your way out of this one. We agreed we were just going to come down here, find out what we could, then go home, right? So that's what I'm going to do—go home—and you're going to have to do the same unless you want the whole thing to unravel."

Robert swore under his breath and made a great show of huffing and puffing with exasperation, but that was the extent of his protesting. I think he knew perfectly well that I was right but would probably never have reined himself in without being nagged into it.

"OK, Peter," he said at last. "We'll go home. But I think it's lousy not to be there at the finish of this."

"We will be, Robert. Believe me, we will be."

O'Sullivan had remained by his kitchen door all this time, waiting for us to sort ourselves out. Now that we had done so, he appeared anxious to wrap our visit up.

"Well, if the two of you have decided what you're going to do, why don't we get out of here now? I want Gaudett brought in ASAP." We filed out ahead of him and headed toward our bikes on the other side of the road while he locked the door and started for his pick-up truck. We were in the middle of the road when I suddenly remembered a detail that would be vital to the delicate game of untruths we were playing with our moms.

"Mr. O'Sullivan?"

"Yes?"

"I just thought—our moms don't know we're here and they'd be megapissed if they found out. If the cops tell you they want to see us again, would you do us a favor and have them kind of... forget to tell our moms we came here?" O'Sullivan chuckled and nodded, then beckoned us back. We returned to the end of his front path and waited while he fiddled clumsily with his truck keys.

"I should have said this before," he said awkwardly. "You two didn't need to come here; you didn't know me from Adam, and for all you knew I had something to do with the killing. But if you hadn't come here and told me everything, Gene Gaudett would probably have found some other way to get at me—maybe without the complicated planning. Maybe he'd have hung around across the street after dark and shot me when I came out of my house; I don't know. Anyway, without being over-dramatic, let me just say you probably saved my life. I want to thank you; you're good kids. That's all I wanted to say."

It was obvious that even saying this much had been a considerable effort for O'Sullivan, not because he was naturally ungrateful but because he was naturally ungifted at dealing with kids of our age. I didn't think any the less of him for it; I felt I could give a lot of latitude to a man whose gray-hued life had been briefly illuminated before being plunged into the kind of darkness to which he now woke up every day. Rather than prolong his embarrassment we quickly biked ourselves out of there while he clambered into his truck and got it started. A minute later he passed us on his way into town and gave us a friendly, but not exactly light-hearted wave.

We split up at the top of Sachem Street and I coasted home, wondering whether our stories had held up or whether the kid cauldron was even now being prepared. I entered the kitchen from the side door to find my mom puttering in the kitchen; she looked up in mid-putter as I entered, and from the tone of her greeting it was obvious that my absence had not aroused her suspicions. I chatted with her for a few minutes, painting a glowing picture of my day at school, then made for my room with a backpack full of homework. I would like to say that I dug right into my homework with energy and dedication but as I explained before, this story is being written as accurately as I can remember it, so... Well, I did at least open my schoolbooks, but then spent half an hour gazing out the window and trying to imagine what was going on at Police Headquarters. Did they believe O'Sullivan, a man who had come close to being charged with the crime forty-eight hours earlier? Had they picked up Gaudett, or had he left town or gone into hiding? Once again my immediate ambition was to be a fly on one of the inner walls of that building.

"Peter! Dinner!"

Dinner was something square and pale; if it had been land-based when alive, my money was on it having been chicken, but if not, then cod was my best guess. When it was mostly off the plates and into our digestive systems I began to clear the dishes and escort them into the kitchen. As I crossed to the sink a movement in the driveway caught my eye; it was a dark green sedan coming to a gentle halt in front of our garage. The car looked vaguely familiar, even in the gathering twilight, and as I peered through the window at its driver I realized why. It was the car in which Robert and I had been driven to the dump on Sunday afternoon, and behind the wheel was the same driver— Jacobson. The detective opened his door, and with the internal light on I could clearly see the passengers in his rear seat. Mrs. Juneau was sitting on the right, an apprehensive frown on her face.

Her only son, however, could hardly be contained within the vehicle; Robert was car-dancing, as likely as not to some lively Reggae tune originating from somewhere between his ears, and beating out a tattoo with his palms on the top of the driver's seat. On his face was the grin that I would have recognized as his if it had been, like the Cheshire cat's, his only discernible feature. I could guess what it meant: our presence had been formally requested at the headquarters of the Gretchyville law enforcement community, and the investigation into the combined crimes of bank robbery and double homicide was about to be neatly wrapped up.

WEDNESDAY, 7:30 PM

It was not so much a room as a large closet, only a little wider than the door by which we had entered and perhaps twice as deep. The wall opposite the door was dominated by a large window giving onto an adjoining room from where, when the door was closed, came the only illumination. I realized immediately where we were, having seen similar set-ups in countless police movies and TV shows; the window was actually a one-way mirror, separating the identification line-up room from the witness room in which we stood. I had never imagined while watching all those pitifully identical shows and movies that I would one day find myself taking part in the process; now that I was, I mused, it was better that I found myself on the dark side of the glass.

Detective Jacobson had explained, as I expected, that Robert and I were needed to identify a suspect at Police Headquarters. Evidently having been tasked by the Chief with following the approved procedure to the letter this time, he had invited both my mom and me to accompany him and the Juneaus downtown. I guess our moms were needed to hover in the background to ensure that we were not corrupted by contact with matters criminal; if only they knew...

C.W. STIMPSON

My mom had parked my sister, under protest, with the Fosdycks' next door, and we proceeded downtown with mom in the front passenger seat and Robert and me in the back with his mom, grinning like idiots and high-fiving each other as surreptitiously as possible. As an aside I should explain that if you are trying to be surreptitious, you should dispense with the high-fiving.

On arrival at Police Headquarters we had been ushered into the Chief's office with some ceremony. The Chief explained that, acting on Mr. O'Sullivan's information, the police were questioning a certain suspect in the recent robbery and homicide case (and no mention of our secret afternoon visit to Bass Point; thank you Chief, thank *you* Mr. O'Sullivan); an identification parade was being arranged and it would greatly assist the police in their enquiries if Mrs. Juneau and Mrs. McLeod would allow their sons to attempt to identify a man who was believed to have been in the vicinity of the town landfill recently.

And now the Chief, Robert and I stood in the cramped witness room, with Raleigh lurking at the door. Bonaventura was explaining that we would shortly see six men walk into the line-up room and stand facing us, one man beneath each of the numbered signs hanging on the far wall. The wall, we were to observe, was marked with horizontal lines at six-inch intervals to help us in gauging the height of each man. We were to take our time, study each face very carefully, and only if we were absolutely sure that we had recognized the man who fired at us in the dump were we to identify him. We were not to make guesses; he would rather we failed to identify the suspect than choose the wrong man. If we wanted to see the line from any other angle we were only to ask, and an officer would instruct the line to turn in the requested direction. We were not to worry about being identified by the suspect; the men in the room would be quite unable to see anyone on our side of the glass. I almost tuned out as the Chief was speaking; it seemed that I had heard this same speech a dozen times before, which just goes to show how much of my life I have wasted watching second-rate cops and robbers shows. Finally the Chief asked if we had any questions, and on hearing nothing from us asked which one of us wanted to be first.

"First?" I repeated.

"You mean we don't get to do this together?" asked Robert, a little breathlessly. The Chief was shaking his head firmly.

"That wouldn't do at all, would it? We need independent identification of the suspect. If you were in here together, one of you might say or do something to affect the decision of the other one, mightn't you? It's what we call collusion, and it could end up with having the case thrown out of court. None of us wants that, right?"

We both shook our heads, but now I was really worried. All three of us knew there was some question about our ability to identify Gaudett— Robert had said as much to the Chief on Monday— and I had been counting on a joint approach with Robert in which we would bolster each other up in case either of us had doubts. But now each one of us was truly on his own for the first time, dependent on his own recollection of those few tense moments in the dump during which we had seen the man we now knew as Gene Gaudett. It really didn't matter, in the circumstances, who went first, and accordingly I raised my hand and stepped across to the glass panel.

From that point, things started to move more quickly. While the Chief remained at my side, Raleigh whisked Robert out, shut the door and called down the corridor. Less than a minute later the door of the line-up room opened and six men, followed by Jacobson, filed in; simultaneously the door behind me re-opened to admit a man whom I had not seen on my earlier visits to this building. The man, a stocky middle-aged specimen in a tired-looking suit, positioned himself behind me and to the side without acknowledging the presence either of the Chief or me. I glanced at Bonaventura, and in the faint light that filtered through from the line-up room saw him purse his lips and set his shoulders more squarely.

A DEATH UNDER SAND

On the far side of the glass Jacobson was arranging the men under the numbers, facing the mirror; I assumed that most of them were other policemen who had been 'volunteered' for the task, but didn't recognize any of them. Finally the detective appeared satisfied with his design and stepped away from the glass; the Chief repeated his earlier instructions to me and I began to concentrate on the men staring at their own reflections in the next room. Following my instructions I examined each man with care, quickly eliminating from contention those who were too short, too fat, too blond, too dark-skinned... Soon only two men were left, numbers 2 and 5, with basic physical attributes that resembled what I remembered of Gaudett. After a few more seconds I decided that number 2 seemed a little too tall and switched my attention to number 5. Which was when my problems really started.

Candidate number 5 was dressed in a conservative, light-colored sports jacket and well-creased slacks. A white shirt and striped tie gave him an air of respectability, as did the new-looking brown wingtips on his feet. He was clean-shaven with no mustache and his hair was cropped close to his head. He looked as unlike the man who had shot at us in the dump as anyone with the same approximate height and build could look. But when I pressed up close to the mirror and fixed my stare on his eyes, which seemed, impossibly, to be boring right through the glass at me, I felt a sudden and uncontrollable shiver. In my heart I knew that these were the eyes that had taken the four of us in for a fraction of a second on Sunday before their owner reached for his gun, but nothing else about him matched. I realized at once that Gaudett had expected this line-up to be arranged and had completely changed his appearance. The unkempt mass of hair that had protruded from under his hat on Sunday had disappeared, to be replaced by a style that would have been acceptable in the U.S. Marine Corps' boot camp, and with his mustache and stubble gone he looked a completely different man. In some consternation I looked at Bonaventura, hoping for guidance.

"Well, Peter? Do you see the man you saw on Sunday?" he asked.

"I think so, but—"

"You have to be sure, Peter. You can't just take a guess to please me." I turned again to the glass and focused on the calm face under the large red '5'; was there any part of it that belonged, without question, to the man in the dump? I found my gaze returning again and again to those eyes and the fury I had seen in them as they took in the presence of four witnesses to murder.

"It's number 5, Chief," I said, and despite my certainty about it there was less iron in my voice than I might have wished. As soon as I finished speaking the unknown man sharing the room with us came to life like a wind-up talking doll and addressed me in a curiously nasal, almost whining monotone.

"I understand, young man, that in the description of the suspect that you originally gave to the police, you noted his long and untidy hair, his mustache and his unshaven appearance. Is that not correct?" Before I could answer, the Chief exhaled noisily and turned to me.

"Peter, perhaps I should introduce Mr. Constantine Arslanian; he's the legal counsel for Mr.… for one of the gentlemen in the next room. The gentleman is entitled to have legal representation during this procedure, and his attorney got here within—what?—ten minutes of your client's phone call, was it, Mr. Arslanian?" It took a few seconds for me to understand the meaning of the Chief's words and contrived tone of politeness, but by the time I had yanked my neck to and fro a couple of times to stare at each of the men in turn I had figured it out. Arslanian was Gene Gaudett's lawyer, and both he and Gaudett must have been expecting the summons to Police Headquarters and were primed for it. I also suspected that the lawyer was well known to the police for representing people who didn't exactly radiate a glow of righteous innocence; if so, he must not have been a popular sight in this building. Ignoring Bonaventura's barb, he repeated his question.

"Well yes, that's true," I admitted. "He's cleaned himself up a lot since then."

"Whether he has or not," continued Arslanian, "may I know the basis of your identification of my client?" I looked to the Chief for a translation.

"How do you know that's the man from the dump?" asked Bonaventura wearily.

"Well... He's the right height, and... I guess it's his eyes. They look just like Black Hat's. It must be him."

"So you're saying that my client looks almost nothing like the man you saw on Sunday except for his eyes, is that not correct?" I again studied the man I now knew to be Gene Gaudett but could not find one more feature that would link him to the man I had known as Black Hat. Without waiting for me to admit as much, the lawyer addressed Bonaventura.

"His eyes, Chief? Is that what you're going to go on? Because I can promise you now, you won't even get *into* court if that's what you intend."

"All right, Mr. Arslanian," said the Chief. "I hear you. That's all right, Peter; you did a good job. Let's see what Robert can do." Within half a minute I found myself in a small waiting room with my mom and O'Sullivan while Robert, who had been waiting in yet another room with his own mom, took his turn at completely fouling up what we had come to do. I briefly explained what had happened, causing O'Sullivan to swear beneath his breath and my mom to make sympathetic noises at me. I relapsed into a gloomy silence, while the two adults talked in a way that suggested they had been striking up a friendship in the short time they had spent in each other's company. When the door re-opened and the Chief ushered the Juneaus in, I only had to look at Robert's face to know that we had both gone through the same experience in the witness room. The Chief closed the door and addressed us.

"I would like you to know that both of you did as well as could be expected in there. They really did, Mrs. McLeod and Mrs. Juneau; you should be proud of them. But I'm afraid that between our suspect changing his appearance and his—" He searched for a suitable adjective for a few seconds before giving up the struggle. "—his attorney being so well prepared, we could not get an identification that would stand up in a court of law. I'm afraid we're back where we were at the beginning. Even if we could establish a link between Gaudett and your car, Mr. O'Sullivan, it wouldn't help us much, since the two of you had dealings with each other long before last weekend. We'll keep probing, of course, but we don't have a whole lot to go on. Perhaps someone saw the car on its way to the dump on Saturday, which could tie him in to the robbery, but this was our best shot—if you'll pardon the expression—and he seems to have been ahead of us. It's a real shame. Speaking confidentially,

Mr. Gaudett is, shall we say, quite well known to this department and it would have given many of us a lot of personal satisfaction to be able to send him down for a crime like this. A real shame."

It was that and more, and Robert and I must have looked as sick as two parrots at the outcome, because before he brought the meeting to a close the Chief put a comforting hand on our shoulders and repeated to our mothers the praise he had given us in the living room on Monday afternoon. Somehow, this time, I felt that he was not putting on an act for their benefit, that perhaps he had shed any last doubts about our motivation and wanted to express his real feelings. Finally he ushered us all out into the corridor, then, apparently remembering something that had slipped his mind, called Robert and me back and closed the door. When he spoke again, his voice was quiet but urgent.

"Now listen, boys. I don't want you to worry your mothers about this, or yourselves for that matter. Gaudett probably feels safe now, and wouldn't risk doing anything stupid. But I don't want to take any chances, so I'm stepping up the patrols where you live and around the school. We'll also be keeping a close eye on his movements, just to be sure."

"Why, Chief?" I asked. "He couldn't see through that mirror, could he? He doesn't know who we are." The Chief grimaced, then spoke as if suddenly very tired.

A DEATH UNDER SAND

"When we knew who we were dealing with today, we contacted the Registry of Motor Vehicles." He paused, looking from me to Robert and back again. "You can probably guess, Peter. Gene Gaudett drives a twelve-year-old black Mercedes-Benz."

THURSDAY, 3:15 PM

I won't bore you with details of the following day in school; suffice it to say that I paid (even) less attention than usual to the parade of educators laboring to improve our minds. I can't speak for Robert, but he also seemed to be present only in body; like me, he was probably depressed and distracted by the events of the previous day. We spoke little, and as if by silent agreement we both avoided contact with our regular group of friends. The day dragged on and dragged us with it until we found ourselves slumped in Celeste's bus on the homeward journey. As we bounced down Compass Avenue Robert turned to me.

"Hey man, you wanna go riding for a while?"

"You think that's a good idea?" My friend let out a noisy, disgusted breath.

"Well, I'm not gonna spend the rest of my life under my bed with the drapes closed, if that's what you mean."

"I know, I know; I didn't mean that. I just—" I twisted round and scanned the road behind us. About three hundred yards back a police cruiser was discreetly following the bus, one of several police cars that I had sighted throughout the day. I felt stupid and scared, and angry with myself for feeling stupid and scared. So Gaudett *had* been scoping us out at school, and it *was* him waiting in Dabney

Street; what was he going to do—run us down with half the cops in town watching him?

"Oh hell, sure. Why not? Where do you want to go?"

"I dunno. Skatepark. Beach, maybe."

"I don't feel much like doing the park. We could hit the beach, I guess."

"OK."

The bus was beginning to slow down as it approached the top of Sachem Street. I reached down for my backpack, and as I pulled it up onto my lap Robert spoke again, as if answering a question I had put to him.

"I just... I just feel like I want to do something, you know? I can't sit around the apartment." I looked him in the eye.

"Yeah, I know what you mean." I punched him lightly on the shoulder, then stood and started down the aisle as the bus squealed to a halt.

"Ten minutes, back here?" Robert called, over the clamor and clangor of afternoon school bus noise. I raised my hand in assent, then descended from the bus two steps at a time.

"Be careful with that leg," Celeste called after me.

A little less than ten minutes later I rode up Sachem Street on my Cozmo to find Robert waiting for me at the top. He was passing the time by riding his bike around in the smallest possible circles he could manage without losing his balance, and as I came up to him he slowed to a stop, keeping himself upright by resting one hand on the Carling's mailbox.

"So," I said as I came up to him. "You want to hit the beach?"

"Yeah, I guess," he replied, sounding as if he were already going off the idea. "I dunno, Peter. Don't you just want to puke?"

"No. We're not having dinner for another couple of hours."

"Come on, man; you know what I mean. The whole thing sucks. Where's the justice?"

"Ah, that. Well, I'll tell you, I don't think we're going to see too much of it."

"I think you're right," he agreed, slapping the empty metal mailbox violently enough to cause the front flap to fly open. "Just damn it to hell."

"Aw, come on," I said suddenly, trying to snap him out of his mood. "Let's forget about it and just go for a ride."

Robert nodded and yanked his Viper around to face Compass Avenue. We both moved up to the curb and were about to cross the street and turn left toward the water when I put my arm out to check Robert's progress. A familiar vehicle was coming down the street from the direction of town; it was O'Sullivan's large black pick-up truck. The truck slowed as if to make the turn into Sachem, but before it could do so the driver recognized us and brought it to a halt opposite our position.

"Hi guys," O'Sullivan called out. "So how are you two doing today?"

"OK, I guess. Kinda bummed out if you really want to know," I replied, as we waddled our machines over to him.

"Yeah, I know; I'm the same way. He's done a screw job on everyone. They let me see him when he was brought in, and the moment I saw what he'd done with his hair and face I knew I was right about him. Gene knew he might end up in an ID parade, and he hasn't looked that clean since his mother used to wash him in the bathroom wash basin." We all laughed, and it felt good; I didn't know about O'Sullivan, but we certainly needed some comic relief at that point. It did, however, raise a new question in my mind.

"I'd have thought you'd have been kind of worried, Mr. O'Sullivan," I said. "Gaudett must know you put the finger on him; won't he come after you now?" O'Sullivan shook his head, grinning.

"Frankly, guys, I believe I'm safer now than at any time since he started figuring out ways to kill me. Gaudett knows the police are watching him closely, and if anything—*anything*—happens to me, they'll be on his case like the 101st Airborne. Same goes for you two." As he was speaking, another cruiser passed us on its way down Compass Avenue toward the Rosario Apartments.

"So what brings you to the classy end of town, Mr. O'Sullivan?" I asked. For the briefest of moments he looked uncertain of himself, as if he needed to rehearse his answer.

"I—er—actually, I was just coming to see your mother, Peter. I wanted to be sure she knew how much I appreciated your involvement—and yours, Robert—in what's happened." I immediately became alarmed.

"Hey, she's not supposed to know we came to see you yesterday, remember? And so far as she's concerned Gaudett never fired at us; we just saw him from a distance."

"I know I know I know," replied O'Sullivan, waving his hands as if to ward off an attack of bees. "Don't worry; I'm not going to get you into the soup at home. As far as your mothers are concerned the police put your description of Black Hat together with my story, and that's what led them to Gaudett. In fact, the three of us did that and told the police what they should have figured out themselves, didn't we?"

"Well, yes... But when it comes to my mom, she's still in the dark and doing very nicely there, thank you. Anyway, you're too early; she's not home yet."

"Oh... Well, that is a shame. I was hoping she'd be there." O'Sullivan looked genuinely disappointed, and as the notion began to form in my mind that his unannounced visit to my house had really very little to do with me I remembered the preoccupied way in which he and my mom had been talking while we waited in Police Headquarters. Was Michael O'Sullivan interested in my mother? It was not completely beyond the bounds of reason, and if I thought hard enough I could recall that I had heard of women even older than my mom—some as old as forty—who had still kept some of their looks and had their admirers. Moreover, while I tried to steer clear of visualizing my mom in a romantic situation (gag), I didn't exactly find it objectionable that she and O'Sullivan might become friendly. From what little I knew of the guy he seemed fairly normal—untidy, but normal. She could do worse and so, for that matter, could he. It also occurred to me that if he continued with his solitary lifestyle and nocturnal work habit without being virtually thrown into the company of someone like my mom, as had happened the previous night, he might just go on grieving for Katie Gaudett forever. And for a basically decent guy like O'Sullivan, that would be a great shame.

"Well, I've got some other errands to do," he remarked disconsolately. "Where are you guys off to?"

"Just taking a ride down to the beach or somewhere," replied Robert, swinging his bike around. O'Sullivan squinted down at a spot on the ground in the vicinity of his rear wheel.

"Looks like you need a squirt of air before you go far," he observed. We followed his gaze downward to see what neither of us had noticed before, that the rear tire of Robert's Viper was in need of an injection of psi. Robert reached down automatically between his legs to unsnap the pump from his crossbar, only to have his hands close around empty air. He remained frozen in his position of discovery like someone who had just realized he had walked out of his house without his pants.

"Lost your pump, Robert?" I asked. "Here, use mine." Still Robert did not move. I began to wonder if he had fallen asleep or suffered a silent seizure when he slowly raised his head, and I saw that his eyes were wide and serious and his mouth had dropped open. He looked twice from O'Sullivan to me and back again before he found his voice.

"No, I haven't lost my pump" he said breathlessly. "I know right enough where it is. It's in the dump, near where it fell when Steven Cardeiro knocked it out of my hand. It'll be where Gene Gaudett threw it right after that, before he started shooting at us *and after he'd picked it up and put his fingerprints all over it.*"

THURSDAY, 4:00 PM

Viewed through the hole in the fence, the dump looked much the same as it had the previous Sunday when we had stood here on our return trip and scanned it for signs of Steven Cardeiro. There was activity on the far side, with the occasional pick-up truck feeding the in-use dumpster and the 'dozer artistically rearranging piles of construction debris. Robert and I straddled our BMXes and observed the activity in silence for a couple of minutes.

O'Sullivan and I had understood the significance of Robert's revelation immediately, although for my part I could not believe that it had not occurred to either of us earlier in the week. Robert was right: it was the sight of his pump on the perimeter track that had alerted Gaudett to our presence in the dump, and he had indeed picked it up and handled it extensively before he saw us. Even if he now shaved off every last frond of body hair it was the one piece of evidence that would place Gene Gaudett in the dump on Sunday afternoon, so long as we could find it and get it to the police.

O'Sullivan had been all for loading our bikes into his truck and barreling down to Bonaventura's office with us to give the police what they needed to put Gaudett away for good, but neither Robert nor I wanted to wait for the Gretchyville Police to put a posse together and lumber over to Silver Hill as they had done on Sunday. Without even discussing it we were of one mind; we wanted to get back to the dump as fast as humanly possible and find that single metal tube that was going to do so much: smash open the door that Gaudett had slammed on the police's case, justify the efforts that Robert and I had expended in ferreting out the truth, avenge the Cardeiro brothers, put Michael O'Sullivan beyond danger and put Gene Gaudett where he could only direct his murderous anger against the walls of an 8' x 10' cell. Pausing only to pump up Robert's tire, we had ignored O'Sullivan's protestations and taken off for Birch Street at high speed. Half-way up Compass Avenue he passed us, shaking his head disapprovingly as he drove, and made a left at the top toward town.

Despite my closeness to Robert, when I look back on it I'm surprised by how much we were of the same mind that day. Mostly Robert's the one who goes off like an artillery shell without thinking of the consequences, and I'm the one who has to drag him back into the cannon so I can get it properly aimed. But that Thursday afternoon we were so much in sync. with each other that one of us could probably have turned his brain off to save energy without affecting our joint actions. After all we had gone through we not only wanted to bring this final, vital act in the drama to a close, we also wanted to do it without assistance, intervention, or—most importantly—delay. That's how it was that we found ourselves, twenty minutes later, scanning the Silver Hill Landfill through the as-yet unplugged hole in the fence.

"OK to go down?" asked Robert. I nodded.

"Let's do it."

Robert crossed the fence line and dropped down, gathering speed, toward the perimeter track. I was close on his tail, checking behind us at intervals, although I did not seriously expect trouble today. There was no reason to suppose that Gaudett would return to the dump again, there being nothing here to interest him now; on the other hand, on our last two unaccompanied trips here we had been both shot at and driven at, so perhaps it was reasonable to take precautions. Before long that part of the dump's periphery that we had come to know so well appeared before us; Robert slowed and waved me forward, and I came up level with him. As we freewheeled on together he pointed to the middle of the track ahead of us.

"About fifty yards more—that's where he was standing."

"Got it. Let's walk from here." We dismounted and walked our bikes forward, closely inspecting the ground. Despite the marks left in it by the tires of the front-end loader on Monday afternoon and the size 13 boots of the police the day before, we could still make out where Gaudett and his partner had swept the sections of matting over the surface to obliterate the marks they had made. There was no sign of Robert's pump, but having been here twice since it was first knocked from his hand without seeing it, we weren't expecting to find it in plain sight. As I approached to within a few feet of where Steven Cardeiro had fallen, however, a desperate thought occurred to me.

"Hey Robert—what if they took it out with them?"

"I know. Maybe they did. I guess this is where we find out."

"Do you remember exactly where it landed when Gaudett threw it away?"

"Pretty close to the outside edge of the track, I think. Near the little ditch at the foot of the cliff."

"Yeah, I think you're right." We laid our bikes down and started shuffling forward through the sand, using our feet to scrape away the top inch or two. When we reached a point that we both agreed was well past the spot where the pump had landed we turned and steered a new course through the search area, repeating the pattern over and over until we had covered every square inch where we thought it might be. Nothing showed up from beneath the surface except stones of various sizes and shapes. Finally I swore in frustration, kicked hard at one of the larger stones, swore in pain, then just swore for the sake of it. Robert waited quietly for me to finish.

"Looks like I was wrong," he said simply. A gust of wind blew down the track, picking up grains of sand and peppering our skins with them. I wiped my face with the back of my hand and looked miserably around us. The sun was well over half-way down to the horizon, the shadows of the nearest trees beginning to creep toward the spot where we stood. I shielded my eyes and squinted up at the treeline.

"How about in the trees? Or on the inside of the track? Maybe he just picked it up and threw it." We expanded our search to cover these areas, but with no success. It was beginning to look quite certain that Gaudett had taken the pump with him, as anyone in his position with an ounce of brains would have done. It was our last hope; it had gone, and worse was to come.

"I just remembered," said Robert urgently, "I scratched my name on the damn thing."

"And Gaudett's got it? Oh my God, Robert." What else was there to say? Move out of the apartment in case he comes gunning for you? No, since our failed attempt to identify him the day before, Gaudett must have thought he was safe, so perhaps that meant Robert was also safe.

We stood on high ground on the inside edge of the track, looking over the ravaged area we had just searched. So far as I could see, we had not missed any spot that could conceivably have concealed the foot-long cylinder, from the car's gravesite to the foot of the sandy cliff on the outer edge of the track.

"Robert."

"What?"

"I thought you said there was a little ditch at the foot of the cliff."

"Yeah, there is. Only a few inches deep. Rain probably makes it."

"There's no ditch there." Robert looked closely at the foot of the cliff.

"Well, there *was*. And there still is, way down there" he observed, pointing to a spot about a hundred yards to the right.

"Sure, but right where we were looking it's disappeared." Understanding dawned on us both at the same moment, and we turned to each other with our mouths open and fingers pointing. The sight was too much; we each broke into laughter at the sight of the other.

"While they were sweeping with the mats—"

"They swept the sand toward the ditch—"

"Probably walking backward and didn't see what was under the mats—"

"—There could be anything in that ditch!" In seconds we were back in the search area, squirming our feet down into the sand where we thought the ditch should be. We moved slowly toward each other from opposite ends of the area, kicking up gouts of sand as we went. We were within five feet of each other when Robert suddenly stopped.

"There's something here," he said, trying without success to keep the excitement out of his voice. I watched, hardly breathing, as he kneeled down and probed with his fingers ahead of where his foot had been. Like an archaeologist unearthing a priceless fragment of pre-MTV era pottery he patiently scraped the sand away until he could grip his find with thumb and forefinger. He raised his hand from the ditch and with it came a twelve-inch metal tube, the sand cascading off the frosted blue exterior marked with crudely scratched lettering: 'R. JUNEAU.'

"My God," I breathed. "They *didn't* see it. They buried it without realizing—" Robert interrupted me in a voice that had quickly regained its composure.

"We got him, Peter. This is all we need. Don't matter if we can't ID him; this'll do it for us." Robert's eyes were glowing with the same light of triumph I had seen in them when he discovered the mutilated bushes in the woods on Monday afternoon.

"Just be careful how you handle it," I cautioned.

"I know. Don't worry—I'm not gonna touch the barrel. That's where the prints'll be. All I have to do is open it out—" As he spoke he lightly gripped the inner end of the hand grip and pulled the pump open far enough to be able to grasp it by the exposed steel cylinder within. We both stood, and he hefted the pump in his right hand for a few seconds.

"This should work," he announced. "I can carry it like this without touching the outside *and* ride my bike back to Police Headquarters."

We returned to our machines. I pulled Robert's upright and held it so that he could mount without using his hands. He looked awkward, straddling the BMX and holding the handlebar with his left hand while his right hand was stretched well away from the bike, clutching the pump.

"You sure you can get back through the fence like that?"

"Hell, if not, I'll walk up dragging the bike behind me!"

"It's a pity we don't have a plastic bag or something to protect it," I muttered, checking around for a suitable candidate. I looked up and down the track without seeing anything usable, then checked its inside edge and finally cast my eyes up to the top of the scarp. As I did so a flicker of movement at the tree line caught my eye, but it wasn't a bag, nor anything inanimate being twitched by the wind. It was a sight I had hoped never to see again without the protection of a two-way mirror and a building full of policemen: it was Gene Gaudett, with a look of murder on his face that I had last seen in a nightmare.

The silence that followed felt timeless; not long, not short, but timeless, because even today I cannot say for certain whether that silence lasted a second or a year. Gaudett and I were like statues facing each other eternally across a museum gallery while generations of visitors came and went around them and the sun rose and set at its own unchanging pace.

And then something happened: the statue atop the scarp broke a twig or rustled the leaves with its foot and time rushed in on us again. I found my voice but not, apparently, my breath.

"Robert!" I croaked. My tone must have told Robert that something was terribly wrong; he shot a look at me, then followed the direction of my gaze up to the tree line. His reaction, unlike mine, was instantaneous.

"GO! GO! GO!"

Three moved at once. As Gaudett burst into movement Robert and I pushed off—fast. In a couple of seconds the man reached the gap between fence and soil through which Robert had escaped on Monday and swung down through it so fast that he almost fell the remaining distance to the track. Once at our level—and barely twenty feet away— he took off after us with frightening speed. Terrified as I was, I somehow found space in my brain to curse myself; we had delivered ourselves to Gaudett in a place where he could permanently silence his accusers and recover the only piece of physical evidence against him. We could not have made a worse mistake.

We were still accelerating, and by the time Gaudett was up to speed we were thirty feet ahead of him. I quickly looked across at Robert. His face was a mask of determination, his eyes fixed on the ground ahead and his right hand clamped around both the shaft of his pump and his handlebar. It was a sight that gave me strength. He could probably have saved both our skins by abandoning the pump, but I understood why he wouldn't. Robert had come too far and fought too hard to surrender this piece of metal and all that it meant. And I knew we had only to keep up this speed for a few minutes to be in safe hands.

Then we rounded a sharp bend in the track and everything changed.

Perhaps the Landfill authorities had chosen this week to re-open an old section for dumping; whatever the reason, fifty feet ahead of us the track was totally blocked by a bank of sand, ten feet high and heavily seeded with discarded dump debris. I knew at once that, even if we could handle the climb and avoid the embedded junk, the newly dumped sand of the barrier would be too soft to negotiate. Nor could we reverse direction without at least one of us being caught by Gaudett. It looked as if our near-certain escape was about to turn into a desperate foot race.

Then Robert pointed to our left. On the inside edge of the track a narrow path snaked between the berms toward the middle of the dump. Without slowing we turned and entered it in closely spaced single file. The path was littered with debris, forcing us to weave our way along it, but I knew that as long as it did not come to an abrupt end, we were still ahead of the game.

Without warning Gaudett burst into sight atop the berm to our left and less than twenty feet back. He was still running hard and now held three feet of jagged, rusty metal in his right hand. He must have veered off to the left as soon as he saw us turn into the path, and by cutting the corner had almost caught up to us.

Suddenly I heard a cry from immediately behind me. I turned my head in time to see the metal shard skittering to the ground by Robert's front wheel. Robert's face creased in pain as he clutched his left shoulder, where an ugly tear had appeared in his shirt. And above him Gaudett, who had drawn first blood with his crude weapon, was less than ten feet away and closing in. And still Robert held on to the pump.

Gaudett was now level with us. I was bracing myself for the moment when he would launch himself down the slope to tackle us when the path took a sudden turn to the right and broadened out to about twice its original width. We accelerated into the turn even as I heard Gaudett stumbling down the steep gradient behind us, and immediately started increasing our lead again.

A few seconds later Robert drew abreast of me, giving me a close-up view of his injury. Gaudett's missile had ripped open Robert's shirt at the very point of the shoulder, and blood was running freely from an ugly two-inch gash in his flesh. It had not slowed him down in the slightest, however, as I discovered when he accelerated right past me.

Fifty yards ahead of us the path disappeared into the face of a high slope. We hit the slope fast and barely slowed down as we climbed. By now I was disoriented enough not to know exactly where we were in the dump, but hoped that the perimeter track lay on the other side of this escarpment. No such luck, of course. We scrabbled to a stop in a flurry of digging feet, sliding wheels and billowing sand as we saw what lay on the far side: a near-vertical drop to a trench full of wire mesh and metal fence palings. Time for Plan B, whatever that was.

"That way!" panted Robert, pointing past me and to the left. We took off at right angles to our previous route along a ridge covered with coarse beach grass, which clung to our wheel spokes as soon as we started into it. We would have to negotiate about two hundred yards of this terrain before the grass died out and we could get back to full speed.

Twenty seconds later, panting hard, I stole a glance behind and saw with horror that we had lost more speed in the grass than I had thought. Gaudett was barely five yards behind Robert's bobbing head! The grass had barely slowed him down, and with another few steps he would be able to reach out and snag Robert's rear wheel. We had to clear the grass immediately.

"TURN RIGHT!" As I yelled, I turned as sharply as I dared. Robert followed. Now we were pointing directly at the edge of the ridge, with no idea of what lay beyond it. That scarcely mattered. Whatever was waiting for us at the foot of this drop had to be a lot better than what was following us, now only a few feet back. We were not even going to be able to slow down to plan our descent before crossing the edge of the fast-approaching scarp.

Seconds later we launched ourselves into space.

Robert and I flew off the near-vertical edge of the ridge side-by-side and immediately found ourselves fifteen horrifying feet from the ground. Then we dropped, fast. I was the luckier one; about five or six feet directly below me was a ledge wide enough to break my descent. But the ledge did not extend more than a couple of feet to my right; Robert's route to Earth was uninterrupted.

I landed briefly on the ledge before my momentum carried me forward and over its edge for the second half of my descent. As I did so Robert flew past me, heading for a heavy landing. His rear wheel hit first and the bike canted forward violently, pitching him over the handlebars to somersault bruisingly onto the ground. He landed heavily on his back with the bike on top of him and the precious pump flying out of his grasp. I landed close to him, still on my wheels, and saw at once what trouble we were in. Robert's fall had quite knocked the breath out of him. It was going to take him several seconds to recover and Gaudett, I knew, was literally right on top of us.

All at once I heard a cry from above me; I looked up to see a welter of cartwheeling arms and legs flying downward past me. Gaudett must have started his descent directly above the point where the ledge disappeared into the face of the scarp, and only been able to hit the ledge with his left foot. His right foot must have missed it entirely, causing him to fall the rest of the way. He came to rest on the valley floor, a half-dozen feet behind Robert and just as winded. Now, once more, we had a chance. Gaudett was sprawled on the ground, panting hard and clutching his left thigh in pain. This was the moment for me to dive in, pull Robert to his feet and drag him to safety, but I was frozen to the spot.

In fact, it didn't matter. To my amazement, Robert was on his feet before the dust had settled around him. I had thought him nearly stunned by his fall, and the way he moved told me he was at the very least in great pain, but his face had not lost an iota of its determination. He grabbed his bike and, gasping with the effort, staggered over to where his pump had fallen and swept it up. Even now, Robert had not forgotten this five-dollar piece of hardware that meant so much to him.

Grimacing still, Robert mounted up and started to pedal. As I fell in behind him I glanced quickly at Gaudett, who had dragged himself upright and was starting after us. He, too, looked as if he was making a speedy recovery, and I wasted no more time in catching up to Robert. We followed the line of the valley, but dangerously slowly— Robert was in no shape to break records. Fortunately, neither was Gaudett. I took the lead, looking back frequently to check on Robert's progress and condition, while Gaudett limped after us, cursing and grunting with effort. Injured as he was, our pursuer had not given up the chase, and I knew that its outcome would still be determined by whether hunter or quarry could keep going longer.

The valley wound around haphazardly between high, steep walls, robbing me of whatever sense of direction I may have had earlier. For all I knew, we might have been pointing back at the fence on the Birch Street side of the dump, but it really didn't matter. What was important was whether the valley path was going to disappear into a sand berm like the last one; if it did, we would be forced to abandon our bikes and climb for our lives. And I seriously doubted whether Robert, in his present state, could stay ahead of Gaudett if it came to that.

After struggling through the valley for a couple of minutes we rounded a bend and found ourselves staring at exactly what I had feared—a blank wall of sand stretching clear across our path. I looked back quickly at Robert and was heartened to see that he was moving a little faster now. Perhaps, God willing, he would be able to make the climb. Then I turned back and saw that we might not have to find out. In the left-hand wall the entrance to a narrow side valley—more of a slot than anything grander— had appeared. We were still alive, and still on wheels. I aimed for the slot, praying fervently that it would lead us out into open ground.

The dump gods must have heard my prayer. The slot was short, straight, and about four handlebars wide, with an open patch of ground at the far end. Was this the perimeter track at last? I traversed the slot as fast as I dared, the walls flashing past within a couple of feet of me, and could hear Robert riding close behind me. The far end of the slot grew larger in my vision with each second until I shot out like a ball flying onto a pinball table. I was in the avenue, with a clear, broad path stretching ahead of me to the dump entrance and safety.

A couple of seconds later, Robert emerged and saw for himself where we were. His face lit up with a mixture of relief and triumph, and an exultant "yeah!" broke from his lips. He seemed to have recovered fully from his fall and was ready to ride shoulder to shoulder with me again, still clutching that precious pump. Looking back, I could see Gaudett entering the slot, still limping but as determined-looking as ever. Now, however, we had all the advantage we needed, and by the time I heard him stumble out of the slot behind us we were far enough ahead to be safe from his murderous hands.

"How you doing?" I panted.

"Hurt like hell," replied Robert, in the same tone he might have used to say "fine 'n' dandy". And that was that.

Ahead of us I could see that a section of the right-hand wall of the avenue had been broken down by the 'dozer and dumped across part of it, which obliged us to put in a kind of tack to port to navigate around it. As we did this I glanced behind us once more. Gaudett, although well behind us now, was still coming on.

I turned forward again just as a front-end loader lurched into sight from behind the sand barrier. The driver saw us and brought the large, four-wheeled yellow vehicle to a halt, blocking the gap at which we were aiming. It was not a cause for panic, however, for now—finally—we had an ally.

"Help!"

"Hey, mister—help us! He's trying to kill us!"

"That guy behind us—he's a killer! Don't let him get near us!"

The driver was not the middle-aged man who had caught us on Monday; this one was young—in his twenties, probably—with stringy blond hair and thin, bony cheeks. As we skidded to a halt a few feet short of the loader and dismounted, he looked uncertainly from us to our pursuer and back to us.

"We mean it—he killed two guys!"

"He's trying to get us too!"

I looked back. Gaudett had slowed to a trot but had not turned away, which seemed strange to me—I had thought he would have wanted to avoid being identified by the newcomer. From the front-end loader I heard the sound of something heavy and metallic being hefted; turning forward I could see the driver picking up a long crowbar as he descended from his high perch. That was a relief; now at least the good guys had some weaponry. Then I heard Gaudett's voice, and the universe turned upside down again.

"Don't let them get away, Billy," he called calmly. We snapped our heads around to Gaudett then back to the driver, who had landed on the ground and was approaching us with the crowbar held aloft in his ham-like fist.

"Don't worry, Gene. They ain't goin' nowhere."

And now the last piece of the puzzle was in place. Of all the people we could have chosen to run into and expect to rescue us, the one we had found was Gaudett's accomplice. The one who had been waiting here at the dump as his partner and Jimmy Cardeiro came crashing through the woods with the robbery proceeds; the one who had prepared the Excalibur's burial site, probably with this very front-end loader, then used it again to hide the car and Jimmy's still-warm body from sight. In

all our deliberations about how Gaudett and his
partner could have buried the car, the clear and
obvious answer had somehow never occurred to
us—that Gaudett had specifically recruited a dump
worker as an accomplice in order to obtain the
earth-moving equipment he needed, complete with
operator. As I looked in horror at his approaching
face, I even remembered where and when I had seen
it before—in the small crowd of dump workers who
had gathered near the main gate to watch Robert
and me being driven out in the Chief's car on
Sunday. He had not needed Gaudett's order to stop
us escaping; he had already identified us and
decided his course of action.

There was no time to mount up, but even if
there had been there was nowhere to go. I looked at
Robert and knew that he understood. They were
about to end: the mystery, the chase, the
adventure... Hell, *we* were about to end. Gaudett's
partner was coming straight for me, his expression
hardening as he came, when I heard the voice of the
man behind us again.

"Get the black kid first—and get that pump!"
The man Gaudett had called Billy changed direction
and headed for Robert.

"I'm gonna take your lousy black head off, you
goddam interfering little nig—" He didn't finish.
Hearing him speak was like having an electric
shock pass through me, and I reacted as if I had. I
was still holding my BMX by the handlebars and

335

seat, and with a sudden desperate strength I launched the machine hard at the man's head. At the same time I heard a bellowing noise that sounded like a large, wounded animal giving voice to its pain and anger. Much later, I figured out that the noise had come from me. As the bike closed with our assailant's face he threw his hand up to protect himself; the crowbar tangled with the wheels and was almost wrenched from his grasp. Now, if we did not want just to stand there and accept our deaths without a struggle, was our chance. It was our only chance.

"RUN, ROBERT!"

As I yelled I turned, ran to the left and started to climb the avenue wall. I reached the top and looked back quickly without slowing. The blond man was following me, the crowbar still in his hand. Robert was running fast up the opposite wall with Gaudett in pursuit. I hit the high ground and turned toward the main gate, although without much hope of reaching it; it was too far, the terrain was too broken, and I was already winded.

I kept running along the high ground as long as I could, hoping I would be spotted by someone in the working area of the dump. All the time I could hear the heavy footfalls and breathing of the man close behind me. Eventually I ran out of high ground and was forced to take another blind leap into a valley. I somehow managed to stay on my feet, and led my pursuer through the serpentine twists and turns of the valley until we were again forced to climb to the backbone of a ridge. By the time I reached it my eyesight was blurred with a film of tears, generated by the effort I was expending... and perhaps by the knowledge that I had little more to give. Gaudett's partner was still as close behind me as ever. My lungs felt close to collapsing, my legs ready to fold under me and my heart about to burst out of my chest. A couple of hundred yards ahead of me I could see, through the mist that covered my eyes, the vague shapes of cars moving between us and the in-use dumpsters. It didn't matter. I couldn't attract the attention of the drivers from here, and I knew I could not reach them before I was overtaken. And for all I knew, Robert was already dead.

I pitched down the far side of the ridge and angled to the right. No more than fifty yards ahead was another steep gradient. The blood was now pounding so loudly in my ears that I could barely hear my pursuer's steps, but I knew he was only seconds behind me. I also knew that the slope ahead of me would be my last, if I could even make it all the way up.

I pounded up the slope, gasping, and somehow managed to reach the crest. As I staggered blindly forward on the ridge top I heard the man with the crowbar, now close enough behind to touch me, snarl out his execution speech.

"Now, you goddam little tick! Get a neck full of THIS!"

"NO!"

The voice came from ahead of us, and below.

"You don't touch him! Don't you DARE!" I tried to focus on the low ground ahead. Four cars stood in a line no more than twenty yards away. Three were official police vehicles, already disgorging more than half a dozen uniformed policemen, and the fourth was a large black pick-up that I recognized at once. From the direction of the pick-up a man in civilian clothes was running and screaming at my assailant; even with my blurred vision I recognized him as O'Sullivan. As I stumbled forward one of my legs gave out and I collapsed down the slope in a series of bruising somersaults. O'Sullivan was still coming on at high speed and screaming at Gaudett's partner like a man possessed. The cops, with Bonaventura at their head, were running toward me, drawing their pistols and aiming at the top of the slope. Suddenly the crowbar flew past well above me, spinning wildly, and struck O'Sullivan hard on the head. He staggered and clutched his right temple, but still kept coming until he fell forward, blood oozing from between his fingers, and covered my body with his. I was unable to see how many of the cops started firing then, but for several seconds it sounded like a machine gun until the Chief barked an order and the world went very silent.

It seemed a long time, then, before they came and pulled O'Sullivan off me. I felt a hand on my arm pulling me upright and heard voices asking me if I were hurt. When my vision cleared I saw that O'Sullivan was sitting awkwardly in the sand opposite me, looking dazed and trying to wipe the blood out of his right eye. I looked around and found myself staring at the Chief, whose broad, lined face carried an expression of deep concern.

"Did you hear me, Peter? Are you all right?" I nodded quickly, somewhat belatedly feeling myself for injuries, and looked back at the top of the slope. Several of the cops were gathered there, examining something on the ground. All I could see of it was a pair of legs in orange overalls and heavy work boots; they lay completely still, and I knew that I had encountered violent death at close quarters once more. Behind me, O'Sullivan was struggling to his feet and asking me something.

"Peter… Where's Robert? Is he OK?"

"Robert… Oh my God—ROBERT!" I spun around, temporarily disoriented, then started up the slope in the direction I had come.

"Where is he?" yelled O'Sullivan after me.

"Gaudett's got him!" I shouted back, without turning or slowing down.

"Wait!" shouted the Chief, although he must have realized I was not going to stop. "You men! Go with the boy. We're looking for Gene Gaudett. The rest of you, come with me."

How long had it been since I saw Robert running from Gaudett? Five minutes? Ten? How long could he stay ahead of him? Perhaps not long enough. And I had no idea where in the dump he would have led him. Perhaps Gaudett had already escaped from the dump, taking the evidence with him. Not that I cared a damn for the evidence now; all I wanted was to find my friend, and find him alive. It didn't even strike me as strange that my exhaustion of only a few moments ago had vanished as I tore back across the high ground toward the avenue, closely followed by four of the cops. I looked back once and saw that O'Sullivan was vainly trying to keep up but, slowed by his injury, was having a hard time of it.

I reached the avenue and crossed it without stopping. As I was half-way across I saw, far to the left, the Chief's car rocketing past the end of the avenue on the perimeter track; he had obviously decided he could cover more ground on wheels than on foot. I scaled the opposite wall at the point where I had last seen Robert and paused, looking for footprints. By the time the patrolmen caught up with me I had found the prints, and was about to follow them when the lead cop grabbed my arm.

"Don't get so far ahead," he panted. "He could be anywhere."

"The hell with that," I retorted, wrenching my arm away. The movement turned me around, just in time to see O'Sullivan descending the far wall of the avenue. Partway down he stumbled, scrabbled his way to the bottom and landed on hands and knees, looking across helplessly at me.

"Go on," he gasped, waving a hand feebly. "Go on; find Robert. Get that damned Gaudett."

I took off again. The four cops and I ran as a group, following the two overlapping sets of footprints. With each turn we made and each rise we topped I held my breath, expecting to see the tracks converging by Robert's lifeless body, and only a single track continuing. When each new vista rewarded me with only a continuation of the tracks, I breathed again. But the trail seemed interminable. I had the sense that it was leading us closer to the area where the four of us habitually rode our BMXes, but could not be sure. In any case, it could not have been intentional on Robert's part. Why would he want to lead his pursuer *away* from the active side of the dump?

Several times as we followed the double trail I called Robert's name, but heard no response. I could see that we were getting close to the perimeter track, and even saw the Chief's car a couple of hundred yards ahead. Had the Chief already picked up the tracks? On an impulse I veered off from the route we were following and climbed the nearest slope; once at the top I filled my lungs and bellowed out the name of my friend.

"Robert! Robert!"

I was still looking directly ahead when something popped up in my peripheral vision. I looked to the right and saw, less than a hundred yards away, the cockily grinning figure of Robert Juneau standing on another section of high ground. Posing there with both arms spread up and out, he resembled a large, dark letter Y in short pants.

"Come join the party!"

"Robert, you idiot! Where's Gaudett?"

"Get over here and see for yourself!" I signaled the cops on the low ground nearby to follow me and took off for where Robert was standing. In less than a minute we were all assembled within a few feet of him, staring in astonishment at his achievement. Robert had not been fleeing blindly from Gene Gaudett; he had known exactly where he was going. He had drawn the killer half-way across the dump to the spot we had christened the Golden Gate Bridge, knowing from experience that it would not support a man of Gaudett's weight. He must have crossed the corrugated iron span first, feeling it tremble under his own weight, then waited on the other side and dared his pursuer to come at him. The two metal strips were lying in separate spots at the bottom of a fifteen-foot drop; stretched motionless between them was an unconscious Gene Gaudett, his head canted at an odd angle where it must have struck the back of an old armchair. As the Chief and the other two patrolmen puffed their way over to where we were standing I looked up at

A DEATH UNDER SAND

Robert in disbelief and admiration, to see him proudly holding like the Olympic torch the object for which he had gone to so much trouble: his blue, shiny, and unmolested bicycle pump.

THURSDAY, 6:30 PM

There were ten of us crammed into our living room: my mom, keeping a firm grip on my little sister, Mrs. Juneau, Chief Bonaventura, Raleigh, two State Police detectives whose names I forgot as soon as they were introduced to us, O'Sullivan, Robert and me. Some of the party looked a little worse for wear than others: we had returned from the dump via the hospital emergency room, where Robert and O'Sullivan were given tetanus shots and had their wounded parts cleaned and dressed. Robert got away with jumbo-sized adhesive dressings, but O'Sullivan needed a couple of stitches and had a dramatic-looking bandage wrapped around his head. Both our moms belonged in the walking wounded category. Since it was no longer possible to downplay our roles in the robbery/homicide case Bonaventura had told them everything, including our close brush with death on Sunday, our visit to O'Sullivan's house and the full-dress version of our canter around the dump a couple of hours earlier. The color had still not returned to my mom's face, and Robert's mom just sat with a handkerchief balled in her hand, her large dark eyes wider and more worried-looking than usual. The two mothers sat at either end of our sofa, with O'Sullivan between them. I noticed that from the time the Chief described how O'Sullivan had burst into Police Headquarters that afternoon demanding that the police descend on the dump immediately and how he had put his own life at risk to protect me, my mom had spent much of the time alternately gazing at him closely enough to count his pores and inconspicuously trying to Do Something with her hair.

The period immediately following Gaudett's capture was almost as hectic as that leading up to it. The Chief had personally taken charge of Robert's precious pump and disappeared with it after instructing his men to get Gaudett into a cell and the rest of us to the emergency room. He must have called both our homes from Headquarters, because as we were coming back down the long hill from the hospital in one of the cruisers we were treated to the unusual sight of both our moms' cars coming the other way at startlingly illegal speed.

Not so speedy, however, that they couldn't observe their offspring lurking in the back of the cruiser.

As viewed through the cruiser's rear window, what had followed was pure Keystone Cops: the two cars went through a performance of braking, reversing, three-point turning, accelerating, getting in each others' way, then going through the whole gamut of maneuvers again. Eventually they had sorted themselves out and fastened themselves on our tail, and the two of us thought it wise to maintain a constant state of grinning and displaying

our upraised thumbs through the window for the
rest of the journey to East Gretchyville. As a result,
we had arrived at Sachem Street with charley horse
of the cheeks and uncontrollable tremors in our
thumbs.

Like a guardian angel, Bonaventura was
waiting at our house to deflect the maternal storm. I
think he realized, however, that the smooth
performance he had given on Monday was not
going to work a second time and reverted to a plan
largely based on groveling apologies and appeals
for mercy. But he had come armed with one nugget
of information which could not help but impress our
moms, namely that it was *entirely* due to the efforts
of their sons that the police now had enough
evidence to convict Gene Gaudett of murder. I
would guess that the Chief had been breathing down
the collective neck of the forensic crew who dusted
Robert's pump for prints and compared what they
found to Gaudett's record. What they had found,
evidently, was that Robert had been right; the
man's guilt was delicately imprinted on a dozen
spots on the housing of the pump, and there was no
army of lawyers large enough to spring him from
police custody on this occasion.

Over the next few minutes Raleigh and the two
Staties arrived to add detail to the story, but by then
the Chief was deep into his explanation of our *real*
involvement in the affair. Hell, there was so much
candor wafting around the living room by the time

he finished that, after a whispered conference with Robert, I even threw in Tony's and Liddy's names to clear my own conscience. In response to our pleas, however, the Chief agreed to leave them where they were—out of the picture.

On balance, I would say that our moms took it all pretty well. There was a lot for them to take on board: Robert's injury, our by-now multiple brushes with violent death and, worst of all, the fact that the Chief, Robert and I had been lying to them all along. At the time, I imagined that they were torn between dreaming up new and original punishments for our behavior and congratulating us on our devotion to truth, justice and the rest of it. Later I learned that my mom, at least, was also having a hard time not giving vent to her relief by clasping me to her bosom. That was close. And things almost took a turn for the worse at one point when Bonaventura backpedaled enough to remind us that we had given him our solemn promise not to return to the dump. Through it all, my mom and Mrs. Juneau looked properly alarmed at the real extent of our perilous activities since Sunday morning, but managed to keep their instinctive reactions (blame dispersal, lecture series, loss of privileges) in check.

Henry Raleigh, who had had the pleasure of giving Gaudett the news about his fingerprints as he sat in a cell downtown, filled in some of the gaps in the Chief's story.

"From Gaudett's point of view, the timing of the whole weekend had to be just right. He had to be sure that Mr. O'Sullivan would be at sea, alone, when he and Cardeiro robbed the bank. That would have—or *should* have—robbed him of an alibi for the important period on Saturday afternoon. But the *really* critical day was Monday. We received an anonymous 'phone tip—presumably from Gaudett—in the early afternoon which led us to find the car on Herring Run Lane. We're fairly sure that his original plan was to retrieve the car from the dump and have it found at exactly the right time, which is what he ended up doing, even though you boys had found it the day before."

"What do you mean, 'exactly the right time'?" I asked.

"Well, it had to be timed so that Mr. O'Sullivan would be back from his fishing trip by the time we had identified the car's owner from the real license plate, but before he would have thought to report his car stolen. When did you think Cardeiro was going to return the car, Mr. O'Sullivan?"

"Oh, probably four-ish, five-ish. I wouldn't have started to get worried until after six."

"Exactly. Gaudett must have known from Cardeiro more or less when you would be returning from sea and gave us a window of two or three hours after he made the call to find the car, trace its owner, and turn up at Bass Point to arrest him. Which, of course, is exactly what we did. I'm sorry if we were kind of brusque with you on Monday, Mr. O'Sullivan, but when we found the Dodgers jacket and the money in your garage we thought we had the whole case wrapped up. You must admit it was damning stuff."

"Yeah, well, you might have given me the benefit of the doubt," responded O'Sullivan dourly. I was pleased to note that he did not seem interested in letting Raleigh off lightly. A general round of throat-clearing and embarrassed coughing from the law enforcement delegation, lapsing into an awkward silence, followed O'Sullivan's remark. I think I did everyone a favor by bringing the silence to an end with a question.

"But when we found the car on Sunday afternoon, didn't that wreck Gaudett's whole plan?"

"Well, not really," Raleigh replied. "Your finding the car forced him to get it out of there earlier than he had intended and find somewhere else to hide it for twenty-four hours. We still don't know exactly what he did with it, but he may even have stashed it in Mr. O'Sullivan's garage until Monday afternoon. In fact, his plan was already wrecked as he was putting it into action thanks to your friend Mr. Graveney seeing you at sea, Mr. O'Sullivan. But Gaudett didn't know that on Sunday, or on Monday for that matter. Having to move the car temporarily was something he obviously hadn't planned on, but at the time he thought his plan was still intact. A little bent at the edges, perhaps, but intact. No, the single most important thing that happened on Sunday was Gene Gaudett picking up the bicycle pump. That's what's going to get us our conviction."

Raleigh's answer irritated me. Had it not been for Robert's action in trying to rescue Tony from Steven Cardeiro's clutches, the piece of hardware that would lead to Gaudett's conviction would not even have been lying in the dump. But more than that, it was Robert who had first realized the importance of finding the pump and delivering it to the police. And it was Robert who had held on to the pump like grim death during the chase, when he could have saved himself from Gaudett's attentions at any time by abandoning it. But Raleigh seemed unwilling to recognize my friend's intellect or courage, or to revise his earlier assessment of his character. Perhaps, I surmised, it was too radical a shift for a man with his prejudices.

"Perhaps I missed something at the start of all this," said Robert's mom, a little helplessly. "Tell me if I'm being stupid, but—" Instinctively, Robert put up his hand.

"Not *you*, Robert!" she finished, all helplessness temporarily banished from her voice. There were grins all around, but I revisited Robert's ankle with my foot anyway; low-profile it, my friend.

"What I mean is, why did they put the car in the dump in the first place? It does seem an awful lot of trouble to go to, if they were going to take it out again."

"I think I know why," answered O'Sullivan. "The one thing Gaudett didn't want was for anyone to find it before Monday afternoon. If he'd put it anywhere else—a back road, a trail, a vacant lot—there would always have been the risk of someone stumbling onto it. Plus, he had to get somewhere really secluded really fast after they left the bank, so he could kill Jimmy without being seen. And, of course... well, let's just say the sand was good insulation for the car, and Gaudett knew he'd be climbing back into it in two days. If it had been exposed to the sun all that time with Jimmy's body in it..." Our moms shuddered in sync. with each other.

"By the way," he added, turning to Raleigh, "he couldn't have used my garage. I keep it padlocked when I'm away, 'cause I had stuff stolen from it once. The side door's another thing; the bolt's on the fritz, which is how they must have got in to take my jacket and plant the money."

"Did Gaudett admit any of this?" Robert asked Raleigh. The detective shook his head.

"No, and I don't expect him to. He's been understandably tight-lipped since he woke up in handcuffs a couple of hours back. And right now he's closeted with Mr. Arslanian, trying to figure out a defense. But somehow I don't think even Ass—er, Arslanian, that is—can find a loophole for him to crawl through this time." Raleigh looked thoughtful for a moment, then continued.

"Chances are, we'll never know who killed Jimmy Cardeiro. It could just as easily have been Tunney as Gaudett, and since Tunney's dead we fully expect Gene to put the blame on him."

"Tunney?" Robert interjected. "The other guy in the dump—Gaudett's partner?"

"That's right. William Tunney. Worked for Gretchyville Waste for the last couple of years. He was no saint, as I'm sure you know, which made him a good partner for Gaudett. Anyway, it's not a vital point. It's Steven's murder we'll get him for."

Raleigh's reminder that Gaudett's partner had been a *bona fide* dump worker finally silenced the buzzer that had been sounding intermittently in my head since O'Sullivan had pointed out to us, the day before, that the dump closes at three o'clock on weekends. Even that made sense now.

"Of course!" I exclaimed, smacking my forehead with the ball of my hand. "That's why he timed it the way he did!"

"What do you mean?" asked the Chief.

"We could never understand how Gaudett got the spot ready to take the car, and how he covered it up afterwards, without equipment. Or, if he had equipment, how he persuaded the guy in charge to let him use it to cover up a murder scene. Now it makes sense. He timed the robbery not just for when he knew you'd be at sea, Mr. O'Sullivan, but for *when the dump would be closed.* I bet this Tunney character hid himself somewhere as all his buddies were going home, then took the front-end loader over to the far side and got the spot ready. When they were ready to bury the car, he used the loader and probably had the whole job done in ten minutes." I looked at Robert, expecting—foolishly—expressions of admiration and praise. What he gave me instead was a look of mild surprise.

"Well, of course, I knew that from the very beginning, Peter," he said, with excruciating politeness. I feinted at his rib cage with my right fist, and when he moved his hands to protect himself I used my left hand to smack him soundly on the skull. Even our moms laughed at that.

"Something else we'll probably never know," mused the Chief when the noise subsided, "is how Gaudett was planning to pay Tunney for his services. He probably agitated the money bags in the car to force the dye bombs to explode, so he'd have some contaminated bills to plant in Mr. O'Sullivan's garage. But that meant he had nothing to pay off his partner with."

"I think you'd have to know Gene," said O'Sullivan. "I knew him better than any of you, and I have no problem believing he was so obsessed with doing me down that he'd use his own money—all of it—to pay Tunney. Of course, he didn't have to make any allowance for paying Jimmy..." My mom shuddered again in the short silence that followed.

"I just can't help thinking of poor Jimmy" continued O'Sullivan, speaking of him with more charity than I would have expected in the circumstances. "I wonder when he started to realize that things weren't going according to the plan he'd been told about. Did he think they would switch cars at the end of Old Kingsleytown? I guess, even if he did, he still had less than a minute to figure out what was going on. Probably died with more questions than answers..." We all became more serious during this speech, but Robert more so than anyone. During the silence that followed, he began shaking his head.

"No, it wasn't like that," he said quietly.

"How do you know?" asked the Chief with a frown. Before he continued Robert looked around the room with the same air of calm self-assurance he had shown in the library on Monday, when he had figured out how the car had entered and left the dump.

"Jimmy knew they were taking the car to the dump right enough. He didn't know he'd be inside it, but he knew they were going to bury it."

"What makes you say that?" asked Raleigh. Robert spread his hands expressively.

"Because he told his brother about it," he said simply. "When we first saw Gumboots—Steven Cardeiro—in the dump on Sunday, he was searching for something in the sand. He was poking around in it with some kind of long metal rod, but he didn't have the first idea where to look. I reckon Jimmy told him all about the bank job *and* what they were going to do with the car. When his brother didn't show up Saturday night, Steven got worried. Sunday afternoon he heads for the dump to try and find the car or Jimmy. Poor guy found both."

"Good thinking, Robert," said Bonaventura, smiling broadly. "Yes, that makes complete sense. In fact, he wouldn't have got to the car at all if you hadn't found it for him."

In my mind's eye Gumboots was back in the crater, probing uselessly every few feet for the Excalibur. There was just one thing still not quite right with the picture.

"But wasn't he wearing dump clothes?" I asked Robert.

"What—the overalls?"

"Yeah; how did he get those, I wonder?" One of the Staties finally piped up.

"Didn't he work at the County Hospital? In the boiler room?"

"Of course!" exclaimed the Chief. "He'd have almost identical clothing. He probably put it on that day in case he was seen by a legitimate dump worker." His remark generated an episode of synchronized nodding in the room.

"Well, Mr. O'Sullivan, I expect you're feeling a lot more comfortable now Gaudett's safely out of the way." Raleigh seemed to be trying to rebuild bridges with O'Sullivan, which started another buzzer going in my head.

"Well, as I said to the boys earlier, I doubt he'd try anything with me knowing the police were on to him," he replied. But if he'd caught up to either of the boys in town, he might have tried to hurt them. *That's* why I'm 'comfortable' with him being behind bars." Out of the corner of my eye I saw my mom's hand moving. There was no mistaking what happened next: she took O'Sullivan's hand in hers and gave it a brief but definite squeeze.

"So, Robert," said the Chief, turning in his chair to face him. "You seem to have worked a lot of this out by yourself. Now tell us: why do you think Gaudett was in the dump at all on Sunday—or today, for that matter?" Robert appeared pleased that he was being treated as an expert witness.

"I don't know about Sunday; maybe he was just paranormal, you know?"

"Er—paranoid, perhaps?" suggested the Chief.

"Right—that one. You know, like you check your pockets for your house keys ten times a day. Maybe he had to keep checking the dump to see that no-one—like us—disturbed the car."

"But that wouldn't explain today," put in his mom. Robert thought for a moment.

"I know it's a helluva coincidence, but I think he remembered the pump about the same time we did." He looked pointedly, but not unkindly, at O'Sullivan. "So if we hadn't gone straight there today it might have been too late." O'Sullivan raised his eyebrows and inclined his head.

"I hate to say it, junior Sherlocks, but you're probably right." Now he had both of us embarrassed, but there was worse to come. The Chief was straightening up, brushing his uniform down and clearing his throat as if preparing to launch into a major policy speech.

"Well, I think we're about done here," he announced. "I just want to say one more time, Peter and Robert, what a magnificent job you've done. It's no exaggeration to say that we simply would not have closed this case without you. You gave me one or two heart palpitations along the way, you know, but it's tough for me to stay mad at you with the end result the way it is. As for your mothers… Well, I hope they'll be as understanding as I am. And if you don't think you can stop your sons from using their God-given brains this way, Mrs. McLeod and Mrs. Juneau, perhaps you'll just have to let them become policemen when they grow up. They would be an asset to any police department they joined, I promise you." There was that ole' honey tongue again, reinforced by a chorus of approval from the Staties.

"Now, this case will be in the hands of the District Attorney's office from now on," he continued. "And when it comes to trial, you *will* be called upon to testify. But don't let it worry you; the D.A.'s office is very good at preparing young people for the court experience; all you have to remember is to tell the truth and keep telling it. I'm sure you'll handle yourselves just fine."

The Chief's speech seemed to be the signal for all the official visitors to prepare to leave. The Staties let themselves out first, shaking hand with our moms and us as they went. Bonaventura did the same but hung around in the doorway, waiting for Raleigh. The detective was attempting one last time to make his peace with O'Sullivan, which the latter finally—and somewhat half-heartedly—accepted. It was now or never, I thought, and as I drew breath to speak the buzzer in my head finally died away into silence.

"Wasn't there someone else you wanted to apologize to, Sergeant Raleigh?"

Like a fart in an elevator.

The general murmur of leave-taking was cut off as sharply as if I had sliced through it with a scythe. My mom's face, to which the color was only just beginning to return, trended right back to pasty white again. Mrs. Juneau looked rapidly from face to face as if she had missed some vital part of the conversation and needed someone to bring her up to date. Robert stared at me questioningly.

A DEATH UNDER SAND

O'Sullivan just looked puzzled and Raleigh was genuinely perplexed. It looked as if I were going to need to spell it out with numbered paragraphs and bullet points when the Chief, standing behind me, finally broke the silence.

"Ah yes, I think I know what you mean, Peter," he said in that deliberate, gentle tone of voice he could command at the appropriate moment. "Henry, it's not for me to tell you what to do in this case, but I do believe Peter is referring to your comments about Robert, his father... Robert's capacity for truth and... well, you know the sort of thing he means. I'll be waiting outside."

Despite his actual words, Bonaventura could not have made his meaning clearer: Raleigh was expected to perform. The detective glanced at Robert's mom, whose expression was beginning to show some hostility, then at me. I think he was hoping I would let him off, but I just looked right back at him without even blinking. Finally—and about bloody time, too—he looked at Robert.

"Yes, well, I guess... I guess I shouldn't have judged you quite so hastily, Robert. As the Chief said, we couldn't have caught Gaudett without your contribution and... well, I suppose the point is, you were telling the truth from the very beginning. I um... I should have given you the benefit of the doubt, I know, and I apologize." Raleigh was rapidly running out of grovel material, and Robert must have figured that if he squirmed any more he'd drill a hole for himself and disappear into the basement; in what I considered an enlightened act of charity he actually let the creep off the hook.

"That's OK, Sergeant Raleigh. But you know—you might have given me the benefit of the doubt," he said, echoing (deliberately, as I later found out) O'Sullivan's words of a few minutes earlier. Raleigh grunted something that might have been another apology, or might just have been a strangled appeal to the gods to get him out of there. And I knew, as did Robert and everyone else within earshot, that what we had heard was about as genuine as WWF wrestling. Raleigh had been forced into the 'apology' and it showed, so I guess Robert felt there was no point in prolonging the agony.

Outside, the police started their cars and swept away past a street full of inquisitive eyes. We stood at the end of the driveway and watched them disappear around the corner and out of our lives—for now, anyway. Looking back on it, that did seem to be the point—when the last taillight passed out of sight behind the Carling's house—at which the story came to an end for me. What lay ahead seemed more like dotting the 'i's' and crossing the 't's' than anything; what had just happened felt like the natural tying up of loose ends in this weird mystery of a robbery that had nothing to do with stealing money.

A DEATH UNDER SAND

My mom was ushering O'Sullivan and Mrs. Juneau out to their cars. After he had said his good-byes and thanks to us (and after I had thanked him for saving my life) O'Sullivan returned to his pick-up and spoke briefly to my mom. All I heard of the exchange was her reply to him.

"Sure, I'd like that. We're in the book."

As Mrs. Juneau was fussing with her car keys I felt a gentle punch on my right shoulder and turned to see Robert looking at me. His face was illuminated not with its usual toothy grin but with a quiet smile and slight frown.

"You know, you didn't have to do that back there, man."

"What—with Raleigh? Sure I did. You wanted him to get away with what he said on Sunday?" Robert shrugged.

"You think he's changed his opinion because of what you said? Or what you made him say?" I consulted the gravel in our driveway for a moment.

"Nah. I doubt it. I think I ambushed him, and he said what he thought he was supposed to say. You don't get people like Raleigh to change just like that. But... Oh hell, I don't know—it's like... Well, it's like when you see a football team that's down twenty points lining up to play thirty seconds from the end. You know it's a waste of time. *They* know it's a waste of time. But they take the snap and try for yards and get beaten up some more anyway, right? Some things you've just got to do, even if you know it makes no difference."

"In other words, you weren't doing it for him, right?" I remembered the feelings of frustration that had washed over me as we sat on the dune four days earlier.

"No, I guess I wasn't. I guess I was doing it for you. Or maybe I was doing it for me. Would that be so bad?" Feeling totally stupid I looked up at Robert. He was still smiling, but without the frown.

"Hey, buddy, come here," he said, approaching me with his arms outstretched. I turned toward him and opened my arms just as he whipped his right hand up and smacked the crown of my head as I had done to him a few minutes earlier.

It took both our moms to disentangle us as we wrestled on the grass, laughing and cursing at each other. When we had dusted our clothing off I accompanied Robert to the car.

"See you tomorrow?" I asked.

"Unless they tear down the school between now and then."

"Hey, one thing, Robert; I've been trying to figure this out since we left the dump. When Gaudett went down with The Golden Gate Bridge, why didn't you just keep going? It must have been about ten minutes before we found you, and you were still hanging around there."

"Yeah, well, I didn't want him getting away, did I?"

"For God's sake, Robert, I'd have thought you'd have been satisfied with not getting strangled and buried in the sand."

"After all we'd been through? No way, man. I wanted him taken down, right enough, and I do mean *down*."

"So what if he'd come to while you were waiting for the cops?" Robert glanced furtively around to make sure his mom was out of earshot.

"Well... He did come to... a couple of times."

"A couple of times? I don't get it."

"Peter, didn't you see the rocks lying around him at the bottom?" I brought up the mental image of Gaudett sprawled out fifteen feet below where the bridge had given way under him. And yes, now that Robert mentioned it, there *were* some lumps of stone scattered around in the sand.

"What about them?"

"Well, what do you think? I couldn't let him wake up and run out of there, could I? I was busy as all hell for ten minutes finding those rocks and getting them up to the top of the slope, so I could-"

"-so you could keep dropping them on his head when he woke up! Oh my God, Robert!" Robert shushed me into silence with some energetic arm-flapping.

"What else was I supposed to do? Go down there and challenge him to an arm-wrestling contest, best out of three?"

"Yes, but—do you mean to tell me you just stood up there and stoned the guy whenever he moved?"

"Mm... kinda. After the second time he kind of did it himself; he fell back and knocked himself out on an armchair frame. It wasn't long after that when I saw you, and believe me, man, I was glad to see you alive. If Tunney had got you and then come after me, I probably wouldn't 've made it. There aren't too many places in the dump where you can pull the kind of trick I did on Gaudett."

By now I was laughing, although I probably shouldn't have been. It didn't seem to have occurred to Robert that he could have killed Gaudett outright with his rock bombing technique; on the other hand, perhaps it had, and he had regarded it as an acceptable risk. I made a mental note to quiz him on his ethics later, but as his mom was getting impatient to leave I figured I would have to be satisfied with the image of him cradling a boulder in his arms and waiting for the prostrate Gaudett to twitch before releasing it over his head. And the more I thought about it, frankly, the more satisfying it became.

O'Sullivan accelerated up the street with a smile and a wave to all of us. Mrs. Juneau started off a little more sedately, and as the Dodge slid past me Robert put his hand out of the window, palm open. I thought he wanted a high-five and started to reciprocate, but when our hands met he gripped mine tightly. As a result I was obliged to walk alongside the car for a few yards, and while I did so Robert held my eyes with what was probably the happiest and most trouble-free look I have ever seen in his. Finally he released my hand and the car sped up, leaving me standing in the middle of the road waving at the two departing Juneaus. Robert's hand was still outside the car, but now the fist was clenched in a triumphant gesture.

The sun was almost on the horizon now, and the elongated shadows of trees and mailboxes reached back toward me all the way up the street. Much of the ground—lawns, driveways and blacktop—was covered by the exaggerated shadows, but outside these areas the dying sun coated objects both still and moving in a layer of almost tangible gold. As I watched the Dodge glide smoothly away up the street I could see that Robert's fist remained bathed in sunlight the whole way and, after the car made the turn, until I could see it no more.

THE END

C.W. STIMPSON